THE ALLIES
OF TREASON

The merest glimpse of the thing set off all his danger instincts—the very presence of it roused primeval horror. In the shadows of the strange black machine, he could see a bulging, glistening surface, translucently greenish, wet, slimy, palpitating with sluggish life—the body surface of something gross and vast and utterly strange.

And then a red avalanche of unendurable pain hurled him to the ground. Black oblivion brought mercy.

**Are there paperbound books you want
but cannot find in your retail stores?**

You can get any title in print in **POCKET BOOK** editions. Simply send retail price, local sales tax, if any, plus 35¢ per book to cover mailing and handling costs, to:

MAIL SERVICE DEPARTMENT
   POCKET BOOKS • A Division of Simon & Schuster, Inc.
   1230 Avenue of the Americas • New York, New York 10020.

Please send check or money order. We cannot be responsible for cash. *Catalogue sent free on request.*

Titles in this series are also available at discounts in quantity lots for industrial or sales-promotional use. For details write our Special Products Department: Department AR, POCKET BOOKS, 1230 Avenue of the Americas, New York, New York 10020.

The
Legion
of
Space

JACK WILLIAMSON

A KANGAROO BOOK
PUBLISHED BY POCKET BOOKS NEW YORK

THE LEGION OF SPACE

Fantasy Press edition published 1947

POCKET BOOK edition published September, 1977

This POCKET BOOK edition includes every word contained in
the original, higher-priced edition. It is printed from brand-
new plates made from completely reset, clear, easy-to-read type.
POCKET BOOK editions are published by
POCKET BOOKS,
a Simon & Schuster Division of
GULF & WESTERN CORPORATION
1230 Avenue of the Americas,
New York, N.Y. 10020.
Trademarks registered in the United States
and other countries.

Printed in the U.S.A.

ACKNOWLEDGMENTS

The Legion of Space was originally published in *Astounding
Stories*, 1935.

DEDICATION

To all the readers and the writers of that new literature called science-fiction, who find mystery, wonder, and high adventure in the expanding universe of knowledge, and who sometimes seek to observe and to forecast the vast impact of science upon the lives and minds of men.

CONTENTS

PROLOGUE

The Man Who Remembered Tomorrow

"Well, Doctor, what's your verdict?"

He sat up on the examination table, with the sheet wrapped around his bent and stringy frame, and firmly commanded my nurse to bring back his clothes. He looked at me, his bright blue eyes sharply curious and yet oddly unafraid—for I knew he expected a sentence of death.

"Acquittal, John," I told him honestly. "You're really indestructible. Remarkable shape, for a man of your age —except for that knee. You'll make me a good patient and a better chess opponent for the next twenty years."

But old John Delmar shook his weatherbeaten head, very seriously.

"No, Doctor." In that same tone of quiet and unexcited certainty, he might have said today was Tuesday. "No, Doctor, I've less than three weeks. I've known for several years that I'm going to die at eleven-seven on the morning of March 23, 1945."

"Nonsense," I told him. "Not likely—unless you jump in front of a truck. That knee may always be a little stiff, but there's certainly nothing else—"

"I know the date." His thin, old voice had a flat, impersonal conviction. "You see, I read it on a tombstone." He didn't seem to regard that statement as remarkable. "I came in this morning just to see if you can tell me what it is that I'm to die of."

He looked entirely too sane and cool to fall victim to any superstitious notion.

"You can forget the idea of that," I assured him heartily. "Physically, you're sounder than most men twenty years younger. Except for that knee, and a few assorted scars—"

"Please don't think I want to question your diagnosis, but I'm really quite positive." He seemed apologetic, and

9

oddly hesitant. "You see, Doctor, I've an unusual—well, call it a gift. I've meant, sometime, to tell you about it. That is, if you'd care to hear—"

He paused, diffidently.

I had wondered a long time, about old John Delmar. A faded, stiff little man, with thin gray hair and blue eyes that were curiously bright, strangely *young*. Still erect and agile, for all the years he owned to, he walked with a slight quick limp from that old bullet wound in his knee.

We had first met when he came home from the war in Spain—he looked me up to bring me word of a friend of mine, not a third his age, who had died beside him, fighting with the Loyalists. I liked him. A lonely old soldier, he didn't talk too much about his campaigns. We discovered a mutual interest in chess, and he made a pleasant companion. He had a youth of heart, an eager and unquenchable vitality, rare in a man so old. My medical interest, besides, was aroused by his durable physique.

For he had endured many things.

He had always been reticent. I was, I believe, his most intimate friend through those last, unwontedly peaceful years, yet he had given me no more than the barest hints of his long and remarkable life. He grew up, he told me, in the frontier West; he rode with a gun in a cattle war when he was only a boy, and somehow he got into the Texas Rangers a little short of the legal age. Later he served in the Rough Riders, and in the Boer War, and under Porfirio Díaz. In 1914 he joined the British Army— to make up, he said, for fighting the British in South Africa. Later he was in China and in the Rif, in the Gran Chaco and in Spain. It was a Spanish prison camp that stiffened his bad knee. His hard-seasoned body began to fail him at last, and he finally came home, too old to fight again. That was when we met.

I knew, too, that he was busy with some literary project—dropping in at his rather shabby rooms for a pipe and a game of chess, I had noticed his desk piled with closely written pages. Until he came to the office that morning in the spring of 1945, however, I had supposed that he was merely writing the memoirs of his colorful past. I had no inkling that his manuscripts dealt with his recollections of the more wonderful future.

Fortunately, no patient was waiting that morning, and his quiet air of matter-of-fact certainty about the moment of his death piqued my curiosity. When he was dressed again, I made him fill his pipe and told him that I'd be glad to hear.

"It's a good thing that most fighting men are killed before they get too old to fight," he began a little awkwardly, settling back in his chair and easing his knee with thin, quivering hands. "That's what I was thinking, one cold morning, the year this war began.

"You remember when I came home to New York—or I called it coming home. But I found myself a stranger. Most people don't have the time that you do, Doctor, for old fighting men. There was nothing for me to do. I was useless as a worn-out gun. That wet, gusty morning—it was April thirteenth, I remember—I sat down on a bench in Central Park, to think things over. I got cold. And I decided—well, that I'd already lived too long.

"I was just getting up from the bench, to go back to the room and get my old automatic, when I—remembered!

"That's the only word I know. Memory. It seems a little strange, though, to speak of remembering things that haven't happened yet. That won't happen, some of them, for a thousand years and more. But there's no other word.

"I've talked to scientists about it, Doctor. A psychologist, first. A behaviorist. He laughed. It didn't fit in, he said, with the concepts of behaviorism. A man, he said, is just a machine. Everything a man does is just mechanical reaction to stimulus.

"But, if that's so, there are stimuli that the behaviorists have never found.

"There was another man who didn't laugh. A physicist from Oxford, a lecturer on Einstein—relativity. He didn't laugh. He seemed to believe what I told him. He asked questions about my—memories. But there wasn't much I could tell him, then.

"What he told me helped to ease my mind—the thing had had me worried. I wanted to talk about it to you, Doctor. But we were just getting to be good chess companions, and I didn't want you to think me too odd.

"Anyhow, this Oxford man told me that Space and Time aren't real, apart. And they aren't really different. They fade one into the other all around us. He spoke of the *continuum* and *two-way time* and a theory of the *serial universe*. I didn't understand it all. But there's no real reason, he said, why we shouldn't remember the future—all of us. In theory, he said, our minds ought to be able to trace *world-lines* into the future, just as easily as into the past.

"Hunches and premonitions and dreams, he believed, are sometimes real memories of things yet to come. I didn't understand all he said, but he did convince me that the thing wasn't—well, insanity. I had been afraid, Doctor.

"He wanted to know more about what I—remembered. But that was years ago. It was just scattered impressions, then, most of them vague and confused. It's a power, I think, that most people have to some degree—it simply happens to be better developed in me. I've always had hunches, some vague sense to warn me of danger—which is probably why I'm still alive. But the first clear memory of the future came that day in the park. And it was many months before I could call them up at will.

"You don't understand it, I suppose. I'll try to describe that first experience, in the park. I slipped on the wet pavement, and fell back on the bench—I had got cold, sitting there, and I wasn't so long back from Spain then, you know.

"And suddenly I wasn't in the park at all.

"I was still falling, all right. I was in the same position —but no longer on the Earth. All around me was a weird plain. It was blazing with a glare of light, pitted with thousands of craters, ringed with mountains higher than any I had ever seen. The Sun was burning down out of a blue sky dark as midnight, and full of stars. There was another body in the heavens, huge and greenish.

"A fantastic black machine was gliding down over those terrible mountains. It was larger than you'd think a flying machine could be, and utterly strange. It had just hit me with some weapon, and I was reeling back under the agony of the wound. Beside me was a great explosion of red gas. The cloud of it poured over me, and burned my lungs, and blotted out everything.

"It was some time before I realized that I had been on the Moon—or rather that I had picked up the last thoughts of a man dying there. I had never had time for astronomy, but one day I happened to see a photograph of the lunar craters—and recognized them, and knew that the greenish crescent had been the Earth itself.

"And the shock of that discovery only increased my bewilderment. It was nearly a year before I understood that I was developing an ability to recall the future. But that first incident happened in the thirtieth century, in the conquest of the Moon by the Medusæ—the man whose last moments I shared was one of the human colonists they murdered.

"The faculty improved with practise, like any other. It's simply telepathy, I'm convinced, carrying thought across Time and not merely through Space. Just remember that neither Space nor Time is real; they are both just aspects of one reality.

"At first I got contact only with minds under great stress, like that of the dying colonist. Even yet, there are difficulties—or I shouldn't have asked you to examine me this morning, Doctor. But I've managed to follow human history, pretty well, through the next thousand years. That's what I've been writing.

"The history of the future!

"The conquest of space is what thrills me most. Partly because it's the most difficult achievement of human engineering, the most daring and the most dangerous. And partly, I suppose, because my own descendants played a big part in it."

An eager ring of enthusiasm had risen in his voice, and now he paused awkwardly, as if suddenly self-conscious because of it. His sharp blue eyes searched my face. I kept silent until he went on, sure that the least show of doubt would stop him.

"Yes, Doctor, I've a son." His thin brown face showed a wistful pride. "I don't see much of him, because he's a very busy young man. I failed to make a soldier out of him, and I used to think he'd never amount to much. I tried to get him to join up, long before Pearl Harbor, but he wouldn't hear of it.

"No, Don never took to fighting. He's something you call a nuclear physicist, and he's got himself a nice, safe deferment. Now he's on a war job, somewhere out in New Mexico. I'm not even supposed to know where he is, and I can't tell you what he's doing—but the thesis he wrote, at Tech, was something about the metal uranium."

Old John Delmar gave me a proud and wistful smile.

"No, I used to think that Don would never accomplish much, but now I know that he designed the first atomic reaction motor. I used to think he had no guts—but he was man enough to pilot the first manned atomic rocket ever launched."

I must have goggled, for he explained:

"That was 1956, Doctor—the past tense just seems more convenient. With this—this capacity of mine, you see, I shared that flight with Don, until his rocket exploded, outside the stratosphere. He died, of course. But he left a son, to carry on the Delmar name.

"And that grandson of mine reached the Moon, Doctor, in a military rocket. After uranium was discovered there, he went back to take command of the American outpost—a little camp of air-tight domes, over the mines. But the ghastly atomic wars, in the 1990's, isolated the Moon. My grandson died there, with the rest of his little garrison, and it was nearly two hundred years before human civilization was far enough recovered from the wars to build another space rocket.

"But it was a Miles Delmar, late in the twenty-second century, who finally went back to the dead mining camps on the Moon, and then set out for Mars. He left too much shielding off his atomic reaction motor, to lighten his ship for that voyage, and the leaking radiations killed him and all his crew. The dead ship carried the bodies on, and crashed in the Syrtis Major.

"Miles's son, Zane Delmar, patented the geodyne—which was a vast advance over the heavy, dangerous atomic reactors. He found the wreck of his father's ship on Mars, and survived an attack from the native Martian beings, and later died of a Venusian jungle-fever. The victory of men over space wasn't easy—quite! But Zane's three sons carried on the war. And they made a huge fortune out of the geodyne.

"In the next century, all the solar system was pretty well explored, as far out as the moon of Neptune. It was fifty years more before a John Ulnar reached Pluto—our family name was changed, about that time, from Delmar to Ulnar, to fit a new universal identification system.

"His fuel exhausted, so that he couldn't return, John managed to keep himself alive for four years, alone on the Black Planet. He left a diary that his nephew found, twenty years later. A strange document, that diary!

"It was Mary Ulnar—a peculiar Amazon she must have been—who began the conquest of the silica-armored desert life of Mars. And Arthur Ulnar, her brother, who led the first fleet to attack the cold, half-metallic beings which had extended their own rule over the four great moons of Jupiter—he died on Io.

"More battles, however, were fought in the laboratory than in space. Explorers and colonists met terrific, endless difficulties with bacteria, atmospheres, gravitations, chemical dangers. As planetary engineers, the Ulnars contributed a full share to that new science, which, with gravity generators, synthetic atmospheres, and climate-controls, could finally transform a frozen, stony asteroid into a tiny paradise.

"And the Ulnars took a generous reward.

"For a dark chapter of the family history begins with the twenty-sixth century. By then, the conquest of the solar system was finished. The Ulnar family had been the leaders, and they seized the spoils. They had controlled interplanetary commerce since the time of Zane and his geodyne, and they finally dominated the whole System.

"One bold tycoon had himself crowned Eric the First, Emperor of the Sun. For two hundred years his descendants ruled all the planets as absolute despots. Their reign, I'm sorry to say, was savagely oppressive. There were endless outbreaks for liberty, cruelly put down.

"Adam the Third, however, was at last forced to abdicate—his great mistake was an effort to suppress the freedom of scientific research. The scientists overthrew him, and the Green Hall Council launched the first real democracy of history. For the next two centuries, a genuine civilization existed in the System, defended by a small body of picked and well-trained fighting men, the Legion of Space."

Wistfully again, old John Delmar shook his lean gray head.

"If I could have lived a thousand years later!" he whispered. "I might have fought with that Legion. For that golden age of peace was broken. Another Eric Ulnar ventured away into space, the first man to circle another star. He reached that strange dwarf sun that astronomers know as Barnard's Runaway Star—the few nearer stars having proved to possess no planets. And he brought back terror and suffering and the shadow of doom to the human planets.

"The mad ambition of that remote descendant of mine

brought war between our System and another," that slow old voice said sadly. "War and invasion, treason and terror. Even the Legion was betrayed.

"And then there was an epic achievement by a few loyal men of the Legion of Space—perhaps the most heroic thing that men ever did. One of those few was another Ulnar. John Ulnar. I like to think that his name came down from me."

My office nurse chose that unfortunate moment to announce another patient. And little John Delmar hastily knocked out his pipe, apologetic for having taken so much of my time. He came to his feet, unsteady on his bad knee, and a vision seemed to fade from his oddly bright, *live* blue eyes.

"I must be going, Doctor." And he added, quietly, "Now you see how I know that I'm due to die on the morning of March twenty-third."

"You're sound as a bell," I insisted again. "And much too sane to let any such notion— But this is a very remarkable thing you've told me, John. I wish you had mentioned it before; and now I'd like very much to see those manuscripts. Why don't you publish them?"

"Perhaps," he promised vaguely. "But so few would believe, and I don't like to expose myself to any charge of fraud."

I let him go, reluctantly. I meant to call at his rooms, to hear the rest of his story and read his manuscripts. But the urgencies of wartime practise kept me busy all that week—until his landlady phoned me, to say that poor old Mr. Delmar had been down sick with a cold, for the last two days, alone in his rooms.

In two hours, in spite of his feeble protests, he was in the hospital. If I had only made the time to call, a few days before—but yet, perhaps, as he quietly believed, it may be that the future is really already determined, as firmly unchangeable as the past.

Influenza, with pulmonary complications. The outlook seemed good enough, the first few days, and I knew that old John Delmar's fighting heart had pulled him through a hundred more desperate situations. But sulfa and penicillin failed. His old heart surrendered. He knew he was going to die, and he did—quite peacefully, under an oxygen tent, on the morning of March 23. I was standing by his bed, and I looked at my watch.

The time was eleven-seven.

Whatever others may decide, I was well enough convinced, even before the proof of death. John Delmar at first wished to have his manuscripts destroyed, because his splendid scheme of a full history of the next thousand years was far from complete, but I persuaded him to leave the finished sections in my hands. As mere fiction, they would be enormously entertaining. As a real prevision of future history, they are more than fascinating.

The selection which follows deals with the adventures of John Star—born John Ulnar—who was a young soldier in the Legion of Space, in the thirtieth century, when human treason sought an alliance with the unearthly Medusæ, and so brought alien horror and black disaster to the unwarned worlds of men.

CHAPTER ONE

A Fort on Mars

"I'm reporting, Major Stell, for orders."

John Star, lean and trim in his new Legion uniform, stood at attention before the desk where the stern, white-haired officer sat toying with the silver model of a space cruiser. He felt the major's merciless eyes come up from the tiny ship to search out every detail of his small-boned, hard physique. Taut and almost quivering, he endured that probing gaze, burningly anxious to know his first assignment.

"Are you ready, John Ulnar, to accept your first order in the Legion as it should be accepted, to put duty above everything else?"

"I hope so, sir. I believe so."

What would it be?

"I hope so too, John Ulnar."

John Star was then called John Ulnar; the "Star" is a title of distinction given him later by the Green Hall. John Star we shall call him, according to the Green Hall's edict.

This day, one of the first in the thirtieth century, had

been the supreme, the most thrilling day of his twenty-one years. It marked the end of his five arduous years in the Legion Academy, on Catalina Island. Now the ceremonies were finished. His life in the Legion was about to begin.

Where, he wondered eagerly, would his first tour of duty be? On some cruiser of the Legion Patrol, in the cold wastes of space? At some isolated outpost in the exotic, terrible jungles of Venus? Or perhaps in the Guard of the Green Hall, itself? He strove to conceal his consuming impatience.

"John Ulnar," old Major Stell spoke at last, with maddening deliberation. "I hope you realize the meaning of duty."

"I think I do, sir."

"Because," the officer continued, as slowly, "you are being assigned to a duty that is peculiarly important."

"What is it, sir?"

He could not resist the desire to hasten the satisfaction of his anxious curiosity, but Major Stell refused to hurry. His keen eyes still scanned John Star pitilessly, while his thin fingers continued to turn the silver toy on his desk.

"John Ulnar, you are being given a duty that has previously been entrusted only to seasoned, chosen veterans of the Legion. It surprised me, I may say, that you were selected for it. Your lack of experience will be a disadvantage to you."

"Not too much of one, I hope, sir."

Why didn't he come to the point?

"The orders for your assignment, John Ulnar, came directly from Commander Ulnar himself. Does it happen that you are related to the Commander of the Legion, and his nephew, Eric Ulnar, the explorer?"

"Yes, sir. Distantly."

"That must explain your orders. But if you fail in this duty, John Ulnar, don't expect any favor of the Commander to save you from the consequences."

"No, sir. Of course not!"

How long could he endure this anxiety?

"The service to which you are assigned, John Ulnar, is not well known. It is in fact secret. But it is the most important that can be entrusted to a soldier of the Legion. Your responsibility will be to the Green Hall itself. Any failure, I may warn you, even if due only to negligence, will mean disgrace and very severe punishment."

"Yes, sir."

What could it be?

"John Ulnar, did you ever hear of AKKA?"

"Akka? Why, I think not, sir."

"It isn't 'akka.' AKKA. It's a symbol."

"Yes, sir. What does it mean?"

At last, was he coming to it?

"Men have given their lives to learn that, John Ulnar. And men have died for knowing. Only one person in the System knows precisely what those four letters stand for. That person is a young woman. The most important single duty of the Legion is to guard her."

"Yes, sir." A breathless whisper.

"Because, John Ulnar, AKKA is the most precious thing that humanity possesses. I need not tell you what it is. But the loss of it, I may say—the loss of the young woman who knows it—would mean unprecedented disaster to humanity."

"Yes, sir." He waited, painfully.

"I could assign you to no duty more important than to join the few trusted men who guard that young woman. And to no duty more perilous! For desperate men know that AKKA exists, know that possession of it would enable them to dictate to the Green Hall—or to destroy it.

"No risk, nor any difficulty, will deter them from attempting to get possession of the young woman, to force the secret from her. You must be unceasingly alert against attempts by stealth or violence. The girl—and AKKA—must be protected at any cost."

"Yes, sir. Where is the girl?"

"That information cannot be given you, until you are out in space. The danger that you might pass it on, unwittingly or otherwise, is too great. The girl's safety depends on her whereabouts being kept secret. If they become known—the whole Legion fleet might be inadequate to defend her.

"You are assigned, John Ulnar, to join the guard of AKKA. You will report at once, at the Green Hall, to Captain Eric Ulnar, and place yourself under his orders."

"Under Eric Ulnar!"

He was astonished and overjoyed to know that he was to serve under his famous kinsman, the great explorer of space, just returned from his daring voyage beyond the limits of the System, to the far, strange planet of Barnard's Runaway Star.

"Yes. John Ulnar, I hope you never forget the overwhelming importance of the duty before you. . . . That is all."

Queerly, John Star's heart ached at leaving the old campus of the Academy, at parting from his classmates. Queerly, for he was a-thrill with eagerness. Mystery lay ahead, the promise of peril, the adventure of meeting his famous kinsman. With native optimism, he ignored Major Stell's grim hints of the possibility of disastrous failure.

From the ports of the descending strato-flier, that afternoon, he first saw the Green Hall—seat of the Supreme Council of the united planets.

Like a great emerald, it shimmered darkly cool in a waste of sun-baked New Mexico mesa—a colossal marvel of green, translucent glass. Three thousand feet the square central tower leaped up, crowned with the landing stage to which the strato-plane was dropping. The four great colonnaded wings spread over a full mile of luxuriantly verdant parkland—a solitary jewel in the desert, under the rugged, mile-high wall of the Sandias.

John Star was a-throb with eagerness to see Eric Ulnar, then in the full radiance of his fame for commanding the first successful expedition beyond the System—if an expedition could be called successful when but a fourth of its members returned, and most of those dying of a fearful malady involving insanity and hideous bodily disfigurement.

Dark chapters, and silent ones, were in the story of the voyage. But the public, like John Star, had ignored them. Honors had been showered on Eric Ulnar, while most of his companions lay forgotten in hospital cells, gibbering of the horrors of that remote solitary planet, while their bodies rotted away unspeakably, beyond the aid or the understanding of medical science.

John Star found Eric Ulnar waiting for him in a private room in the vast Green Hall. Long golden hair and slender figure made the young officer almost femininely handsome. Burning eyes and haughty airs proclaimed his passion and his insolent pride. Retreating chin and irresolute mouth betrayed the man's fatal weakness.

"John Ulnar, I believe you are a relative of mine."

"I believe I am, sir," said John Star, concealing the stab of disappointment that pierced even through his admiration. He stood at attention, while the arrogant eyes of Eric Ulnar boldly scanned his lean body, hard and capable from the five grinding years of Academy training.

"You are under some obligation, I believe, to Adam Ulnar?"

"I am, sir. I am an orphan. It was the Commander of the Legion who got me the Academy appointment. But for that, I might never have been able to enter the Legion."

"Adam Ulnar is my uncle. He had me select you for the duty ahead. I hope you will serve me loyally."

"Of course, sir. Aside from the obligation, you are my superior in the Legion."

Eric Ulnar smiled; for a moment his face was almost attractive, in spite of its weakness and its pride.

"I'm sure we shall get on," he said. "But I may require services of you as a kinsman that I couldn't ask of you as my subordinate in the Legion."

John Star wondered what such services might be. He could not hide the fact that Eric Ulnar was not all he had hoped of the heroic explorer of space. Something about him roused a vague distrust, though the man had been his idol.

"You're ready to start for our post?"

"Of course."

"We shall go aboard the cruiser, then, at once."

"We're leaving the Earth?"

"You'll serve yourself best, John," Eric Ulnar said with an air of cutting superiority, "by obeying orders and asking no questions."

An elevator lifted them to the glittering confusion of the landing stage on the green glass tower. The *Scorpion* was waiting for them there, a swift new space cruiser, taperingly cylindrical, a bare hundred feet long, all silver-white save for black projecting rockets.

Two Legionnaires met them at the air-lock, and came with them aboard. Vors, lean, stringy, rat-faced; Kimplen, tall, haggard-eyed, wolfish. Both years older than John Star, both, he soon learned, veterans of the interstellar expedition—among the few who had escaped that mysterious malady—they displayed for his inexperience a patronizing contempt that annoyed him. It was strange, he thought, that men of their type should have been chosen to guard the infinitely precious AKKA. He would not, he thought, care to trust either of them with the price of a meal.

The *Scorpion* was provisioned, fueled, her crew of ten aboard and at their posts. Her air-lock quickly sealed, her multiple rockets vomiting blue flame, she flashed through the atmosphere into the freedom of the void.

A thousand miles off, safe in the frozen, star-domed vacuum of space, the pilot cut out the rockets. At an order from Eric Ulnar, he set the cruiser's nose for the far red spark of Mars and started the geodyne generators. Quietly humming, their powerful fields reacting against, altering, the curvature of space itself, the geodynes—more technically, electro-magnetic geodesic deflectors—drove the *Scorpion* across the hundred million miles to Mars, with an acceleration and a final velocity that science had once declared impossible.

Forgetting his uneasy mistrust of Vors and Kimplen, John Star enjoyed the voyage. The eternal miracles of space fascinated him through long hours. Ebon sky; frozen pinpoints of stars, many-colored, motionless; silver clouds of nebulae; the supernal Sun, blue, winged with red coronal fire.

Three meals were served in the narrow galley. After twenty hours, the geodynes—too powerful for safe maneuver in the close vicinity of a planet—were stopped. The *Scorpion* fell, checked by rocket blasts, toward the night side of the planet Mars.

Standing by the navigator, Eric Ulnar gave him directions from some private memorandum. About the whole proceeding was an air of mystery, of secret haste, of daring unknown dangers, that mightily intrigued John Star. Yet he had the sense of something irregular; he was troubled by a little haunting fear that all was not as it ought to be.

On a stony Martian desert they landed, far, apparently, from any city or inhabited, fertile "canal." Low, dark hills loomed near in the starlight. John Star, with Eric Ulnar and rat-faced Vors and wolfish Kimplen, disembarked; beside them was lowered their meager baggage and a little pile of freight.

Four Legionnaires came up presently through the darkness, the part of the guard, John Star understood, that they had come to relieve. The four went aboard, after their leader had exchanged some documents with Eric Ulnar; the valve clanged behind them. Blue flames jetted from the rockets; the *Scorpion* roared away, a dwindling blue comet, soon lost amid the blazing Martian stars.

John Star and the others waited in the desert for daylight. The Sun burst up suddenly, shrunken and blue, after the briefest yellow dawn, flooding the red landscape abruptly with harsh radiance.

Under violet zenith and lemon-green horizons, the ancient planet lay weirdly and grimly desolate. Lonely wastes of ocher drift-sand, rippled with low crescent dunes. Cruel, jutting ridges of red volcanic rock, projecting from yellow sand like broken fangs. Solitary boulders, carved by pitiless, wind-driven sand into grotesque scarlet monsters.

Crouching above the plain were the hills. Low, ancient, worn down by erosion of ages immemorial, like all the mountains of dying Mars. Tumbled masses of red stone; broken palisades of red-black, columnar rock; ragged, wind-carved precipices.

Sprawling across the hill-top was an ancient, half-ruined fort. Massive walls rambled along the rim of the precipices, studded here and there with square, heavy towers. It was all of the red volcanic stone characteristic of the Martian desert, all crumbling to slow ruin.

The fortress must date, John Star knew, from the conquest of the weird, silica-armored Martians. It must have been abandoned a full three centuries ago. But it was not now deserted.

A sentry met them when they climbed to the gate, a very fat, short, blue-nosed man in Legion uniform, who had been dozing lazily on a bench in the warm sunlight. He examined Eric Ulnar's documents with a fishy eye.

"Ah, so you're the relief guard?" he wheezed. " 'Tis mortal seldom we see a living being, here. Pass on, inside. Captain Otan is in his quarters beyond the court."

Within the crumbling red walls they found a large, open court, surrounded with a gallery, many doors and windows opening upon it. A tiny fountain played in a little garden of vivid flowers. Beyond was a tennis court, from which a man and a slender girl vanished hastily as they entered.

John Star's heart leaped with excitement at sight of the

girl. She must be, he felt immediately certain, keeper of the mysterious AKKA. She was the girl he had been ordered to guard! Recalling Major Stell's warning of desperate, unknown enemies anxious to seize her, John Star had a pang of apprehension. The old fort was no real defense; it was no more than a dwelling. There were, he soon found, only eight men to guard her, all told. They were armed only with hand proton-blast needles. Truly, secrecy was their only defense. Secrecy, and the girl's secret weapon. If those enemies discovered she was here, and sent a modern, armed ship—

During the day he learned no more. Eric Ulnar, Vors, and Kimplen remained insolently uncommunicative; the four men left of the old guard were oddly distant, cautious in their talk, unmistakably apprehensive. They were busy bringing up the supplies from where the *Scorpion* had landed—provisions, apparently, to last many months.

An hour after dark, John Star was in the individual room he had been assigned, which opened on an ancient court, when he heard a shouted alarm.

"Rockets! Rockets! A strange ship is landing!"

Running into the yard, he saw a greenish flare descending athwart the stars; he heard a thin whistling that increased to a screaming bellow, deafeningly loud. The flame, grown enormous, dropped beyond the east wall; the bellow abruptly ceased. He felt a sharp tremor underfoot.

"A great ship!" cried the sentry. "It landed so near it shook the hill. Its rockets burned green, a thing I never saw before."

Could it be, John Star wondered, with an odd little pause of his heart, that the girl's mysterious enemies had learned where she was? That this ship had come to take her?

Captain Otan, the commander of the tiny garrison, evidently had some such apprehension. An elderly thin man, very much agitated, he called out all the Legionnaires to station them about the old walls and towers with hand proton guns. For three hours John Star lay on his stomach, watching a crumbling redoubt. But nothing happened; at midnight he was dismissed.

The old officer, however, must still have been alarmed over the strange ship's arrival. He ordered the three others of his own relief—Jay Kalam, Hal Samdu, and

Giles Habibula—to remain on guard. From him, John Star caught a sense of terror and impending doom which he was not to escape for many dark and dreadful days.

CHAPTER TWO

An Eye and a Murder

John Star found himself abruptly sitting bolt upright in his bunk, staring at his open window, beyond which lay the great courtyard. It was no alarm that he could name which had aroused him; rather, a sudden chill of instinctive fear, an intuition of terror.

An eye! It must be, he thought, an eye, staring in at him. But it was fully a foot long, ovoid, all pupil. Thin, ragged black membranes edged it. It was purple, shining in the darkness like a great well of luminescence, somehow infinitely malignant. Mere sight of it shook him with an icy, elemental dread.

For only the briefest instant it gazed at him, unutterably evil, and then it was gone. Trembling, he scrambled out of bed to give the alarm. But the shock of it had left him doubtful of his senses. When he heard one sentry hail another in the court, as if nothing were amiss, he decided that the frightful eye had been no more than nightmare.

He wasn't given to nightmares. But after all, he had heard nothing; and the thing had vanished the very instant he glimpsed it. It was sheer impossibility; no creature in the System had eyes a foot long, not even the sea-lizards of Venus. He went back to bed and tried to sleep—unsuccessfully, for the image of that fearful eye kept haunting him.

He was up before dawn, anxious to know more of the strange ship. Passing the weary sentries in the court, he climbed the spiral stair in the old north tower, and looked out across the crimson landscape just as the sun rose abruptly above the horizon.

Dunes of yellow sand—shattered, weirdly eroded rock —he saw nothing else. But crumbling walls, eastward, shut off his view; the vessel, he thought, might lie beyond them. His curiosity increased. If it were a friendly, Legion ship, why had the rocket-blasts been green? If it carried enemies, why had they not already struck?

The girl was behind him when he turned: she whom he had glimpsed on the tennis court, and guessed to be keeper of AKKA. He saw again that she was very lovely. Slim and straight and cleanly formed; eyes cool gray, sober and honest; hair a lustrous brown that made magic of flame and color in the new sunlight. She wore a simple white tunic; her breast was heaving from the run behind him up the stairs.

It surprised him that the keeper of AKKA should be so young and lovely.

"Why—why, good morning." He felt confused, for Legion cadets have little time for the social graces, yet very delighted and eager to please her.

"It must be very near!" she cried, breathless. Her voice, he perceived, was adorable—and alarmed.

"Beyond the walls, perhaps."

"I think so." Her gray eyes studied him frankly, weighed him—warming, he thought, with approval. She said abruptly, voice lower: "I want to talk to you."

"I'm quite willing." He smiled.

"Please be serious," she appealed, urgently. "You are loyal? Loyal to the Legion? To the Green Hall? To mankind?"

"Why, of course I am. What——"

"I believe you are," she whispered, gray eyes still very intent on his face. "I believe you really are."

"Why should you doubt me?"

"I'll tell you," she said swiftly. "But you must keep this to yourself. Every word. Even from your officer, Captain Ulnar."

Her face, when she spoke the name, tensed with a dislike that was almost hate.

"If you say. Though I don't see——"

"I shall trust you. First, do you know why you're here?"

"I've orders to guard a girl who knows some mysterious secret."

"I'm the girl." Her voice was more deliberate, more confident. "I don't matter. But the secret, AKKA, is the most valuable and the most dangerous thing in the System. I must tell you a little more about it than you seem to know. For AKKA is in terrible danger. You must help us to save it!"

Quietly, then, she asked a question that seemed odd:

"You know the history, I suppose, of the old wars between the Purples and the Greens?"

"Why, I think so. Purple was the color of the Emperors. The Greens were the faction led by the research scientists that revolted and set up the democratic Green Hall. The last Emperor, Adam the Third, abdicated two hundred years ago."

"Do you know why he abdicated?"

"No. No, the books didn't say. I used to wonder."

"I must tell you. It's important. The Emperors, you know, enjoyed despotic power. They were vastly wealthy; they commanded private space fleets, and owned whole planets, outright. They ruled with an iron cruelty. The enemies they didn't liquidate were deported to Pluto.

"An ancestor of mine, Charles Anthar, was shipped out—because of a chance remark in favor of free speech and free research, made to a man he thought a friend! The finest physicist in the System. He spent fourteen years in the cold dungeons of the Black Planet.

"On Pluto, he made a scientific discovery. The theory he worked out in his dungeon by pure mathematics. That took him nine years. Then his fellow prisoners smuggled materials to him, to build the apparatus he had planned. It was very simple, but he was five years finding the parts.

"When it was finished, he destroyed the prison guard. Sitting in his cell, he forced Adam the Third to obey his orders. If the Emperor had refused, Charles Anthar could have wrecked the solar system.

"Since, his discovery has defended the peace of the Green Hall. It is so very dangerous that only one person at a time is permitted to know it. Only this much of it has ever been put in writing—an abbreviation."

She showed him, tattooed on a white palm, the letters AKKA.

"And now you are in danger?" John Star whispered.

"I am. The Purples didn't lose their wealth and influence, you see, and they've always plotted to restore the Empire. The terrible power of AKKA is all that restrains their schemes. They want the secret, but it has always been safely kept for the Green Hall, by the descendants of Charles Anthar.

"My name is Aladoree Anthar. I had the secret from my father, six years ago, before he died. I had to give up the life that I had planned, and make a very solemn promise.

"The Purples, of course, have known about AKKA from the first. Endlessly they have conspired and bribed and murdered to get possession of it for themselves. With it, they'd be supreme, forever. Now I think Eric Ulnar has come to take it!"

"You must trust Eric!" protested John Star. "Why, he's the famous explorer—and the nephew of the Commander of the Legion!"

"That's why I think we're betrayed."

"Why, I don't see——"

"Ulnar," she said, "was the family name of the Emperors. Eric Ulnar, I believe, is the direct heir, the pretender to the throne. I don't trust him, or his scheming, plotting uncle——"

"Adam Ulnar, scheming, plotting!" John Star was outraged. "You call the Commander that?"

"I do! I think he used his wealth and influence to become Commander, so he could find where I am hidden. He sent Eric here! That ship, last night, brought the traitor reinforcements, and a way to escape with me!"

"Impossible!" gasped John Star. "Vors, perhaps, and Kimplen. But not Eric!"

"He's the leader." Her voice was cold with certainty. "Eric Ulnar slipped out of the fort last night. He was gone two hours. I think he went to communicate with his allies on the ship."

"Eric Ulnar is a hero and an officer of the Legion."

"I would trust no man named Ulnar!"

"My name is Ulnar."

"Your name—Ulnar," she whispered, shocked. "You're kin——"

"I am. I owe my commission to the Commander's generosity."

"Then I see," she said bitterly, "why you are here!"

"You are mistaken about Eric," he insisted.

"Just remember," she whipped out furiously, "that you are a traitor to the Green Hall! That you are destroying all liberty and happiness!"

With that she whirled and ran back down the old
stone stairs. He stared after her, breathless and discon-
certed. Even though he had defended Eric, he was left
with a haunting doubt. Vors and Kimplen he mistrusted
deeply. The proximity of the strange ship had alarmed
him. And he was very sorry, just now, that he had lost the
confidence of Aladoree Anthar. It would make her
harder to protect—and, besides, he liked her!

Eric Ulnar met him when he came back to the court,
and told him with a grim, sardonic smile:

"It appears, John, that Captain Otan was murdered
during the night. We've just found his body in his room."

CHAPTER THREE

Three Men of the Legion

"Strangled, apparently," said Eric Ulnar, pointing to a
swollen purple mark. In the soldierly bareness of his
quarters, the dead commander lay face upward on his
narrow cot, limbs rigid in agony, thin face contorted, eyes
protruding, mouth set in an appalling grin of terror and
pain.

Bending over the corpse, John Star discovered other
strange marks, where the skin was dry, hardened into little greenish scales.

"Look at this," he said. "Like the burn of some chemical. And that bruise—it wasn't made by a human hand.
A rope—perhaps—"

"So you're turning detective?" cut in Eric Ulnar, with
his thin, superior smile. "I must warn you that curiosity is
a very dangerous trait, John. But what's your theory?"

"Last night," he began slowly, "I saw something rather
—dreadful. I thought afterwards it was just a nightmare,
until now. A huge, purple eye, staring into my window
from the court. It must have been a foot long! It was evil
—pure evil.

"Something must have come into the court, sir. It looked
in my window. And murdered him. And left those stains.

That mark about the throat—no human hand could have made that."

"You aren't going space-happy, are you, John?" There was a little, sharp, angry edge to the amused scorn in Eric Ulnar's voice. "Anyhow, this thing happened while the old guards were on duty. I'm going to hold them for questioning." His narrow face set coldly. "John, you will arrest Kalam and Samdu and Habibula, and lock them in the old cell block under the north tower."

"Arrest them? Don't you think that's extreme, sir, before they've had a chance to speak—"

"You are presuming on our kinship, John. Please remember that I am still your officer—now in sole authority here, since Captain Otan is dead."

"Yes, sir." He subdued his haunting doubt. Aladoree *must* be wrong.

"Here are the keys to the old prison."

Each of the men he must arrest occupied a single room opening upon the court. John Star tapped on the first door, and it was opened by the rather handsome, dark-haired Legionnaire whom he had seen on the tennis court with Aladoree Anthar.

Jay Kalam was in dressing gown and slippers. His gravely thoughtful face showed weariness; yet he smiled at John Star, courteously but silently invited him in, motioned him to a seat.

It was the room of a cultured man, quietly luxurious, reserved in taste. Old-fashioned books. A few select pictures. A case of shining laboratory apparatus. An *optiphone,* now filling the room with soft music, its stereoscopic vision panel aglow with the color and motion of a play.

Jay Kalam returned to his own chair, his attention back on the drama. John Star did not like to arrest such a man for murder, but he took his duty very seriously. He must obey his officer.

"I'm sorry——" he began.

Jay Kalam stopped him with a little gesture.

"Please wait. It will soon be done."

Unable to refuse such a request, John Star sat quietly until the act was ended, and Jay Kalam turned to him with a slow dark smile, reserved and yet attentive.

"Thank you for waiting. A new record that came on

the *Scorpion*. I could not resist the temptation to see it before I went to bed. But what do you wish?"

"I'm very sorry——" began John Star. He paused, stammered, and then, seeing that the thing had to be done, went on swiftly: "Sorry, but I am ordered by Captain Ulnar to place you under arrest."

The dark eyes met his in quick surprise; there was pain in them, as if they saw some dreaded thing.

"May I ask why?" The voice was low and courteous, unsurprised.

"Captain Otan was murdered last night."

Jay Kalam stood up quickly, but did not lose self-possession.

"Murdered?" he repeated quietly, after a time. "I see. So you are taking me to Ulnar?"

"To the cells. I am sorry."

For an instant John Star thought the unarmed man was going to attack him; he stepped back, a hand going to his proton gun. But Jay Kalam smiled a hard brown smile, without amusement, and told him quietly:

"I shall go with you. A moment, to pick up a few articles of clothing. The old dungeons are not famous for comfort."

John Star nodded, and kept his hand near the needle.

Crossing the court, they descended the spiral stair to a hall cut through red volcanic rock. With his pocket light-tube, John Star found the corroded metal door; he tried it with keys Eric Ulnar had given him, and failed to open it.

"I can turn it," offered his prisoner.

John Star gave him the key; he opened the door after a little effort, gravely returned the key, and stepped through into dank darkness.

"I'm very sorry about all this," apologized John Star. "An unpleasant place, I see. But my orders——"

"Never mind that," said Jay Kalam quickly. "But remember one thing, please!" His tone was urgent. "You are a soldier of the Legion."

John Star locked the door and went after Hal Samdu.

To his astonishment, this man met him in the dress uniform of a general of the Legion, complete with every decoration ever awarded for heroism or distinction in service. While silk, gold braid, scarlet plume—his splendor was blinding.

"It came on the *Scorpion,*" Hal Samdu informed him. "Very good, don't you think? Though the shoulders are not quite——"

"I'm surprised to see you in a general's uniform."

"Of course," Hal Samdu said seriously, "I don't wear it in public—not yet. I had it made, to be ready for promotion."

"I regret it," said John Star, "but I've been ordered to place you under arrest."

"To arrest *me?*" The broad, red face showed ludicrous amusement. "What for?"

"Captain Otan has been killed."

"The Captain—dead?" He stared in blank incredulity that changed to slow anger. "You think I——"

His great fists knotted. John Star stepped aside, whipped out his proton gun.

"Stop! I'm just obeying orders."

"Well——" The big hands opened and closed convulsively. Hal Samdu looked at the menacing needle, and John Star saw simple contempt of danger in his eyes. But he stopped.

"Well——" he repeated. "If it isn't your fault—I'll go."

The third man, Giles Habibula, did not open the door when John Star knocked, but merely called out for him to enter. The massive, blue-nosed sentry of the day before, he was now sitting, comfortably unbuttoned, before a table burdened with dishes and bottles.

"Ah, come in, lad, come in," he wheezed again. "I was just eating a mortal taste of lunch before I go to bed. A blessed hard night we had, waiting for trouble in the cold.

"But draw up, lad, and have a bite with me. We got new supplies on the *Scorpion.* An agreeable change from these mortal synthetic rations. Baked ham, and preserved candied yams, and some ripe old Dutch cheese—but look it over for yourself, lad."

He nodded at the table, which, John Star thought, bore food enough for six hungry men.

"No, thank you. I've come——"

"If you won't eat, you'll surely drink. We're mortal fortunate, lad, in the matter of drink. A wine cellar left full when the fort was abandoned in the old days. Aged precious well—the best wine, I dare say, in the System. A full cellar—when I found it. Ah——"

"I must tell you that I've orders to place you under arrest."

"Arrest? Why, lad, old Giles Habibula has done no mortal harm to anybody. Not here on Mars, anyhow."

"Captain Otan has been murdered. You are to be questioned."

"You aren't jesting with poor old Giles, lad?"

"Of course not."

"Murdered!" He shook his head. "I told him he should drink with me. He lived a Spartan life, lad. Ah, it must be terrible to be cut off so! But you don't think I did it, lad?"

"Not I, surely. But my orders are to lock you in the cells."

"Those old dungeons are mortal cold and musty, lad."

"My orders——"

"I'll go with you, lad. Keep your hand away from that proton gun. Old Giles Habibula wouldn't make trouble for anybody."

"Come."

"May I eat a bite first, lad? And finish my wine?"

John Star somehow liked old Giles Habibula, for all his grossness. So he sat and watched until the dishes were clean and the three bottles empty. And then they went together to the dungeons.

Aladoree Anthar met him as he returned to the court, her face shadowed with worry and alarm.

"John Ulnar," she greeted him, and winced at the name, "where are my three loyal men?"

"I have locked Samdu and Kalam and Habibula in the old prison."

Her face was white with scorn.

"Do you think they are murderers?"

"No, I really doubt their guilt."

"Then why lock them up?"

"I must obey orders."

"Don't you see what you have done? All my loyal guard are murdered or locked up. I'm at the mercy of Ulnar—and he's your real murderer! AKKA is betrayed!"

"Eric Ulnar a murderer! You misjudge——"

"Come! I'll show him to you, a murderer and worse. He has just slipped out again. He's going back to that ship that landed last night—to his fellow traitors."

"You're mistaken. Surely——"

"Come!" she cried urgently. "Don't be blind to him."

She led him swiftly along ramps and parapets to the eastern flank of the old fortress, up to a tower platform.

"Look! The ship—where it came from, I don't understand. And Eric Ulnar, your hero of the Legion!"

Age-worn precipices and tumbled red boulder-fields fell away from the foot of the wall to the lurid plain. There, not a mile from them, lay the strange ship.

John Star had seen nothing like it. Colossal, so vast it stunned his mind. Intricate and strange. All shining, jet-black metal.

The familiar space-craft of the System were all spindle-shaped, trimly tapering; all of them silvered mirror-like to reduce heat radiation and absorption in space; all comparatively small, the largest liners not four hundred feet long.

This machine had a spidery confusion of projecting parts—beams, braced surfaces, vast, wing-like vanes, massive, jointed metal levers—all jutting from the hull, which was a gigantic black globe. It was incredibly huge; the metal skids on which it rested lay along the red desert for a full half mile, the sphere was a thousand feet thick.

"The ship!" whispered the girl. "And Eric Ulnar, the traitor!"

She pointed, and John Star saw the man's tiny figure, scrambling down the slope—dwarfed to the merest insect in the shadow of that machine, so huge and strange and queerly black.

"Now do you believe?"

"Something is wrong," he admitted reluctantly. "Something . . . I'm going after him! I can overtake him, make him tell me what's going on. Even if he is my officer."

He plunged recklessly down the stairway from the old tower.

CHAPTER FOUR

"Well, John, I Am a Traitor!"

The black mass of the strange flier filled the eastern sky, the central globe looming like a dark moon fallen in the red desert. The black skids, lying for half a mile upon the debris of boulders they had crushed, were like tall metal walls. In the shadow of that incredible machine, the toiling man ahead was shrunken to the merest human atom.

Midway to the black hull—almost under the top of the dark wing that covered an eighth of the sky—he still had not looked back. John Star was within forty yards of him, breathing so hard he feared the other would hear. He gripped his proton gun, shouting:

"Halt! I want to talk to you."

Eric Ulnar stopped, looking back in astonishment. He made a slight movement as if to draw the weapon in his own belt, but stopped when he saw John Star's face.

"Come here," John Star ordered. He waited, getting his breath, and trying to control the nervous tremor of his weapon, while his famous kinsman walked slowly back, with sharp annoyance on that narrow, weak, and handsome face.

"Well, John." Eric Ulnar gave him a tolerant, superior smile. "You're exceeding your duty again. I'm afraid you're too zealous to make a successful Legionnaire. My uncle will be sorry to hear of your failure."

"Eric," said John Star, surprised a little at his own deadly calm, "I'm going to ask you some questions. If I don't like the answers, I'm afraid I'll have to kill you."

White fury mounted to Eric Ulnar's girlish, passionate face.

"John, you'll be court-martialed for this!"

"Probably I shall. But now I want to know where this ship came from. And why you are slipping out here."

"How should I know where it's from? Nothing like it was ever seen in the System before. Simple curiosity was enough, John, to bring me out here."

Eric Ulnar tossed his bare, golden head, and smiled mockingly.

"I'm afraid, Eric, that you are planning treason to the Green Hall," said John Star quietly. "I think you know why this flier came, and why Captain Otan was killed. Unless you can convince me that I am wrong, I'm going to kill you, release the three men I locked up, and defend the girl. What have you to say?"

Eric Ulnar looked up at the great black vane above them, and smiled again, insolently bold.

"Well, John," he said deliberately, "I am a traitor."

"Eric!" John Star was dazed with shock and anger. "You admit it!"

"Of · course, John. I've never planned to be anything else—if you call it treason to take what is mine by right. I suppose you don't know you have imperial blood in your veins, John—your education seems to have been neglected. But you have.

"I am the rightful Emperor of the Sun, John. In a very short time I shall take possession of my throne. As a prince of the blood, I had hoped that you might claim a high place under me. But I doubt, John, that you will live to enjoy the rewards of the revolution. You are too independent."

"Just what have you done?" demanded John Star. "And where did this flier come from?"

He kept his eyes, and his menacing weapon, fixed on the other.

"That ship came from the planet of Barnard's Star, John. You've heard, I suppose, of the dying men we brought back from the expedition? Heard what they babble of? They aren't as insane as men think they are, John. Most of the things they talk about are real. Those things are going to help me crush the Green Hall, John."

"You brought back—allies?"

Eric Ulnar smiled mockingly at the horror in his tone.

"I did, John. You see, the masters of the planet we found—they are as intelligent as men, though not at all human—the things we found need iron. It doesn't occur on their world—and it's priceless to them—for magnetic instruments, electrical equipment, alloys, a thousand things.

"So I made an alliance with them, John . . .

"They sent this ship, with some of their weapons—

they have fighting machines that would surprise you, John; their scientific achievements are really remarkable. They sent this ship to help crush the Green Hall, and restore the Empire. In return, we agreed to load the ship with iron.

"Iron is cheap. We may do it. But I rather think we'll wipe them out, after we have AKKA, and the Purple Hall is safely in power again. They're not too pleasant to have about. Worse than you might imagine. Those insane men—yes, John, I'm sure we should destroy them, after we get the secret weapon.

"The girl must have told you about AKKA, John?"

"She did! And I thought—I trusted you, Eric!"

"So she suspects, already! Then we must get the chains on her, before she has a chance to use AKKA. But I suppose Vors and Kimplen have her safe, by now."

"You . . . traitor!" whispered John Star.

"Of course, John. We're taking her away. I suppose we'll have to kill her, after she's told us about her little secret gadget. Too bad she's such a luscious beauty."

John Star stood paralyzed with unbelieving shock, and Eric Ulnar smiled.

"I'm a traitor, John—by your definition. But you're something worse. You are a fool, John. I brought you along because I had to have a fourth man, to complete the guard. And because my uncle insisted that you must have a chance in life. He appears to have an exaggerated idea of your ability."

A sudden, high-pitched, girlish giggle burst from Eric Ulnar.

"You've been a fool, John. If you want to know how big a fool, just look up above you." And the handsome golden head made a mocking little bow.

John Star had kept his eyes on the other, expecting some ruse to distract him. Glancing warily upward now, he saw his danger. Some fifty feet above him swung a sort of gondola, a car of bright black metal suspended on cables from a great, jointed boom that reached out of the flier's confusion of titanic ebon mechanisms.

Inside it, he glimpsed—*something!*

Beyond the black sides of the gondola he could not see it clearly. But the little he did see made the short hair rise on his neck. It sent up his spine the cold, electric tingle of involuntary horror. His breath was checked, his heart pounding, his whole body tense and quivering. The merest glimpse of the thing set off all his danger-instincts —the very presence of it roused primeval horror.

Yet, in the shadows of the queer black car, he could see little enough. A bulging, glistening surface, translucently greenish, wet, slimy, palpitating with sluggish life —the body surface of something gross and vast and utterly strange.

Staring malignly from behind the shielding plates, he met—an eye! Long, ovoid, shining. A well of cold purple flame, veiled with ancient wisdom, baleful with pure evil.

And that was all. That bulging, torpidly heaving green surface. And that monstrous eye. He could see no more. But that was enough to set off in him every reaction of primal fear.

Fear held him frozen. It stopped his breath and squeezed his heart. It poured the choking dust of terror down his throat. It washed his rigid limbs with icy sweat. He broke free at last and threw up his weapon.

But the half-seen thing in the gondola struck first. Reddish vapor puffed from the side of the swinging car. Something brushed his shoulder, a mere cold breath. And then a red avalanche of unendurable pain hurled him to the sand. Black oblivion brought mercy.

When consciousness came back, he contrived to sit up. He was miserably sick, his body trembling and wet with perspiration, his arm and shoulder still paralyzed and aflame with scarlet agony. Dizzy, still half-blinded, he looked anxiously about.

Eric Ulnar had vanished, and at first he couldn't find that black gondola. But the Cyclopean ship still loomed monstrous against the greenish Martian sky. He searched its maze of vanes and struts and levers, until at last he saw the swinging car.

That titanic boom had reached out, over the fort. The car was just rising above the red walls when he found it. Swiftly the cables were drawn in. The mile-long lever telescoped itself, and the gondola was swallowed through a huge valve in that black, spherical hull.

It must have picked up Eric Ulnar, he thought, and then swung over the fort to take aboard Vors and Kimplen, with Aladoree. The girl, he realized, heart utterly sick, was already taken inside the enemy machine.

Very soon it rose. Cataracts of green flame thundered

from cavernous jets. Endless ebon wings tilted and spread to catch the tenuous air of Mars. The ground trembled under him as those vast black skids lifted their burden fom the yellow desert. A monstrous, evil bird, the black machine lifted obliquely across the greenish sky, into the violet zenith.

The noise of it beat about him, mauled him with raging seas of sound. A furnace-hot wind whipped up curtains of yellow sand, dried his sweat, stung his eyes and burned his skin.

He watched it shrink to a grotesque black insect. The green flame faded; the thunder died. It dwindled, grew dim with distance, at last was lost.

He lay in the sand, ill, agonized, and bitter with self-reproach. It was late afternoon before he could rise, still weak and faint. His shoulder and upper arm, he found, were strangely burned, as if some mordant fluid had been squirted on them. The skin was stiff, lifeless, covered with hard, greenish scales.

The corpse of Captain Otan had been marked like that. And the eye of that greenish, heaving monster in the black gondola—it was like the nightmare eye that had stared through his window! Yes, *something* from the ship had killed Otan.

Driven by a faint spark of irrational hope, he staggered back up the hill to the old fort, to search the inhabited section. It was silent, utterly deserted. Aladoree was really gone, and AKKA lost. Aladoree, so freshly lovely, was in the hands of Eric Ulnar and those monstrous beings from the dark planet of Barnard's Star.

Only black self-accusation remained to haunt him. Admiration of his famous kinsman had blinded him too long. A misplaced sense of a Legionnaire's duty had driven him to actual treason. However unwittingly, he had helped betray the Green Hall and the Legion.

CHAPTER FIVE

The "Purple Dream"

"Ah, lad, it's time you thought of us!" wheezed Giles Habibula plaintively from the gloom behind the bar of the old prison. "Here we've been, life knows how long, locked up in the cold and dark of a mortal tomb! My old bones will ache with this wicked damp, lad.

"Ah, but I'm famishing, lad. Faint with mortal hunger. How could you leave us so long, lad, without a blessed bite to eat? Mortal me, lad, have you never known the gnawing agony of starvation?"

John Star was unlocking the rusty door. Here was one thing that he could do to repair the traitorous work of his kinsman—though the greater deed, the rescue of Aladoree and her mighty secret, was all but hopeless.

"Can you bring us some broth, lad?" whined the old Legionnaire. "And a bottle of old wine from the cellar? Something to revive us and give us strength for stronger victuals?"

"I'm going to turn you out," said John Star, adding bitterly: "That much I can do, to make up for the fool I've been!"

"You must help us creep out, lad, and up to the blessed sun. Don't forget we're mortal weak. Ah, me, we're starving, lad. Not a bite to eat since the day you locked us up. Not a morsel, lad, for all that mortal time. Though I cut off the uppers of my boots, and chewed them, for the bit of precious nourishment in the leather."

"Ate your boots? Why, it was just this morning that I brought you here!"

"Don't jest with poor old Giles Habibula, lad! Don't be so heartless, when he's had nothing but his blessed boots to eat, rotting in a dungeon for mortal weeks. Ah, and wasting his precious skill trying to pick a lock that's ruined with wicked rust!"

"Weeks? It wasn't ten hours ago! And I let you eat

all that breakfast in your room, just before—enough to
provision a fleet!"

"Don't torture me with your jokes, lad! I'm starved to
a blessed bag of bones! For life's sake, lad, help old Giles
Habibula out into the sunshine, and find him a drop of
wine, to warm his poor old blood again."

The rusty bolt at last shot back, the door creaked open.
Giles Habibula waddled out, Hal Samdu stalked behind
him, and Jay Kalam walked deliberately.

"We are free?" asked the latter.

"Yes. The least I can do. I've been a total idiot! I'll
never be able to undo the crime I helped Eric Ulnar carry
out—though I'm going to spend the rest of my life trying
to!"

"What has happened?" Taut anxiety edged Jay Kalam's
voice.

"Eric Ulnar was a traitor, as Aladoree thought. After
I had locked up you three, he had the way clear. The
ship—the one that landed last night—came from that
planet of Barnard's Star. Monstrous creatures aboard,
allies of Eric's—it was one of them that murdered Captain
Otan. He's promised them a ship-load of iron, to pay for
their part. Iron is precious to them. The ship took Eric
away, and Aladoree. I was—hit. Can just now walk
again."

"It's the Purples?"

"Yes. As Aladoree thought. The plot is to restore the
Empire, with Eric on the throne."

They entered the courtyard, bright with the afternoon
sun. Giles Habibula stood with his thick hands stretched
out in front of him, staring in amazement. He fingered his
heavy-jowled face, slapping his bulging paunch.

"For life's sake, lad!" he gasped. "Tell me, was that
no joke? Is this the same mortal day? . . . All that suffering! . . . My blessed boots!"

"Forget your belly, Giles!" shouted Hal Samdu, the
slow and homely giant; and he turned to John Star with
helpless anger on his broad red face.

"That Eric Ulnar——" He was panting, incoherent in
his rage. "Aladoree—he has taken her, you say?"

"Yes. I don't know where."

"We'll find out where!" he promised savagely. "And
bring her back! And Eric Ulnar——"

"Of course." It was the low, calm voice of Jay Kalam.

"Of course we shall attempt her rescue, at any risk. The safety of the System demands it, if it were not our simple duty to Aladoree. The first thing, I suppose, is to find where she is—which won't be easy."

"We must get away from here," added John Star. "Is there a radio?"

"A little ultra-wave transmitter. We must report to Legion headquarters, at once."

John Star winced, and added bitterly:

"Yes, of course. Report what a fool Eric Ulnar made of me!"

"Don't blame yourself," Jay Kalam urged him. "Others, higher up, were deceived, too, or he wouldn't have been sent here. You could have done little alone. Your only guilt was obedience to your officer. Forget your regrets, and let's undo the harm!"

"But I can't help feeling——"

"Come on. We'll send a message to the base—if they didn't smash the transmitter before they left!"

But the little transmitter, located in a small tower room, had been systematically and utterly destroyed. Tubes were smashed, condensers hammered to shapeless metal, wires cut to bits, battery jars emptied and broken.

"Ruined!" he said.

"We must repair it!" cried John Star.

But with all his optimistic determination, he soon had to admit the impossibility of the task.

"Can't be done. But there must be something. The supply ship?"

"Won't be back for a year," said Jay Kalam. "They came seldom, to avoid attracting attention."

"But when the station here remains silent, won't they know something is wrong?"

"It was only for emergencies. We had never used it. The signals might have been picked up, and located. We depended on absolute secrecy—together with the power of AKKA itself. And of course Aladoree didn't keep her weapon set up, for fear it would be stolen—that was what gave the traitors time to take her. We weren't prepared for treason."

"Could a man walk out?"

"Impossible. No water in the desert. This is the most isolated spot on Mars. We wanted no accidental visitors."

"But there must be *something*——"

"We must eat, lad," insisted Giles Habibula. "Even if it is the same mortal day. Nothing like good food to quicken the mind. A good supper, lad, with a bottle of the old wine to wash it down, and you'll have us away from here this blessed night!"

And, indeed, it was while he sipped a glass from the old man's precious cellar that inspiration came.

"We've light-tubes!" he cried. "We can step up the output—it doesn't matter if they soon burn out. Flash a distress signal. Against the dark background of the desert, somebody would see it from space!"

"We'll try that," agreed Jay Kalam. "Might not be a Legion cruiser, but it would have a transmitter to call one."

"Ah, lad, what did I tell you? What did poor old Giles Habibula tell you? Didn't a drop of wine sharpen your brain?"

When the green afterglow was gone, and the cold, clear dark of the Martian night crashed down on the red landscape, John Star was ready on the platform of the north tower, his pocket light-tube in hand, its coils rewound to increase its brilliance a thousand-fold.

Into the purple, star-shot night he flashed it, forming again and again the code letters of the Legion signal of distress. The tube burned his hand, as the electrodes fused and the over-loaded coils went dead. But Jay Kalam was ready with another, its potential stepped up in the same way; he kept flashing the silent appeal for aid.

It seemed incredible to him, as he stood there, that Aladoree had been with him that morning on the same platform. Incredible, when now she was lost somewhere in the black gulf of space, perhaps ten million miles away. With a little ache in his heart, he pictured her as she had stood—slender and straight and cleanly molded; eyes candid and cool and gray; sunlit hair a splendor of brown and red and gold.

His determination to restore her to safety could hardly be less, he knew, were she just an ordinary bit of humanity, not the keeper of the System's priceless treasure.

It was long after midnight when the last light-tube went out.

Then, until the lemon-green dawn, they waited on the platform, scanning the star-sifted purple, anxious for the blue rocket-exhausts that would brake the descending ship. But they saw no moving thing, save the faint tiny spark of

Phobos, rising in the west and creeping swiftly eastward.

Giles Habibula was with them, lying on his back, peacefully snoring. He woke with the dawn, and went down to the kitchen. Presently he called up that breakfast was ready. The others were about to leave the tower in despair, when they heard the roaring rockets of a ship landing.

A long silver craft, an arrow of white flame in the morning sun, it dropped across the fort, pushing ahead the blue flare of its rockets.

"A Legion cruiser!" John Star exulted. "The latest, fastest type."

His blue eyes keener than they appeared, Hal Samdu read the name on its side:

"Purple—something—she's the *Purple Dream!*"

"Purple Dream?" echoed Jay Kalam. "That's the flagship of the Legion fleet. The ship of the Commander himself!"

"If it's the Commander's ship," John Star said slowly, his high spirits falling, "I'm afraid it won't bring us much good. Commander Adam Ulnar is Eric Ulnar's uncle. The real leader of the Purples.

"It was Adam Ulnar who sent Eric on that interstellar expedition and Adam Ulnar who found that Aladoree was hidden here, and sent Eric to be commanding officer of her guard. I'm afraid we can't expect much but trouble from the Commander of the Legion."

CHAPTER SIX

The Empty Throne

The four of them went out of the old gate. Giles Habibula still eating morsels he had stuffed into his pockets, and down the red boulder slope to the *Purple Dream*, lying amid the yellow dunes of the sand desert.

Her officer, a man too old for his rank, thin and stern, with a jaw like a trap, appeared in the open air-lock.

"You flashed a signal of distress?"

"We did," said John Star.

"What's your difficulty?"

"We must leave here. We have an urgent matter to report to the Green Hall."

"What's that?"

"It's confidential."

"Confidential?" the officer repeated, looking down with frosty eyes.

"Very."

"Come aboard, then, to my stateroom."

They climbed the accommodation ladder to the great valves, and followed him down the narrow deck into his cabin. Closing the door, he turned on them with sharp impatience.

"You need keep nothing back from me. I'm Captain Madlok of the *Purple Dream.* I enjoy Commander Ulnar's full confidence. I know that you men were stationed here to guard a priceless treasure. What account have you to make of it?"

All his companions hesitated, Jay Kalam habitually taciturn, Hal Samdu, slow with words, Giles Habibula overly cautious. John Star spoke out bitterly:

"That treasure is lost!"

"Lost!" snapped Madlok. "You've lost AKKA?"

John Star nodded, sick at heart. "A traitor was sent here——"

"I don't care for alibis!" rapped Madlok. "You admit that you have betrayed your trust."

"Aladoree Anthar has been kidnapped," John Star said stiffly, Madlok's stern face recalling his lectures in military courtesy. "I suggest, sir, that she must be rescued. And I believe, sir, that the news should be communicated to the Green Hall."

Madlok's voice had a brittle snap: "I shall take care of any reports necessary."

"Sir, the search must begin at once," said John Star, urgently.

"I'm accepting no orders from you, if you please. And I shall take the four of you at once to Commander Ulnar, at his estate on Phobos. You can report your failure to him."

"May I go back, sir, just a few minutes?" appealed Giles Habibula. "Some things I must bring——"

"What things?"

"Just a few mortal cases of old wine, sir."

"What! Wine! We're taking off at once."

"If you will pardon me, sir," gravely offered Jay Kalam, "our mission gives us a peculiar position in the Legion, regardless of military rank. We are not under your command."

"Your signals were seen from Commander Ulnar's private observatory on Phobos," snapped Madlok. "Inferring—and rightly—that you had betrayed your trust and lost AKKA, he sent me to bring you to the Purple Hall. I trust that you will condescend to obey the Commander of the Legion. We take off in twenty seconds!"

John Star had heard of the Ulnar estate on Phobos, for the magnificent splendor of the Purple Hall was famous throughout the System.

The tiny inner moon of Mars, a bit of rock not twenty miles in diameter, had always been held by the Ulnars, by right of reclamation. Equipping the barren, stony mass with an artificial gravity system, synthetic atmosphere, and "seas" of man-made water, planting forests and gardens in soil manufactured from chemicals and disintegrated stone, the planetary engineers had transformed it into a splendid private estate.

For his residence, Adam Ulnar had obtained the architects' plans for the Green Hall, the System's colossal capitol building, and had duplicated it room for room. But he had built on a scale an inch larger to the foot, using, not green glass, but purple, the color of the Empire.

The *Purple Dream* dropped upon the landing stage atop the square, titanic tower. Beyond the edge of the platform, when they disembarked, John Star could see the roofs of the building's great wings, glistening expanses of purple stretching out across the vivid green of lawn and garden. Beyond, the woods and hills of the tiny world appeared to drop with an increasing, breath-taking abruptness, so that he felt as if he were perched insecurely on the top of a great green ball, afloat in a chasm of starry purple-blue.

They dropped in an elevator three thousand feet, escorted by Madlok and half a dozen alert armed men from the cruiser, and entered an amazing room.

Corresponding to the Green Hall's Council Chamber, it was five hundred feet square, arched with a tremendous dome. The lofty vault and columned walls were illuminated with colored lights to secure effects of ineffable vastness and splendor.

In the center of the floor, all grouped in a tiny-seeming space, were a thousand seats, corresponding to the seats of the Council of the Green Hall—empty. Above them, on a high dais, stood a magnificent gem-canopied throne of purple crystal—vacant. On its seat lay the old crown and sceptre of the Emperors—waiting.

They marched, astonished and awed, across the vast floor, under the whispering vault, and around the dais. Behind the throne they entered a small room, beyond a guarded door. There Adam Ulnar, Commander of the Legion of Space, master of all this splendor and the immense wealth and power it represented, was sitting at a simple table.

Though twice Eric Ulnar's age and almost twice his weight, Adam Ulnar was as handsome as his nephew. Square-shouldered, erect, he wore a plain Legion uniform, without insignia to show his rank. The calm strength of his face—nose prominent; mouth firm; blue eyes deepset, wide apart, steady—contrasted with the reckless girlish weakness of Eric's narrow face. His long hair, nearly white, lent him the same distinction that Eric had from his flowing yellow locks.

John Star, to his surprise, felt an immediate instinctive admiration for this man of his own blood, so generous to an unknown relative—but now, it seemed, a traitor to the Legion he commanded.

"The men, Commander," Madlok reported, briefly, "who lost AKKA."

Adam Ulnar looked at them, without surprise, a faint smile on his distinguished face.

"So you were the guard of Aladoree Anthar?" he said, his voice well-modulated, pleasant. "Your names?"

John Star named his companions. "And I am John Ulnar."

Smiling again, the Commander stood up behind the table.

"John Ulnar? A kinsman of mine, I believe?"

"So I understand."

He stood still, coldly unsmiling; Adam Ulnar came around the table to greet him, warmly courteous.

"I'll see you alone, John," he said, and nodded to Madlok, who withdrew with the others.

Then he turned to John Star, urged cordially:

"Sit down, John. I wish now that we had met sooner, and under less awkward circumstances. You made a brilliant record at the Academy, John. I've a career planned for you, equally brilliant."

John Star, remaining on his feet, his face taut, said stiffly:

"I suppose I should thank you, Commander Ulnar, for my education and my commission in the Legion. A few days ago I should have done so very gratefully. Now it seems that I was intended merely for a dupe and a tool!"

"I wouldn't say that, John," Adam Ulnar protested softly. "It's true that events did not take place just as I had planned—Eric is taking affairs too much into his own hands. But I had you placed under his direct command. I was planning——"

"Under Eric!" John Star burst out hotly. "A traitor! Much as I once admired him, that's what he is. Obeying his orders, I helped betray the Legion and the Green Hall."

"Traitor is a harsh word to use, John, just because of a political difference."

"Political difference!" Shocked outrage shook John Star's voice. "Do you admit to me openly that you are false to your own trust as an officer of the Legion? You, the Commander himself!"

Adam Ulnar smiled at him, warmly, kindly, and a little bit amused.

"Do you realize, John, that I am by far the most wealthy man in the System? That I am easily the most powerful and influential? Doesn't it occur to you that loyalty to the Purple Hall might be more to your advantage than support of the democracy?"

"Are you trying, sir, to make a traitor out of *me?*"

"Please, John, don't use that word. The form of government I stand for has a historic sanction far older than your silly ideas of equality and democracy. And, after all, John, you are an Ulnar. If you will consider just your own personal advantage, I can give you wealth, position, and power, which your present impractical democratic attitude will never earn for you."

"I will not consider it."

John Star was still standing stiffly in front of the table. Adam Ulnar came around beside him to take his arm persuasively.

"John," he said, "I like you. Even when you were very small—I suppose you don't remember when we were ever together—you displayed qualities I approve. Your courage, and that stubborn determination which is about to keep us apart now, was one of them—something left out of my nephew's disposition.

"I've been interested in your career, John—I've followed it more closely than you ever knew. Your progress at the Academy—everything you have done—was reported to me in detail.

"I had no son of my own, John. And the family of Ulnar isn't very large—just Eric, the son of my unfortunate elder brother, and you and I. Eric is twelve years older than you are, John. He was pampered in his youth. He was always told that one day he would be Emperor of the Sun; he was spoiled.

"And I don't quite like the results, John. Eric is weak; he's headstrong, and yet a coward. This alliance with the creatures from the planet of the Runaway Star was a coward's device—he made it without my knowledge, because he feared my own plans for the revolution would fail.

"Anyhow, with you, I tried a different way. I put you in the Academy and left you ignorant of your high destiny. I wanted you to learn to depend on yourself, to develop some character and resource and courage of your own.

"This last experience has been a sort of test, John. And it has proved, I think, that you have everything I had hoped for. Besides, I like you, John."

"Yes?" said John Star, coldly, and he waited.

"The Empire is going to be restored. Nothing can halt our plans, now, John. The Green Hall is doomed. But I don't want to set a weakling back on the throne. Ulnar is an old name, a proud name, John. Our ancestors paid for the Empire, with blood and toil and brains. I don't want our name disgraced, as such a man as Eric might disgrace it."

"You mean——" cried John Star, astounded. "By all this, you mean that I——"

"That's it, my boy!" Adam Ulnar was smiling at him with pleasure on his proud, distinguished face, and a fond hope. "That's it. I don't want Eric to be Emperor of the Sun, when the Green Hall surrenders.

"The new Emperor shall be you!"

John Star stood motionless, staring dumfounded into that fine strong face, with its crown of snowy hair.

"Yes, you shall be Emperor, John," Adam Ulnar repeated softly, warmly smiling. "Your claim is really better than Eric's. You are in the direct line of descent. I have proof."

John Star shook off his hand then, and moved back a step, laughing incredulously.

"What's the matter, John?" The tall Commander seemed deeply concerned. "You don't——"

"No!" John Star caught his breath, and spoke decisively. "I don't want to be Emperor. If I were ever Emperor, I'd abdicate. I'd restore the Green Hall."

Adam Ulnar went slowly back behind the table, and sat down heavily, wearily. A long time he sat silently, watching John Star's tense, determined figure with a frown of painful thought.

"I see," he said at last. "I see you're in earnest. An unfortunate result of your training, which I had not anticipated. I suppose it's too late to change you, now."

"I'm sure it is."

Again Adam Ulnar mused awhile, and then he stood up suddenly, his lean face imperious with decision.

"I hope you understand the situation, John. Our plans are going ahead. If you won't be Emperor, Eric will. Perhaps, with my advice, he won't do too badly. Anyhow, the Green Hall is doomed. I suppose, with your foolish attitude, you'll be against us?"

"I will!" John Star promised warmly. "I hope for nothing more than a chance to smash your crooked schemes."

Adam Ulnar nodded; for an instant he almost smiled.

"I knew you would." The family pride rang briefly in his sad, slow voice. "And that means, John—I'll be as honest with you as you have been with me—that means that you must spend your life in prison. Unless it becomes necessary to kill you. I have far too much confidence in your ability and your determination to set you at liberty."

"Thank you," said John Star, his tone more friendly than he intended.

Something softened the proud authority of the old Commander's face.

"Good-bye, John. I'm sorry we must part, this way."

He laid his hand a moment on John Star's shoulder,

and showed a sudden concern at his involuntary shudder of pain.

"You've been hurt, John?"

"Some weapon from the black ship. It made a greenish burn."

"Oh, the red gas!" The Commander was suddenly very grave. "Open your tunic, and let me see. The stuff is believed to be an air-borne virus, really, though the bio-chemical reports brought back by the expedition are in-complete and extremely confusing. The effects of it are rather distressing, but my experts in planetary medicine have worked out a treatment. Turn, and let me see . . . You must go right to the hospital, John, but I think we can catch it in time."

"Thank you," said John Star, less stiffly—for he remembered terrifying rumors of men insane and rotting alive from that red gas.

"I'm sorry, my boy, that I'll never be able to do more for you. I'm really sorry that you choose to go to prison from the hospital—not to the empty throne in the Purple Hall."

CHAPTER SEVEN

Giles Habibula's Higher Calling

In a hospital room in the south wing of the colossal Purple Hall, a gruffly capable, tight-mouthed doctor washed John Star's injury with a blue, palely luminescent solution, cov-ered it with a thick salve, bound it and made him go to bed. Two days later the old skin began to peel off in hard, greenish flakes, leaving new healthy flesh beneath it.

"Good," said the laconic physician, bending to examine him. "Not even a scar. You're lucky."

John Star practised one of the wrestling holds he had learned in the academy. He walked out of the room in the doctor's clothing, leaving him gagged and bound, furious but unharmed.

Four men in Legion uniform met him at the door, armed, unsurprised, and warily courteous.

"This way, please, John Ulnar, if you are ready now to go to the prison."

With a taut little smile, John Star nodded silently.

The prison was a huge space, square and lofty, beneath the north wing of the Purple Hall. Its walls were white metal, shining and impregnable. The triple doors were massive, sliding slabs of armor plate, with guards in the short halls between. The mechanism permitted only one door to open at a time, so two always sealed the way to freedom.

The cell block stood in the center of that great room, a double tier of big, barred cages, partitioned with sheet metal. Each cell had a hard, narrow bunk, and the barest necessary facilities for a single occupant. One guard was always on watch, pacing endlessly around the block of cells.

John Star, locked in alone, threw himself hopelessly on the bunk. His heart was set on escape. For the Legion, under Adam Ulnar, would get no orders to attempt the rescue of Aladoree. The Green Hall, he realized bitterly, wouldn't even be informed that AKKA was lost.

But how escape? How leave the locked cell? How evade the sentry outside—who carried only a club, lest some prisoner snatch his weapon? How pass the triple doors, with guards between? How get through the endless, labyrinthine corridors of the Purple Hall, a veritable fortress? How finally get away from the tiny planet, which was virtually a private empire of Adam Ulnar, policed by his loyal retainers? How accomplish the sheer impossible?

He heard a wheedling voice from the next cell:

"Ah, have you no heart, man? We've been locked in this evil place a blessed time, on bread and water, or precious little more. Is your heart of stone, man? Surely you can bring us something more for supper. Just an extra morsel, to edge our appetite for the regular prison fare. A thick steak with mushroom sauce, say; and a hot mince pie for each one of us. Just to give us an appetite."

"An appetite, you bag of tallow?" retorted the sentry, good-naturedly, walking past. "You eat more now than seven men."

"Of course I eat," came the whining plaint. "What else can a man do, a devoted old soldier of the Legion, rotting in this black dungeon, accused of murder and betrayal of duty and life knows what other crimes he didn't do?

"Ah, come, man, and bring me a bottle of wine. Just one blessed bottle. It'll bring a bit of warmth into a poor old soldier, against the cold of these iron walls. It'll help me forget the court-martial that's coming, and the lethal chamber beyond it—life knows they mean to kill the three of us!

"How can you be so heartless, man? How can you re-fuse one little drop of happiness to a man already doomed and as good as dead? Come, for life's sake! Ah, just one bottle, man, for poor, starved, beaten, condemned old Giles Habibula——"

"Enough! Keep quiet! I bring you all I can. Six bottles, you've already had today! No more, the warden said. At that, I never knew such generosity! It's only by the special order of the Commander himself that you get a drop. And no more talking, now! That's regulations."

John Star was glad to hear again of his companions, though it was no good news that they were waiting trial. Adam Ulnar would be ruthless with these loyal men, whose real crime was only the knowledge of his treason.

He still lay hopeless on the narrow cot, when a low, cautious tapping on the metal partition by his head abruptly recalled him from his apathy of despair. For the muted rapping formed letters, in the Legion code:

"W-H-O?"

Quickly, cautiously, he replied: "J U-L-N-A-R."

"J K-A-L-A-M."

He waited for the sentry to pass again, and tapped: "E-S-C-A-P-E?"

"C-H-A-N-C-E."

"H-O-W?"

"G-U-A-R-D-S C-L-U-B."

For the most of a day and a night John Star watched that club, as it passed at regular intervals outside the bars. A simple, eighteen-inch stick of wood, the grip taped, the slender part above wrapped with green-enameled wire, for reinforcement. He did not see how it could be very useful, but evidently it was part of some plan for escape conceived by Jay Kalam's deliberate, analytic mind.

Each guard was locked in the great room with them four hours at a time, pacing around the cell block, reporting through a speaking tube at fifteen-minute intervals.

Their habits differed. The first, good-natured man carried the club safely in his farther hand. The next walked a precise, cautious beat, well out of reach. The third was not so careful, swinging the club by a leather thong, sometimes from one wrist, sometimes the other. He would swing it sometime, John Star thought, within a foot of the bars. He waited, unobtrusively alert, until the guard was changed again. And his chance had not yet come.

Again the good-natured man. And the precise, cautious man.

Then, again, the one who swung the club. John Star waited an hour, sprawled on the cot with gloom on his face, aimlessly picking the lint from his blanket—and the chance did come.

Every minutest motion of it he had planned, rehearsed in his mind. He was keyed up, ready; his trained body reacted with lightning quickness. He sprang, soundlessly, when the club began its swing. His arm slipped through the bars. His straining fingers snapped around the wood. He braced knee and shoulder against the bars. His arm came back.

It was all done before the guard could turn his head.

The leathern thong on his wrist jerked him against the cell; his skull struck the bars; he went down silently.

John Star slipped the thong over his limp hand, whispering:

"Jay! I have the club!"

"I hoped you might," spoke Jay Kalam, quietly, quickly, from the cell to his right. "If you will please hold it out to Giles—"

"Outside here, lad!" The fearful, wheezing gasp came from his left. "Quick, for life's sake!"

He thrust the club back through the bars, felt Giles Habibula's fingers grasp it.

"Shall I search him?" he whispered. "For keys?"

"He had none," said Jay Kalam. "They knew this might happen. We must depend on Giles."

"My father was an inventor of locks," came the absent nasal whine from the cell on the left. "I learned a higher calling. Giles Habibula was not always a crippled old soldier in the Legion. In his nimbler days . . ."

The voice drifted away. John Star restrained his curiosity, waiting silently. There was nothing else to do. In the next cell, Giles Habibula was busy. His breath became audible, panting. John Star could sometimes hear a fearful muttering:

"Mortal minutes! . . . This wicked wire! . . . Life's precious sake! . . . Ah, poor old Giles . . ."

"Hurry, Giles!" implored Hal Samdu, from the cell beyond. "Hurry!"

There were tiny, metallic sounds.

"We've another five minutes." Jay Kalam's voice was calm and low. "Then the guard's report is due."

The sentry groaned. John Star silently restored him to unconsciousness with a trick he had learned at the Academy—one quick blow with the edge of his open hand.

His door swung open. He stepped out to join Giles Habibula. The short and massive body of the old Legionnaire seemed to quake with apprehension, but his thick hands were oddly sure and steady. Already he was feverishly busy at the door of Jay Kalam's cell, with a bit of twisted green wire—the winding which had reinforced the club.

"Poor old Giles wasn't always a lame and useless soldier in the Legion, lad," he wheezed abstractedly. "Things were different when he was young and bold—before mortal disaster overtook him, back on Venus, and he had to join the blessed Legion——"

That door let out Jay Kalam; the next gave freedom to Hal Samdu.

Breathless, John Star whispered, "Now what?"

They had four minutes, before the guard would fail to report. The great room that housed the cell-block was massively metal-walled, windowless. It had one opening —with armed men waiting between the three locked doors across the single passage.

"Up!" said Jay Kalam, as urgently as he ever spoke. "On top of the cells."

John Star swarmed up the bars. The others swiftly followed, Giles Habibula puffing, hauled by John Star from above, pushed by Hal Samdu beneath. They reached the metal net that covered the second tier of cells, the white-painted metal ceiling still fifteen feet above.

"Now!" whispered Jay Kalam. "The ventilator."

He pointed to the heavy metal grating in the ceiling above, from which a cool draft struck them.

"Your part, Hal! If your strength was ever needed, it is now."

"Lift me!" cried the giant, great hands ready.

They lifted him.

Puffing Giles Habibula and Jay Kalam stood on the netting, John Star, lightest of the four, on their shoulders, while huge Hal Samdu stood upon his.

The ventilator grille was strong, though it had been placed where men were not likely to reach it. Hal Samdu's immense hands closed about its bars; he strained; John Star heard mighty muscles cracking. His breath came in short, laboring gasps.

"I can't——he sobbed. "Not this way!"

"We've one minute longer, perhaps," Jay Kalam told him softly.

The giant lifted himself from John Star's shoulders, and doubled his body, planting one foot on each side of the grating, hanging by his arms.

"Catch him!" cried John Star.

Hal Samdu straightened, with his feet on the ceiling. Strained metal snapped. He fell down, head foremost, fifteen feet, the grate torn out in his hands. The tube yawned black, above, a cold stream of air pouring down from it.

The three caught him in their arms.

A whirring from the door of the great room. The lock mechanism was opening the inner valve. In seconds, the guardsmen would come, to find why the speaking tube was silent.

"You first, John," said Jay Kalam. "The lightest. Help us."

They lifted him to the opening. He hung his knees over the edge, and swung down his body, hands reaching.

Giles Habibula came first, wheezing, hoisted from beneath. Then Hal Samdu, who lowered John Star, a living rope, so that Jay Kalam could catch his hands.

"Halt!" rang the order from the opening door. "As you are! Or we fire to kill!"

They scrambled upward into the narrow black mouth of the ventilator tube. Another rapped command. The blast of a proton gun lit the dark tube with brief, intense violet, and spattered fused metal behind them. It reached them all with numbing electric shocks.

They tumbled ahead into cramped black spaces.

CHAPTER EIGHT

With Death Behind

The horizontal passage they followed was formed of heavy sheet metal, square, not three feet high, and as Giles Habibula put it, "black as the gut of a mortal whale."

They scrambled along on all fours, bruising limbs and heads upon rivets and interior braces. Giles Habibula was ahead, then Jay Kalam, and Hal Samdu, with John Star behind.

The guards must have delayed to get a ladder—escape into the ventilation system must have found them unprepared—for at first there was no sound of pursuit. The four dragged themselves through the narrow dark, the strong wind from the fans rushing about them, Giles Habibula puffing like an engine.

"If it branches," gasped Jay Kalam, "we must turn against the air current. That will guide us toward the fans, away from the small dividing passages. We must get past the fans, and out through the intake. If we lose the way, they'll have us trapped like rats——"

He stopped. The wind against their faces had abruptly ceased.

"They've shut off the fans," he whispered bitterly. "Now we haven't the air to guide us."

"I hear voices," John Star breathed. "Behind us. Following."

"Sweet life's sake!" wheezed Giles Habibula, later. "A mortal wall! I bumped my old head into it."

"Go on," said Jay Kalam, behind him, quietly urgent. "Feel about. There must be a way."

"My blessed head! Ah, yes, there is a way. Two ways. 'Tis another passage we're entering. Right or left?"

"A blind chance, since they stopped the fans. Say, right!"

They hastened on for another while, on hands and bruised knees.

A gasp from Giles Habibula. "My mortal life! A fear-

ful pit! I half fell into it. For life's sake, don't push so!
I'm sprawling on the edge!"

"The shaft turning down, it must be," said Jay Kalam.
"We turned wrong, I'm afraid—the intake must be
above. But it's too late to turn back. Feel about. There
should be rungs, a ladder—in case the shafts should need
to be cleaned, or repaired."

"Ah, yes, right you are, Jay. I've found them—and
precious flimsy they are, for such a man as I. Ah, Jay, I
should have stayed back in the cells, to let them torture
me and starve me and use my poor old body as they
would, court-martial me and seal me in their ghastly lethal chamber. Old Giles Habibula is too old, Jay, too ill
and lame, to be running through black and filthy rat-holes
on his knees, and dancing up and down flimsy little lad-
ders in the dark. He's no mortal monkey!"

Yet he had slipped over the edge in a moment; he was
already tumbling down the dark ladder, the others behind
him, punctuating his phrases with the gasps of his panting
breath.

"A floor!" he wheezed presently. "Ah, it's all up now,
I'm afraid. I've struck bottom. No way out but tiny pipes
a rat himself couldn't creep through."

They explored with anxious, bleeding fingers, but found
no branching passage large enough for a man to enter.

"We should have turned left," Jay Kalam said.

"We must go back," John Star cried. "If we hurry,
perhaps we can beat them."

Now ahead, he rushed back up the ladder. He reached
the horizontal shaft, and plunged down it, reckless of
bumps and bruises. Hal Samdu kept close at his heels, Jay
Kalam not far behind. Giles Habibula, heaving and gasping frantically, called out from far in the rear:

"For dear life's sake, you can't abandon poor old Giles!
Wait for me, lad! Jay, Hal, you can't leave an old com-
rade alone, to be starved and tortured and done to his
death! Wait just a second, for poor, lame and suffering
old Giles Habibula to snatch a breath of blessed air."

John Star saw the white flicker of a pocket light-tube
on the wall ahead; again he heard voices. The pursuing
guards, then, were just approaching the intersection. He
scrambled desperately to reach it first.

The light flashed briefly, out of the intersecting tube, to
strike the wall. He oriented himself by it, and waited,

crouched behind the angle, breathing quietly as he could. Hal Samdu came up behind, and he cautioned the giant to silence with a pressure of his foot.

Far back, he heard Giles Habibula's plaintive appeal:

"Just one blessed second! For life's own sweet sake! Ah, a poor old soldier, sick and crippled, imprisoned and unjustly sentenced to a wicked traitor's death, deserted by his comrades and caught like a dying rat in this stinking hole——"

The light flashed again, close now. The leading man came out of the side tunnel. John Star caught his groping arm, and hauled him around the metal corner, into deadly combat.

A fight in utter darkness, for the dropped light-tube went out. A savage battle; the unknown guard fought for his life, John Star for more than his. And brief; it was over before the next man in line could reach the cross-passage.

The Legion Academy had trained John Star. He knew every weak point of the human machine. He knew the twist that snaps a bone, the jab that pulps a nerve, the shift that kills an opponent with his own fighting strength. He was light, but the Legion training had made him hard and quick and sure enough to fight the Legion, now.

The other man tried first to use the heavy little proton gun in his right hand, and found that his wrist was broken. With his left hand, then, he struck into the darkness, and his own blow hurled him against the wall of the shaft. He twisted back, tried to butt, and broke his neck.

That was all.

When the next man flashed his light, to see how the battle went, John Star had the proton gun the first had dropped, pointed ready down the tube.

A thin, searing jet of pure electricity, the proton blast fused metal, ignited combustibles, electrocuted flesh. It was a narrow, killing sword of intense violet incandescence—not quite a toy!

A matter of split seconds.

The other men had similar weapons, also ready. But they must have held themselves a moment, must have waited to aim. John Star did not delay.

And five men died in the shaft, the three foremost by direct, searing contact with the ray, the two others electrocuted by current conducted through ionized air—the proton gun was not a toy; and John Star pulled hard on

the lever, to exhaust all the energy of the cell on one terrific blast.

The blinding violet flame went out. There was darkness in the shaft again. Stygian, complete. Silence. The
pungence of ozone in the air, from the action of the ray.
The acrid smell of seared flesh and smoldering cloth.

Such swift spilling of life sickened John Star. This was
the first test of the deadly arts he had learned; he had
never killed a man before. He was abruptly trembling,
faint.

"John?" whispered Hal Samdu, uncertainly.

"I'm—I'm all right," he stammered, and tried to get
possession of himself. There had been no choice. He had
had to kill as he would surely have to kill again. A few
lives, he told himself sternly, were nothing against the
safety of the Green Hall. Or—whispered another part of
him—the safety of Aladoree!

He fumbled weakly for the dropped light-tube.

"The guards——"

"They're all dead!" he whispered dully. "I killed them
—all."

"You've a proton gun?" Hal Samdu did not sense his
horror.

"Dead!" But the question brought him back to the
needs of the moment. "Yes. Useless, though, until I find
an extra cell. Burned out."

Forcing himself to it, he searched the body by him,
found no extra, and moved on to those the ray had slain.

Jay Kalam came up.

"You used the proton-blast? Full power? No use, then,
to look for weapons, or light-tubes either. Anything electrical. Burned out."

He found another proton gun; half fused, reeking with
burned insulation, it was still so hot it seared his fingers.

Far down the shaft, toward the prison, he heard a command; he saw a flicker of warning light.

"They're coming again. We must get on. To the left,
this time."

Giles Habibula came noisily up; he blundered into Jay
Kalam, wheezing:

"Time we rested! I've lost ten mortal pounds, already,
scampering through these foul and endless rat-holes. Ah,
but I'm hot as——"

"Come on!" retorted Hal Samdu. "You'll be hotter when a proton blast catches you in the rear!"

On they tumbled, desperate, bruised, gasping for breath, again without a weapon—save for the useless proton gun—still without light. Running on all fours. Colliding painfully with rivets and flanges. "Playing an evil game of rat-and-ferret," sobbed Giles Habibula.

John Star, now ahead, reported suddenly:

"Another shaft! Larger. Runs both up and down."

"Up, then!" said Jay Kalam. "The intake must be above us. Probably on the roof."

They ascended flimsy metal rungs, in close-walled, smothering dark.

"The roof!" John Star whispered suddenly. "Can we get to the landing stage, above the tower? There are ships on it."

"Possibly," said Jay Kalam. "But we must pass the fans—easy to do if they keep them stopped. But there are guards on the landing stage, and we've no weapon."

They climbed rungs without end, up through rayless gloom. Breath came with painful effort. Muscles screamed and quivered with the agony of fatigue. Worn, blistered hands left blood on the metal.

Giles Habibula, lagging a little behind, puffing noisily, yet found breath for complaint.

"Ah, poor old Giles is dying for a drink. Perishing for one blessed sip of wine! His precious throat is dry as leather. Poor old Giles; lame, feeble, sick old Giles Habibula—he can't stand this any longer. Climbing till he feels like he's turned into a mortal mechanical monkey!"

"I've been counting the rungs," Jay Kalam said calmly, at last, breaking the silence of endless, tortured effort. "We must be in the tower."

A current of air presently struck them, blowing down the shaft.

"The fans, again!" muttered John Star. "I wonder why——?"

He soon knew. The downward wind increased. It became a tempest, a howling hurricane. It yelled in their ears with demoniac voices. It ripped garments from their bodies. It snatched at them with prankish hands, hammered them with savage blows.

"Trying——" screamed Jay Kalam above the roar of it, "to blow us—off the ladder! Climb on—stop—fans—"

The wind whipped his voice away.

John Star climbed on, against the relentless pressure of howling air, fighting the tearing demon talons. The flimsy metal rungs quivered, bent beneath the strain. Steadily, painfully, he won his way against the narrow storm.

Another sound was at last in his ears, above the shrieking air—a whine of gears, a whirring of great rushing vanes. The purring of the over-driven fans, deadly in the dark.

Upward he battled, inch by hard-won inch, to the top of the trembling ladder, to a wide platform of vibrating metal bars. There he paused to play a game with death. Somewhere in the dark above, those great blades were racing, and he knew they would never pause as they split his skull and splashed his brain.

Cautiously he moved, feeling his way. He was out of the main air-current, now; he could move more easily. Yet sudden, freakish blasts still drove at him savagely; they were demon hands jerking him toward the racing unseen vanes.

Toward the whine of gears he moved. With cautious fingers he explored the frame of the vibrating machine. He tried to shape a mental image of it. At last he found the end of a rotating shaft; and he thrust, slowly, carefully, with the heavy little gun, three times in vain.

Then metal teeth snapped it from his hand. The purring changed to anger. The gears snarled and screamed. They chewed metal, and spit the fragments savagely. And they broke. The unloaded motor whined briefly with rage.

Silence, then. Peace. The whirring, invisible vanes slowed, and stopped. The demoniac air was stilled. John Star waited in the quiet dark, panting, resting his trembling muscles, while the others climbed up to his side.

"Now, the intake," softly urged Jay Kalam. "Before they come!"

"Wait a mortal moment," wheezed Giles Habibula, sobbing for air. "For sweet life's sake, can't you wait for a lame, old soldier, climbing like a dog in a treadmill, with his hair blown out by the roots!"

They climbed again, up a huge, still blade, and out along the massive, motionless axle. They ran upright into the vast, horizontal intake tube and came to the bottom of another vertical pit.

"Light!" exulted John Star. "The sky!"

A square bright patch, at the top of the shaft, shone like a beacon of welcome. It was not the sky, however, but only the undersurface of the great landing stage.

Up the last short ladder, and over a low metal wall, and they stood at last upon the tower's roof. Flat, and tiled with purple glass, the enormous roof was spaced with the openings of other ventilator shafts, and crowded with the forest of gigantic piers that supported the immense platform of the flying stage, yet another hundred feet above.

"They will know we're up here," Jay Kalam reminded them gently. "From the fan. No time to waste."

They ran to the edge of the roof, and climbed again, up the diagonal lattice-work of an enormous vertical member. The last five feet, around the edge of the gigantic metal platform, John Star climbed alone. Clinging like a human fly, he peered cautiously over the edge of the immense flat table.

A mere hundred feet away lay the nose of the *Purple Dream*. A slender bright arrow, the flagship was a-shimmer under the small sun which burned hot through the thin air of Phobos.

The *Purple Dream!* Only thirty yards away, it was freedom and safety and the means to search for Aladoree. Trimly slender, beautiful; the newest, finest, fleetest cruiser of the Legion fleet. A splendid hope, and hopeless.

Her air-lock was sealed, her bright armor impregnable. Twelve Legionnaires, armed, stood in line beneath her valves, wearily alert.

What madness, for the four to think of taking her! Four tattered fugitives, bruised, exhausted, with not one weapon save their bodies, and a thousand hunting them. What madness, when the cruiser was the System's most powerful fighting machine!

John Star knew it was madness, yet he dared to plan.

CHAPTER NINE

"To the Runaway Star!"

He climbed back to the others, mutely eager Hal Samdu, cool, composed Jay Kalam, wheezing, groaning Giles Habibula.

"The *Purple Dream* is there. Her valve toward us, sealed. A dozen men guarding her. But I think I see a way—a chance."

"How?"

He explained, and Jay Kalam nodded, offering quiet suggestions.

"We'll try it. We can do no better."

They climbed down the pier to the roof again, Giles Habibula complaining bitterly at the new effort. They ran diagonally across the purple tiles among the maze of beams, and clambered wearily up again to the platform, to the edge behind the *Purple Dream*.

Again John Star looked above the surface.

No sentry, no searcher, was now in view. That herculean climb up the shaft, three thousand feet, the last thousand against a hurricane, the escape through the blades of the fan—all that must not have been comprehended in the plans of their pursuers.

The flat platform. The side of the *Purple Dream*, fifty feet away, a shimmering curve of armor. Purple-blue sky above and beyond.

"Now," he whispered. "All clear!"

In seconds, he was over the edge, although even for his trained body it was an awkward scramble. Hal Samdu, with his help, came more easily. Giles Habibula, hauled limp and green-faced over the edge, looked once three thousand feet down, to the purple roofs of the wings and the green convexity of the tiny planet, and grew suddenly and amazingly ill.

"Sick!" he groaned. "Mortal sick and dying. Hold me, lad! For poor Giles is faint and dying—and he feels he's falling off the whole blessed moon!"

For all her fleetness and her fighting power, the *Purple Dream* was not large; one hundred twenty feet long, twenty feet her greatest diameter. Yet it was not easy to get silently and unobserved on top of her, as John Star's plan demanded.

They ran beneath the black, projecting muzzle of her port stern rockets, and lifted John Star to it. And he, again, helped the others up. From the rocket, over the glistening smoothness of her silvery hull, they inched a slow and perilous way up and forward.

Once Giles Habibula fell. He started to slide down her polished shell, croaking in mute terror; John Star and Hal Samdu caught him, drew him back. At last they were safely amidships.

There they lay, waiting, atop her flattened hull.

At first they were glad enough to rest, from that superhuman climb. But the sun beat down on them, through the thin artificial atmosphere of Phobos, blinding, intense, and terrible. It drove back upon them from the mirror of the hull. They were blistered, gasping with heat, and thirst came to torture them.

They dared not move; they could only wait. And their position held a mounting peril.

True, they were invisible from near the ship. But the bright metal platform, at a distance, was visible, shimmering and dancing in the heat—and any chance searcher there could easily see them on the cruiser.

Two hours, perhaps, they had been broiling on that flat silver grille, when they heard a bell below, and taut, excited voices:

"From the Commander. He's going aboard in five minutes. The cruiser will be ready to take off at once."

"Have the valve unsealed. Inform Captain Madlok."

"Wonder where he's bound?"

"Wants to get away, I guess, until these escaped prisoners are captured."

"Legion men, they say. One an old criminal. All desperate fellows, dangerous."

"Hiding in the ventilation shafts, they say."

"Don't blame the Commander, if he's going away. Men clever enough to break out of that prison——"

"They've already killed six, in the tubes."

"Twelve, I heard it—with their own guns!"

The sound of hurried feet on the stair from the eleva-

tor. A ringing clang of metal, as the great outer valve
dropped to form a tiny deck under the air-lock. Feet on
the accommodation ladder, entering the vessel. At last
the crisp order:

"All clear! Close the valves!"

"Now!" whispered John Star.

He rolled swiftly off the hull, and slid down feet first,
to the little platform of the lowered valve. The jar shook
him, but he caught his breath and darted inside the air-
lock. Hal Samdu was a second behind him, then Jay
Kalam; Giles Habibula, for all his bulk, was very little
later.

In the struggle that followed, they had the advantage
of complete surprise. The first man, at the control mechanism of the valves, was not even armed. He gasped at
sight of John Star, his face abruptly white with panic—
for the new reputation of the four had preceded them
aboard. And he tried to run.

John Star caught him. A sharp jab to a vital plexus,
a flat-handed blow near the ear. He slumped, limp and
silent.

Giles Habibula stumbled wheezing over the flanges, and
John Star shot at him:

"Close the valves!"

Once the air-lock was sealed and secured from within,
he knew, the *Purple Dream* was armored well against outside danger.

With the gigantic Hal Samdu close behind him, and
Jay Kalam, he burst upon the narrow deck.

Two uniformed men appeared before them, gasped,
started, and tried to reach their weapons. The first of them
met Hal Samdu's fist, rebounded against a bulkhead, and
crumpled slowly to the deck. A proton gun fell spinning,
and Jay Kalam scooped it up in time to meet a third attacker in the Legion green.

John Star met his own opponent, briefly. They both
had Legion combat training, but John Star fought for
AKKA—and Aladoree herself. The other snatched for his
gun, and staggered back screaming, arm snapped, back
broken. Seizing his weapon, John Star turned in time to
meet Captain Madlok, just emerging from his cabin.

Madlok came out crouched and snarling, a proton needle ready in his hand. But once again John Star was first
—merely the hundredth of a second, perhaps, but enough.

A white blade of electric fire stabbed out, and the *Purple Dream* had a new commander.

They divided, then. Giles Habibula remained to guard the air-lock. Hal Samdu ran toward the crew's quarters, in the stern. Jay Kalam plunged down into the generator rooms, below the deck. John Star darted forward, toward the Commander's cabin and the navigation bridge.

The four were still outnumbered two to one—the full complement of the *Purple Dream* had been twelve; and such a crew was ample, since the cruiser was handled almost completely by automatic mechanisms, needing men chiefly for inspection and navigation. But they had not completely lost the advantage of surprise.

John Star found two men forward. The navigator came out of the bridge-room with a proton gun in his hands. He saw John Star and tried to fire. But he lacked the peril of AKKA and its keeper to nerve his urgency. By a few fatal thousandths of a second, he was too late.

John Star flung open the door marked COMMANDER, and found Adam Ulnar in his cabin, hanging up the coat that he had worn aboard.

For a long second, the tall, white-haired master of the Legion and the Purple Hall stood quite motionless, breathless, staring at the menacing needle of the proton gun, his handsome face frozen into absolute lack of expression. He breathed suddenly. The coat fell out of his hands. He sat down heavily in the single chair.

"Well, John, you surprised me," he said with a short, husky little laugh. "I had learned you were too dangerous to keep alive. I was going away until you had been disposed of. But I was hardly expecting this."

"I'm glad you value your life," John Star snapped harshly. "Because I want to trade it to you."

Adam Ulnar smiled, defensively, recovering his suave self-possession. Again he was the shrewd elder statesman of the Purple Hall.

"You have the advantage, John. Your men, I suppose, have control of the cruiser?"

"I imagine so, by now."

"You know, this adds piracy to your long list of crimes. All the Legion fleets will be hunting you, now."

"I know. But that doesn't save your life. Shall we trade?"

"What do you want, John?"

"Information. I want to know where you have Aladoree Anthar."

Adam Ulnar smiled in faint relief, and spoke more easily:

"Fair enough, John. Promise me my life, and I'll tell you—though I don't think the information will give you any satisfaction."

"Well?"

"I didn't approve the thing, John. I wanted her brought here, to the Purple Hall. I think Eric is trusting his strange allies too far. . . . She wasn't disposed to talk, you see. It was difficult to persuade her, without the danger that she would die, and her secret with her. And we still have to deal with a few stubborn fools in the Legion—men like you are, John—still loyal to the Green Hall."

"But where is she?"

"They took her on the Medusæ flier, John, back to the Runaway Star."

"Not there!" he gasped. "Even Eric wouldn't——"

"Yes, John," his famous kinsman told him soberly. "I didn't think you'd find much comfort in the fact."

"We'll go after her!"

"Yes, John, I believe you would do that." There was a note, almost, of admiration in Adam Ulnar's voice. "I believe you would. But you couldn't possibly hope to succeed."

"No?"

"Our allies, John, are a pretty efficient race. They've had a longer existence than the human race. I don't like them, myself—I've had contact enough with them. I don't approve the alliance. And I didn't approve taking the girl there. I don't trust them so far as Eric does.

"They aren't human, at all, you understand—not like any form in the System, though Eric called them Medusæ. They have a queer psychology. Unpleasant. Frankly, I'm afraid of them.

"But they're scientific, able, advanced. They have the accumulated knowledge of ages I can't estimate. Weird as they are, they've splendid brains. Cold, emotionless intelligence. They're more like machines than men. They get what they want, quite efficiently, with no human scruples.

"So I think, John, that they will be able to guard the girl, on their own planet—and make her tell the secret. They have set up very effective defenses, to guard their own strange world. That Belt of Peril, that the insane survivors of Eric's expedition keep babbling about.

"And even if you keep me helpless, John, our plans will go ahead. The Medusæ will come back. The Legion will go over to them—our Purple organization controls it now. The Green Hall will be wiped out—the Medusæ have amazing weapons, John. And Eric will take the throne.

"The throne you might have had yourself, John."

CHAPTER TEN

Farewell to the Sun

Giles Habibula made queer noises. He gasped, strangled, sputtered. Fragments of food flew out of his mouth. His face—save for the ample purple protuberance of his nose —had faded to a greenish, sickly pallor. His fat hands trembled as he tilted up the big flagon of wine, and cleared his vocal organs sufficiently to permit articulate speech.

"My dear life!" he sputtered, rolling a fishy eye about the little bridge-room. "My mortal life! We can't go there!"

"Probably we can't," John Star agreed soberly. "The chances are against us—a hundred to one, I suppose. But we can try."

"Bless my bones! We can't go there, lad. 'Tis beyond the System—six light years, and more. That's a frightful distance, when it takes a precious ray of light six long and lonely years to cross it!

"Ah, there are ten thousand mortal dangers, life knows! I'm a brave man—you all know poor old Giles is brave enough to deal with any common peril. But we can't do that. Of all the doomed and dismal expeditions that ever dared to fly outside the precious System, only one ever came back!"

A tiny red light glowed suddenly on the geodesic telltale screen; a warning gong rang out.

"Another Legion cruiser," observed Jay Kalam, tautly quiet. "Scouring space for the *Purple Dream*. That makes five, in the range of the telltale. Hunting pirates was always a popular sport, with the Legion."

"And the nearest within ten thousand miles," added John Star, with a glance at the dials. "Though they probably won't discover us until we contrive to get the generators repaired, and start moving."

"And to the Runaway Star!" Giles Habibula wheezed on, dolefully. "Sweet life's sake, to the green Medusæ's dark and evil world! The expedition the Legion sent there had five fine fighting ships. The best the System could build. Full, trained crews. And look what came back, after a whole eternal year!

"One crippled ship! The men on her, most of them, blessed babbling lunatics, chattering to freeze your blood about the horrors they had found on the dark and hideous planet of that evil star. And rotting away, all the fearful while, of some frightful virus the doctors never saw before —the flesh of their mortal bodies turning green and flaking off.

"Mortal terrors! And you want us to go there, in one poor and lonely little ship, with her geodynes already wrecked. Just four men of us, against a whole planet full of green and cunning monsters!

"You can't ask old Giles Habibula to go out there, lad. Poor old Giles, half dead from scampering like a hunted rat through the ventilator tubes in the Purple Hall. Old Giles is too feeble for that. If you three idiots want to go out to your death of madness and howling horror, why then you must let poor old Giles off the ship on Mars."

"To be tried and put to death for a pirate?" asked John Star, smiling grimly.

"Don't joke so with old Giles, lad! He's no swaggering, red-handed pirate, lad. Old Giles is just a poor——"

"The whole Legion is hunting us, Giles," Jay Kalam broke in quietly. "Ever since we took the *Purple Dream*. The agents of the Legion would soon have you—you'd never disguise that nose!"

"Good life's sake, Jay, don't talk so! I hadn't thought of that. But we *are* blessed pirates now, with the hand of every honest fighting man against us. Ah, every man looks on us with trembling and horror, and seeks to strike us down to death!"

His fishy eyes glistened with tears; his wheezing voice broke.

"Poor Giles Habibula, aged and crippled in the loyal service of the Legion, now without a place on any planet to rest his mortal head. Hunted through the black and frozen deep of space, driven out of the System he has given his years and his strength to defend. Driven out to face a planet full of green inhuman monsters. Ah, me! The ingrate System will regret this injustice to a mortal hero!"

He wiped the tears away, then, with the back of a great fat hand, and tilted up the flagon.

He had found opportunity for a raid on the galley, since they took the ship. His capacious pockets were stuffed with slabs of synthetic Legion rations, sweet-cakes, and fragments of baked ham, which now flowed again toward his mouth in a stream of traffic interrupted only by the trips of the wine-flagon to the same destination.

The *Purple Dream* was adrift in space, a hundred thousand miles off the huge, tawny, ocher globe of Mars. Tiny Phobos had long been lost among the million, many-hued points that pierced the black sphere of vacant night. They lay with lights and signals dead, helpless; and the avid fleets of the Legion hunted them.

Commander Adam Ulnar safely locked in the brig, their other prisoners released through the air-lock, they had driven the cruiser away from the landing stage on the Purple Hall under rocket power. John Star had felt freedom in their grasp.

But then a dying engineer—true to the Legion traditions —had thrown a switch, burned out a geodyne unit. With generators useless and rockets inadequate to move the vessel fast or far through these hostile immensities, the four had gathered for a council of desperation.

"She's in the hands of those monsters?" huge Hal Samdu asked again, his big hands knotting. "The monsters that Eric Ulnar's crazy veterans kept talking about?"

"Yes. Except that I doubt that those things are enough like men to have hands."

"With care," began Jay Kalam, "organization——"

"Ah, that's the word," broke in Giles Habibula. "Organization. Regularity. Four good meals, hot on the moment; twelve hours of good sound sleep. Organization— though a blessed man might still take a cat-nap now and then, or a cold bite and a sip of wine between meals."

"There's the matter of navigation," Jay Kalam went on. "I know the rudiments, of course, but——"

He looked doubtfully about, at the walls of the bridge-room, bewilderingly crowded with all the shining, intricate mechanism of telescopic periscopes, geodesic telltales, meteor deflectors, rocket firing keys, geodyne controls, gyroscope space-compasses, radar, thermal and magnetic detector screens, star-charts, planetary maps, position-, velocity-, and gravitation-calculators, atmosphere and temperature gauges—all the apparatus for the not quite simple business of taking the cruiser safely from planet to planet.

"I can handle her," offered John Star quietly.

"Good. Then we must have an engineer. To repair the geodynes—we *must* somehow get them repaired!—and then to run them."

Giles Habibula grunted, sputtered crumbs, failed to speak.

"That's right, Giles. I'd forgotten that you were a qualified technician."

He swallowed, tilted the flagon, found his voice.

"Sweet life, yes, I can run the precious geodynes. Giles Habibula can fight, when fighting has to be done, old and lame and feeble as he is. Ah, me, no man is braver than old Giles—all of you know that. When fighting must be done. But, as a matter of choice, he'll always stick to his blessed generators. It's safer—and there's nothing else but wisdom in a blessed bit of caution."

"You can fix the burned-out unit?"

"Ah, yes, I can re-wind it," promised the new engineer. "But it will be hard to synchronize it with the others. Those units are matched when they are made. When one is off balance, it makes the whole system mortal hard to tune. But I'll do my blessed best."

"And, Hal," went on Jay Kalam, "you've been a proton gunner. You can handle the big proton blast needle, if the Legion stumbles on us—though we can't afford a fight, with just four men on a crippled ship."

"Yes, I can do that," gigantic Hal Samdu nodded slowly, his red face very grave. "That's simple. I can do it."

"That leaves you, Jay," spoke up John Star. "We need you to do just what you're doing now. To plan, organize. You will be our commander."

"No——" He started a modest objection, but Hal Samdu and Giles Habibula added their voices; and Jay Kalam became captain of the *Purple Dream*.

The new officer gave his first orders immediately, with the same gravely quiet manner he always had.

"Then, Giles, please get the geodynes into operation as soon as you can—our only chance is to get away before one of these ships catches us in a search beam, and calls the rest of the fleet to wipe us out."

"Very good, sir."

Giles Habibula threw back his head, held up the flagon until the last drop had trickled from it, saluted too elaborately, and rolled out of the bridge-room.

"John, you may be plotting our course. First we must outrun these ships around us. We'll keep above the asteroid belt, and well away from Jupiter and Saturn and Uranus, with their Legion bases—we can't risk running into another fleet. As soon as we get beyond the danger of their search-beams, we'll head on out toward Pluto."

"Very good."

"Hal, if you please, check the big proton gun. We must have it ready—though we can't risk a fight."

"Yes, Jay."

"And I shall keep watch."

"How many, now?" asked Jay Kalam, hours later. They were still drifting helpless in the void. Watching the betraying red sparks on the telltale screen, John Star answered slowly:

"Seven. And I believe—I'm afraid, Jay, they've found us!"

"They have?"

Intently he studied the instruments, and he agreed at last, his voice edged with apprehension:

"Yes. They've found us. They're moving in, all seven."

Jay Kalam spoke into his telephone:

"Hal, stand by for action. . . . Yes, seven Legion cruisers, all converging on us." He gave positions.

"Giles, the geodynes? . . . Not ready, yet? . . . And you can't depend on the re-wound unit? . . . They've seen us. We must move soon, or never."

A few minutes, and the nearest cruiser came into range, or almost into range, of the proton blast. Jay Kalam spoke into the telephone, and a tongue of blinding violet darted at it, from the great needle in its turret above.

"It's drawing back," whispered John Star, his eye fastened to a tele-periscope. "To wait for the others. But they'll all soon be close enough to fight."

"Ah, Jay, we can try them," whistled Giles Habibula's voice from the receiver, thin and shrill. "Though this crippled unit is still a poor, uncertain crutch!"

Jay Kalam nodded, sharply, and John Star turned to the dials and keys. The musical humming of the geodynes rose, filling the ship with a song of power. Swiftly he advanced them to their utmost output; their sound became higher, keener, until it was a vibrant whining which quivered through every member of the ship.

"Away!" he cried exultantly.

His eyes on the dials, on the red flecks glowing on the telltale screen, he saw that the *Purple Dream* was moving, ever faster, away from the center of that hostile crimson swarm. His own heart responded to the keening whine of the generators; he could almost feel the terrific thrust of the geodynes.

"We're gone!" he cried again. "Off for the Runaway Star! Away to——"

His voice fell. Another note had broken the keen musical whine of the generators—a coarse, nerve-jarring vibration.

Giles Habibula's voice came from the receiver, tiny and metallic and afraid:

"Ah, these wicked generators. I re-wound the unit. But they're off-balance. They won't stay synchronized. That evil oscillation will creep back. It bleeds away the power —and it may shake the mortal ship to fragments!"

"We've lost speed," John Star reported apprehensively from the instruments. "The Legion ships are gaining."

"Adjust them, please, Giles," Jay Kalam pleaded into the telephone. "Everything depends on you."

Giles Habibula toiled. The pure power-song came back, and broke again. The *Purple Dream* flashed on, gaining upon the seven pursuing ships when the geodynes hummed clear and keen, but always losing, falling sluggishly back, when the harsh, disturbing vibration returned.

John Star studied his instruments long and anxiously. "We're holding them just about even," he decided at last. "We can keep ahead so long as the generators do no worse—though we can't escape them altogether. Anyhow, we can say farewell to the Sun and the System. Even if they follow us out . . ."

"No," Jay Kalam objected quietly, "we aren't ready yet to leave."

"What's the matter?"

"We must have more fuel for the trip out to Barnard's Star—six light years and back. We must have every foot of space on board packed with extra cathode plates for the geodyne generators. And, of course, we must check the supplies for ourselves—food, and oxygen."

John Star nodded slowly.

"I knew we needed a captain. Where——"

"We must land at some Legion base, and get what we need."

"At a Legion base? With all the Legion fleets hunting us for pirates? The alarm will be spread to the limits of the System!"

"We'll land," Jay Kalam said, with his usual quiet gravity, "at the base on Pluto's moon. This is the farthest on our way, and the most isolated Legion station in the System."

"But even it will be warned and armed."

"No doubt. But we must have supplies. We're pirates now. We shall take what we need."

CHAPTER ELEVEN

The Trap on Pluto's Moon

It was five days' flight to Pluto, most distant outpost of the System; so far that even its sun was but a bright star, its daylight eternal twilight.

Five days—with the full power of the geodynes, whose fields of force reacted against the curvature of space itself, warped it, so that they drove the ship not *through* space, to put it very crudely, but *around* it, and so made possible terrific accelerations without any discomfort to pas-

sengers, and speeds far beyond even the speed of winged
light. Apparent speeds, a mathematician would hasten
to add, as measured in the ordinary space that the vessel
went *around;* for both acceleration and velocity were quite
moderate in the hyper-space it really went *through.*

Giles Habibula nursed the hard-driven generators with
amazing care and energy—his thick hands proved to
have an astounding sureness and delicacy and skill; and
he had an enormous respect for the ever-increasing swarm
of Legion cruisers racing astern, with their threat of suc-
cessfully prosecuted charges of piracy, if not immediate
destruction of the *Purple Dream* and all on board in the
consuming flame of their proton blasts.

He adjusted the injured unit until it was all but perfect.
For an hour at a time, perhaps, the song of the generators
would be clear and keen—but always the harsh discord
of the destructive vibration returned.

One by one, the far-flying patrol cruisers of the Legion
had joined the pursuing fleet, until sixteen ships were
chasing the *Purple Dream.* But, little by little, they were
left behind, until, near Pluto, John Star estimated them
to be nearly five hours astern.

Five hours, that meant, in which to land at the hostile
base, overcome its crew, force them to bring aboard some
twenty tons of supplies, and get safely away into space
again.

In those days of the flight, John Star found himself
thinking often of Aladoree Anthar—and his thoughts
were soft music and sheer agony. Though he had known
her but a day, memory of her brought a glow of joy to
him, and a bitter throb of pain at thought of the human
traitors and the monstrous half-known things that held her
captive.

The *Purple Dream* hurtled down on Pluto's moon.

Pluto itself, the Black Planet, was naked rock and ancient ice, killing cold and solitude. Its only people were
a few hardy miners, mostly descendants of the political
prisoners shipped there under the Empire, lonely exiles
of eternal night.

Cerberus, moon of Pluto, was a tiny, cragged rock,
more desolate and cruel to man than even its dark planet.
A dead satellite, it had never lived. Save for the crew of
the lonely Legion station, it had no inhabitants.

John Star had more than half expected that the Pluto

Squadron of the Legion fleet would be warned and waiting for them, but the field seemed deserted as they came down. He began to hope that the evil web of Adam Ulnar's treason had not been spun so far.

Cerberus Station was a square field, leveled, between ragged black pinnacles. Red-glowing reflectors, spaced along the perimeter, radiated heat enough to keep the air itself from freezing into snow. A long, low building of insulating blocks armored with white metal, housed barracks and storerooms. The power plant, which gave energy to fight the enemy cold, must be somewhere underground. The spidery tower of the ultra-wave radio station rose from a black peak beyond the building. Farther, there was only frowning desolation: broken, ugly teeth of mountains, yawning crater-maws, cracked and riven and blasted rock, and strata of ice as old as the stone, all forever dead.

In a uniform which had belonged to Captain Madlok, John Star stepped out into the thin and bitter air, upon the little deck formed by the lowered outer valve. Assuming a confidence which he hardly felt, he waited while two men approached, with a manner of apprehensive hesitation, from the low white building.

"Cerberus Station, ahoy!" he hailed them, his manner as sternly official as possible.

"*Purple Dream*, ahoy," one of them responded, doubtfully—a very short man, very bald, very stout, very red of face, his appearance showing the careless neglect that sometimes comes of long isolation. There was, John Star thought, the equivalent of an entire meal accumulated on the front of his tunic. He wore the tarnished insignia of a Legion lieutenant.

"I am Captain John Ulnar," John Star said briskly. "The *Purple Dream* requires supplies. Captain Kalam is making out the requisitions. They must be aboard without delay."

The short man scowled suspiciously, pig-eyes narrowed.

"John Ulnar?" His voice was a nasal snarl. "And Captain Kalam, eh? In command of the *Purple Dream*, eh?"

His dirty, yellow-stubbled face held a smirk of sullen cunning. John Star watched his shifty-eyed hostility, and suddenly knew that he must be one of Adam Ulnar's men

—knew that the web of unguessed treason in the Legion had reached out even to this cold forgotten rock.

"We are." Boldness was the only way. "We're on a top emergency mission, and we must have these supplies at once."

"I'm Lieutenant Nana, commandant of the station." The sullen voice was devoid of military courtesy. With a knowing leer, Nana added cunningly: "The special orders in my file show the *Purple Dream* under Captain Madlok and Commander Adam Ulnar. She's listed as the Commander's flagship."

John Star didn't pause to wonder what his game could be. If he had been warned against them, it seemed strange that he had stayed to meet them peaceably—an unfortified supply base, Cerberus Station showed no evidence of any weapons heavy enough to challenge the *Purple Dream*. If he had received no warning—but there was no time for puzzles.

"There has been a change of command," John Star informed him curtly. "Now here is Captain Kalam."

Jay Kalam appeared beside him, in another borrowed uniform. They swung down the accommodation ladder from the tiny deck, and Jay Kalam offered a document, rapping sharply:

"Our requisition, Lieutenant!"

Glancing up at the ship's low turret, John Star made a quick motion with his hand. The ship's long proton gun lifted instantly out of its housing, and swung out above their heads to cover the long white building. Hal Samdu was at his post.

Nana looked up at the needle with small, blood-shot eyes. His unwashed face showed neither surprise nor any great alarm. He gave John Star a narrow-eyed glare of sullen hostility, and then reluctantly took the requisition.

"Sixteen tons of cathode plates!" His astonishment sounded unconvincing. "Not for one ship!"

"Sixteen tons!" John Star rapped. "Immediately!"

"Impossible!" Nana scowled again at the menacing gun, and muttered evasively: "I can't let you have them without first reporting to Legion Headquarters, for confirmation of your orders."

"We've no time for that. Our mission is top emergency——"

Nana lifted his untidy shoulders, in defiance.

"I'm the commandant of Cerberus Station," he snarled. "I'm not accustomed to accepting orders from——" He paused, and his red eyes narrowed. "——from pirates!"

"In this case, however," Jay Kalam said softly, "I should advise you to do so."

Nana shook his fist, in a rage that looked like bad acting, and Jay Kalam waved a signal to Hal Samdu. The great needle above their heads lifted toward the radio tower on the peak, and blinding incandescence jetted out. The tower crumpled instantly, into hot ruin.

And Nana was suddenly trembling, his unshaven face white and twitching with a fear that looked more genuine than his wrath had been.

"Very well," he whispered hoarsely. "I'll accept your requisition."

"Go with him, Captain Ulnar," said Jay Kalam. "See that there is no mistake or delay."

Nana complained that he did not have all the supplies required. Most of his men were too ill to help with the loading. The cranes and conveyors were out of order. He was doing his utmost, John Star recognized, to delay them until the sixteen pursuing Legion cruisers should have time to arrive.

Yet, four hours later, under John Star's stern supervision and the menace of the great proton gun, all the cathode plates were aboard. The cylinders of oxygen were safely loaded, and the supplies of food and wine that Giles Habibula had added to the requisitions. Only the black drums of rocket fuel remained piled beneath the air-lock, and it was still an hour before the pursuing ships should reach them. Yet John Star had caught a gleam of sullen satisfaction in Nana's red pig-eyes, that sharpened his uneasiness.

Then Jay leaped from the valve, and came running across the field.

"Time to go, John!" His voice was low, urgent.

"Why? We ought to have an hour——"

Jay Kalam glanced at the curious, staring men gathering to load the rocket fuel, and dropped his voice. "The 'scopes show another ship, John. Nearer. Headed here from Pluto."

"So that was Nana's game!" John Star nodded in bleak understanding. "A nice little surprise for us. Anyhow, we've got to have the fuel. We'll have to take a chance on outrunning Nana's friends."

Jay Kalam's lean dark face was taut with a rare concern.

"This isn't a Legion cruiser, John—it's moving a good deal too fast." Beneath his calm, John Star could sense his deep alarm. "I never saw the like. A black spider of a ship, with things jutting out of a round belly of a hull."

John Star staggered back from the cold apprehension that hit him in the pit of his stomach.

"The Medusæ!" he gasped. "That's the sort of ship that took Aladoree. Nana must have sent for them, to ambush us here. I don't know what sort of weapons they would have——"

"We'll have to go," Jay Kalam cut in. "We can't risk fighting."

"The rocket-fuel?"

"Leave it. Come aboard."

They ran up the accommodation ladder.

Lieutenant Nana stared after them with narrowed red eyes, and muttered something to his men about the drums. They all retreated toward the long metal building —with a haste that was ominous.

The air-lock was sealed. Levers flicked down under John Star's fingers. Blue flame should have screamed from the rockets, to send them plunging spaceward—but the *Purple Dream* lay dead!

Puzzled and dismayed, he tried the firing keys again— and nothing happened.

"We're somehow—stuck!" Incredulous, he scanned the dials. "Magnetism!" he exclaimed. "Look at the indicators! A terrific field. But how——? The ship is non-magnetic. I don't see——"

"A magnetic trap," said Jay Kalam. "Our friend Nana has somehow got magnets rigged, somewhere close to the ship. Our hull is non-magnetic; but still the field holds the rocket-firing mechanism and the geodynes, out of control. He's trying to hold us, until the ships get here, and——"

"Then," broke in John Star, "we must stop their dynamos."

"Hal," Jay Kalam spoke into his telephone, "destroy the building."

The tongue of roaring violet flame reached again from

the shining needle. It swept the long, low metal building from end to end, and left it a flattened tangle of smoking metal and broken brick, flung off its foundations by the sheer thrust of the blast.

"Now!"

Again John Star tried the rockets; again only silence answered.

"The magnets still hold us. The dynamos must be underground, where our blast didn't reach them."

"I can, then!" cried John Star. "Open the lock."

He snatched two hand proton guns, besides the two in his belt already and darted out of the bridge-room.

"Wait!" called Jay Kalam. "What——?"

But he was already gone; Jay Kalam touched the controls to open the valve for him.

He dropped to the field, ran across to the smoking wreck of the long building, and searched the bare foundations until he found the stair, a shaft hewn through dark rock and strata of old ice. Down the steps he plunged, proton guns in his hands, leaping stray fragments of still-glowing metal.

A hundred feet below, in the cold crust of Cerberus, a heavy metal door loomed in front of him. He turned a proton-blast on it, at full force. It flashed incandescent, sagged, caved in. He leaped over it, into a long, dim-lit hall. He heard the drum of machinery ahead, the hum of dynamos; but another door stopped him. He tried the gun and it was dead—exhausted by that first full blast. Before he could level another, a violet lance stabbed at him from a tiny wicket.

Alert, he flung his body under that blade of killing fire, flat on his stomach. Even though he escaped the searing ray, the conducted shock of it numbed him. But his own blast answered at the same instant, and the glowing wreck of the door was flung back upon the man behind it.

On his feet at once, though his shoulder was blistered and throbbing, he sprang for the door, tossing away his discharged gun and snatching the two from his belt.

A square room was before him, rock-hewn, great dynamos humming in the center of it. Five men stood about it in attitudes of petrified dismay, only Lieutenant Nana's hand groping mechanically for his weapon.

Both John Star's guns flamed—at the generators.

Unarmed now, but sure the dynamos were wrecked, he flung his discharged guns in Nana's sullen, blinking, yellow-stubbled face, and ran back down the hall and up the stair, hoping surprise would give him time to get back aboard.

It did. The air-lock clanged again. The rockets washed black pinnacles with roaring blue flame, and the *Purple Dream* flashed upward from Pluto's cragged moon—off at last, John Star exulted savagely, off at last for far-off Barnard's Star, to the aid of Aladoree!

"The delay——" whispered Jay Kalam. "Too long, I'm afraid. That black spider-ship has got too close—we can hardly escape it, now!"

CHAPTER TWELVE

Storm in Space

Cerberus, Moon of Pluto, fell behind, a cold gray speck, and vanished.

The Black Planet itself was swallowed in the infinite black abyss, and the splendid star that was the sun began to fade and dwindle in Orion.

They passed the speed of light. The Sun and the stars behind were visible now only with rays they had over-taken; picked up and refracted in the lenses and prisms of the tele-periscopes, to correct the distortion of speed.

Giles Habibula lived, now, in the generator room. Under the care of his fat and oddly steady hands, the geodynes ran almost perfectly. That ominous snarl of destructive vibration went unheard for hours at a time.

And the *Purple Dream* drove on. The tiny worlds of men were lost behind. Ahead, the stars of Ophiuchus slowly spread, but still not even the highest powers of the tele-periscopes could show the faint point of Barnard's Star —so dim in stellar death that it was only the tenth magnitude, as seen from Earth. And only their haunted minds could picture its lone evil world, where Aladoree had been taken.

They drove on, day after day, at the utmost speed of straining generators—and the black flier followed. Light from it would never overtake them, now. The teleperiscopes failed to show its monstrous spider-shape. Only the geodesic telltale screen betrayed it—for the telltale mechanism registered geodesic over-drive fields, instantaneously.

John Star begged Giles Habibula to nurse more thrust from the over-loaded geodynes, and he watched the faint red fleck on the screen. It seemed to stand motionless, now. Whether the generators ran well or ill, its distance never changed.

"They're playing with us," he muttered once, uneasily. "No matter how fast we go, we never gain an inch."

"Just following." Gnawing worry was apparent, even in Jay Kalam's calm. "They can catch us when they like. Or maybe—if their communications equipment is up to it—they'll just signal their friends at home to have our welcome ready."

"I wonder why they don't attack us, now?"

"Waiting to see our plans, I suppose. Or, more likely, they're still hoping for a chance to get the Commander back, alive."

For Adam Ulnar was still locked in the brig, a cheerful and philosophic prisoner with no apparent remorse for his treason; he had asked for paper and was busy writing the memoirs of his long career, for the proud archives of the Purple Hall.

Hopefully now, John Star whispered, "If they won't attack, perhaps we can give them the slip."

Jay Kalam shook his dark head, slowly. "I can see no way."

On they drove, into the star-glittering crystal black of interstellar space. All four of them grew haggard, from want of sleep, from the tension of effort and dread. Only Jay Kalam appeared almost unchanged, always deliberate and cool, always gravely pleasant. John Star's face was white, his eyes burning with anxiety. Hal Samdu, grown nervous and irritable, muttered to himself; he knotted his huge and useless fists, and sometimes glared at imaginary enemies. Even Giles Habibula, incredibly, lost weight until the skin hung in pouches under his hollowed, leaden eyes.

Day by day the Sun grew smaller, until it was dwarfed by Betelgeuse and Rigel, until it was a faint white star, lost amid the receding splendors of Orion.

In the tele-periscopes, Barnard's Star appeared and grew.

Runaway sun! Red, feeble, dying dwarf. Racing northward out of the constellation Ophiuchus, in mad flight from the Serpent and the Scorpion. Long ago christened "Barnard's Runaway Star," from its discoverer and its remarkable proper motion, it was the nearest star of the northern sky and the nearest found to have a habitable planet.

Habitable—so the censored and fragmentary reports of Eric Ulnar's expedition had described it. But the mad survivors of the expedition, rotting away in guarded hospital wards of maladies that the Legion specialists in planetary medicine could neither understand nor cure, had shrieked and whispered of a weird domain of half-known horror. The rulers of that planet were the monstrous Medusæ, and it was scarcely habitable for men.

John Star was watching that ancient, expiring sun one day, an eye of dull red evil in the tele-periscope. Its hypnotic glare brought him foreboding thoughts of Aladoree, imprisoned on its terror-haunted planet. He seemed to see her clear, honest gray eyes, horror-distended, and filmed with soul-searing fear. A cold and helpless wrath accumulated in him.

He started when Jay Kalam spoke:

"Look! Ahead of us—a green shadow!"

Even then his low, restrained voice was tense with dread of the cosmic unknown.

Ahead of them, the tele-periscopes showed that ominous and eerie shadow, swiftly growing. It shone with the strange dim green of ionized nebular gases, and the dark spreading wings of it blotted out the stars of Ophiuchus, and slowly grew to hide the Serpent and even the Scorpion.

John Star stepped up the magnification of the 'scopes, until he could see the ugly, crawling motion of its vast writhing streams, and the angry currents of strange matter and stranger energies boiling within it.

"An uncharted nebula," he whispered at last. "We had better turn away."

Star-gazing nomads of the Earth, from the beginning, had wondered at those dark clouds against the firmament.

Star-roving nomads of space, more recently, had sometimes perished in them. Even yet, however, they were little-known, and all prudent spacemen kept well away from their vast maelstroms of fire and cosmic fury.

Back at the Legion Academy, John Star had listened to a renowned astrophysicist lecturing learnedly on "Intranebular Dynamics." He knew the fine-spun theories of counter-space, of inverse curvature, of pseudo-gravitation and negative entropy. The nebulæ, according to the theories, were the wombs of planets and suns and even of future galaxies; the second law of thermodynamics was somehow circumvented in their anomalous counter-spaces, and radiation trapped in their mysterious depths somehow re-integrated into matter; their final awesome destiny was to re-wind the run-down universe itself. So that famous astrophysicist believed—but he had never ventured near the dark, supernal fury of such a storm in space.

John Star gulped, and his voice came faint with awe. "We're running too near—I'll change our course."

"No," Jay Kalam protested quietly. "Drive on toward it."

"Yes?" Wondering, taut with mounting dread, he obeyed.

The mass ahead tripped the gravity detectors. They had to drop below the speed of light, so that their search beams could guard them from collision. And that strange cloud grew.

Utterly insignificant it may have been, in the scale of cosmic space, so tiny that the System's astronomers had never discovered or charted it. The vast and little-known forces of it could make no threat to the System itself, for the inverse inflection of the counter-spaces was held to cause repulsion from the gravity-fields of suns. On the galactic scale, it was the merest fleck of curious dust.

On the human scale, however, it was big enough—and deadly.

Enormously, its dark and dimly shining arms twisted out across the stars ahead. The 'scopes began to show the terrible detail of it: black dust-clouds, hurtling streams of jagged meteoric fragments, dark banners of thin gases, all whipped with the raging winds of half-guessed cosmic forces, angrily aglow with the eerie green of ionization.

John Star stood rigid with dread, and he felt a chill of icy sweat. But he kept their course on toward it, until they were flashing along no more than a thousand miles from the side of a darkly burning greenish streamer, which seemed to reach out for them like a kind of monstrous pseudopod.

"If it caught us——" His dry throat stuck, and he had to swallow. "Those meteor-streams—hurtling boulders! Those whirlpools of shining gas! The forces inside it—unknown!" He wiped sweat off his set, white face. "I don't think we'd last five seconds."

But Jay Kalam told him, gently:

"Steer a little closer."

"Eh?" John Star muttered, hoarsely. "Why?"

Silently, Jay Kalam pointed at the red forgotten spark on the telltale screen, which marked the position of the black ship behind them. It was visibly creeping up, to close the distance which had been fixed so long.

John Star caught his breath. "So they're trying to overtake us, now?"

"More than trying," Jay Kalam reminded him softly. "I suppose they're afraid we'll try to shake them off, in the edges of the nebula. Steer a little closer."

He touched the controls again, with stiff and icy fingers. The racing ship veered slightly, toward that appalling cloud of dim green fire and darkness. A cosmic storm, in very truth—for mad winds of unseen force ripped and twisted black dust and glowing gas into shredded streamers and wild vortices and sprawling tentacles that seemed to writhe and whip with elemental fury.

"Steer a little closer," urged Jay Kalam gently. "And we'll soon find out how much they value Commander Ulnar's life."

John Star moved the controls again, with numb, unwilling fingers, and then turned a tele-periscope on the black ship behind—for even laggard light from it could overtake them, now that they had slowed. A colossal thing, strange as the green and wetly heaving monsters that made its crew. With black rods and vanes and levers jutting in baffling array from the round black hull, it looked like a black spider flying. The main wings had been somehow retracted, but certain smaller vanes moved slightly, now and again, as it came, as if reacting against some unseen medium to control its flight. Perhaps, he guessed, it made use of radiation-pressures.

It grew large in the lenses—dark and strange as the spatial storm ahead.

"They can't attack!" John Star gulped to moisten his throat. "Not if they want to save Commander Ulnar's life."

And Jay Kalam murmured softly: "Try it just a little closer, now."

John Star touched the helm again—and his heart grew sick.

The bright clean song of the geodynes had been ringing like a peal of living power through the ship; he had almost felt the thrust that sent them ahead. But that song changed. Suddenly, now, the snarling vibration of unmatched units came back. Their speed fell off again— and the red spark in the telltale screen came up almost to touch them.

Tense and desperate, John Star guided the sick vessel closer to that stormy wall of dust and green fire and grinding stone, and Jay Kalam watched astern. He said suddenly:

"I'm afraid the Commander won't save us, after all. They're firing—something!"

Out of the belly of that black spider-ship came a little ball of misty white. It followed them, more swiftly than the crippled geodynes could take them, and grew as it came. They watched it in the lenses, frozen with a new wonder and a breathless terror, for it was utterly inexplicable.

A ball of opalescence. It wasn't matter, John Star knew —for no material projectile could have overtaken them so swiftly, even crippled and lagging as they were. It was a swirling globe of milky flame, splendid with rainbow sheens. It swelled behind them. It hid the spider-ship. It covered the belt of bright Orion. It filled the void behind them like a new star born.

A glowing sun—flung after them!

That was quite fantastic, John Star knew. But it grew vast in space, and the hot image of it in the lenses hurt his eyes. And still it swelled, ever more terribly bright.

And it *drew* them!

The *Purple Dream* lurched, rolled toward it.

A sudden dizzy nausea, an intolerable vertigo, overwhelmed John Star. He staggered, stumbled back from the controls, and clutched a handrail. He clung to it, sick and trembling, while the ship spun helpless in the grasp of that pursuing sun.

They fell toward that blinding opalescence. Grimly, his jaw set against that nausea, John Star fought the spin of the stricken ship, battled his lurching way back to the controls—and found the geodynes utterly dead.

The ship dropped, unchecked.

Tossing seas of white opalescence spread out to drown them, vast as the surface of a very sun. Angry, flaming prominences reached out to snare them—and then the thing was gone.

White, exploding fire half-blinded them—and it had vanished like a punctured bubble. John Star's baffling sickness ended. Space was black once more behind them, and soon his dazzled eyes could see the belted splendor of Orion. The song of the geodynes came back, and the ship answered to her controls.

John Star mopped weakly at his face.

"Never felt—such a thing!" he whispered. "Space itself—dropped from beneath us!"

"A sort of vortex of disintegration, I imagine," Jay Kalam commented softly. "Some such thing was mentioned in the secret reports of the Ulnar Expedition, that were sent out to Aladoree at the fort on Mars. Only a hint —they were careful not to tell her much. But there was some reference to an energy vortex weapon—a frightful thing that warped the space-coordinates, making all matter unstable, growing from the energy of the atoms it annihilated, and creating an attraction to draw more matter in. A kind of pseudo-sun!"

John Star nodded, shaken.

"That must be it," he agreed. "The distortion of space must have made the geodynes go dead." He caught a long, uneasy breath. "We can't fight them with the proton gun—not when they start throwing suns!"

"No," Jay Kalam said quietly. "I see only one thing to do—drive straight into the nebula."

"Into that storm!" John Star blinked. "The ship couldn't live a minute, there."

"A minute is a long time, John," Jay Kalam told him gently. "They've fired another shot."

"Another——"

His dry throat seized his voice.

"Turn straight in," Jay Kalam said. "I don't think they'll follow."

For a moment his mind rebelled. He stood frozen at the controls, staring at the angry banners of the nebular storm. One sick instant—and then he had mastered himself. He accepted the danger, and turned the *Purple Dream* into that appalling cloud of dim green fire and darkness.

Death grew behind them. Again a milky ball came from the belly of the black spider-ship, and swelled into a pseudo-sun of devouring atomic flame. Again the cruiser pitched and spun, with geodynes dead, helpless in that greedy grasp. Again John Star was ill.

But the abrupt turn had saved them. That hurtling globe of expanding opalescence missed them, too narrowly, and exploded far beyond them. The released geodynes pealed out again, and the ship sprang ahead—into the nearest angry arm of the nebula.

Into fury and enigma.

John Star had listened to the theories. All positive-entropy processes should be suspended or reversed, the theorists said, in the inverse-inflexure of the nebular counter-spaces. That meant that power-tubes could yield no power, and geodynes could give no thrust. It meant that rockets couldn't fire. It meant that clocks and chronometers would run backwards—and that human machines, very likely, would stop altogether.

That was what the theoretical astrophysicsts said—but none of them had ever been inside a nebula, to observe the birth of matter. Only two or three daring spacemen had ever ventured on nebular explorations, into a smaller counter-space lying on the route to Proxima, and they had never emerged.

John Star caught his breath again and tried to nerve himself to meet emergency. The repulsion fields of the meteor deflector would serve to protect the hull from the nebular drift—if the masses were not too large, too numerous, or coming too fast. For the rest, the life of the ship depended on his skill.

The *Purple Dream*, with his quick fingers on the keys, sought a path through the spinning fringe of spiral arms. Whether the theorists were right or wrong, he knew the ship couldn't survive in the nebula's heart. Nothing stronger than grinding boulders would be needed to destroy them. Mysterious womb of worlds, or merely a pinch of common cosmic dust, it could also be their grave.

His flying fingers touched the keys, and the cruiser spun and darted through a dance with black and shining death. It found rifts in the curtains of dust. It recoiled from green, grasping arms. It swam through rivers of hurtling stones. It defied the grasp of the nebula, and fought like a thing alive for life.

From some remote distance, John Star heard Jay Kalam's gentle voice:

"Good work, John! I don't think they'll follow."

And the *Purple Dream* threaded onward through the mazes of the nebula. Walls of green flame were suddenly ahead; the drift lurked in the black dust-clouds, and leaped out with naked fangs of tearing stone. Hurricane-like, the half-known forces of the cosmic storm battered and tore at the ship—forces akin to the dread vortices of sun-spots, John Star suspected, and even to the deadly drag of the Medusæ's pseudo-suns.

Right or left, up or down, he drove the ship with sure fingers. The radar and the thermal detectors made a continual, useless clamor, until he shut them off. Only human skill and quickness could serve them now.

For a moment he thought they were free. The black ahead was deadly dust no longer, but the frosty dark of open space. Through that glow of eerie green, he saw the beacon of red Antares—and then the geodynes failed again.

The bright keening of the generators was broken suddenly, with that old, heart-breaking vibration. The precious thrust was lost. A black and jagged mass of rock—a nascent world, perhaps—came at them suddenly. John Star's fingers dropped on the keys, but the sick ship failed to answer.

That black-fanged rock came on through the screens. It struck the hull with a clang that reverberated like the very knell of doom. Then there was a silence. John Star listened. He couldn't hear the geodynes—but there was no hiss and roar of air escaping. He knew the staunch hull had held.

Then the ship began to spin. The bright beacon of Antares was suddenly gone, and the rift in the nebula closed. The same wind of force that had hurled the boulder had caught them now. It dragged them back, toward the mysterious heart of the nebula.

John Star tried the dead controls again, and stared fearfully at the chronometer—though he knew that his human mechanism would surely be stopped, quite permanently, before the anomalous forces of the counterspace set time to running backward.

"Giles!" It was Jay Kalam, queerly calm, speaking into the ship's telephone. "We must have power, Giles!"

And Giles Habibula's voice came back from the speaker on the bulkhead, plaintive and abstracted:

"For sweet life's sake, don't bother me now. For poor old Giles is ill, Jay. His head can't stand this wicked spinning—and his precious geodynes never acted so before! Let him die in peace, Jay."

That mad wind of energy swept them on. John Star frantically studied his dials and gauges, and failed to analyze it. Neither magnetic nor gravitic, it must be something of the nebula's own. Here at the unknown borderland of space and counter-space, he thought, even such familiar terms as magnetism and gravitation could have no certain meaning. He watched the chronometer again, waiting fearfully for it to turn backward and knowing he would be dead before that could happen. There was nothing else to do.

"Ah, my poor old head," came the faint and weary plaint of Giles Habibula. "Deadly ill, and spinning like a silly top. Ah, poor old Giles is sick, sick, sick——"

But the sound of the geodynes came back, at first a harrowing growl.

"Sick, sick, sick!" sobbed Giles Habibula. "Ah, a poor old soldier of the Legion, hunted out of the precious System on a lying charge of wicked treason, and dying like a dog in a mortal storm in space. Sick and—ah, *there!*"

The geodynes, abruptly, were humming clear and sweet.

The *Purple Dream* was alive again. John Star turned her out of that savage, sucking current. She nosed through a river of hurtling stones, and drove through a cloud of greenish gas; and ahead was the rift again. The black of space, and bright Antares.

They came out of the last thin streamer of the storm, into the clear dark of space. Ahead were the cold diamond stars; and the greenish shadow of the nebula swiftly dwindled behind—in the vaster cosmic scale, it was just a speck of curious dust.

"Safe!" John Star exulted.

"Safe!" Jay Kalam repeated the word, and smiled a slow, ironic smile. "And there ahead is Barnard's Star."

In the field of the tele-periscope, John Star found the Runaway Sun. It was a red and solitary eye, watching their approach with a cold, steady stare of unblinking menace.

"Yes, we're safe enough, for now," Jay Kalam smiled, a dark taut smile. "I think we're rid of that spider-ship. I think we can reach the planet, now—if we can pass the barrier the Medusæ have set up to defend it."

John Star merely looked at him, with a weary, dim dismay.

"There was something about that barrier belt in the secret reports that came to Aladoree on Mars," Jay Kalam explained. "Not much—Commander Ulnar let her know just enough so she wouldn't suspect his plot. Perhaps he could tell us something more. But I believe the Medusæ have their planet very effectively defended."

He smiled again, gravely.

"Anyhow, John, we're safe enough for now."

CHAPTER THIRTEEN

The Belt of Peril

They went to the cruiser's brig.

"Welcome, John." Adam Ulnar called that cheerful greeting to them, through the bars of the tiny cell. Elder statesman of the Purple Hall, Commander of the Legion, and traitor against mankind, he sat on the edge of the narrow bunk, busy with his memoirs.

"Just a moment, John." Deliberately he finished the sentence he was writing, laid his pen and manuscript aside on the neatly folded blanket, and stood up to meet them. A tall, distinguished statesman. His wide shoulders were proudly erect; his fine head, with the long white hair well-combed and flowing, was bowed to no visible burden of guilt.

"A pleasure, gentlemen." He smiled, and his fine blue eyes held a spark of ironic amusement. "I've too few guests. Come on in. Rough weather we've been meeting, by the feel of the ship."

"But we'll find rougher weather ahead," John Star told him. "Or so I imagine—from all I hear of the Belt of Peril."

That phrase had rather a remarkable effect on Adam Ulnar. His face lost its smile of wary mockery, and froze to a rigid mask. Behind the mask, John Star sensed something like consternation. His hands clenched white on the bars of the cell. He stared from one to the other of them; and seconds had passed before he could speak.

"The Belt——" he swallowed. "You mean we're bound for Barnard's Star?"

"We're going after Aladoree," John Star said crisply. "I understand that Eric's expedition reported some kind of defensive barrier zone around the Medusæ's planet. We want to know what it is—and how to get through it alive."

The fine wrinkles bit deeper into Adam Ulnar's face, and all the cheerful color had ebbed from it. The pupils of his blue eyes were black and big with a sick dismay.

"I don't know what it is." His voice was slow and dull with fear. "I don't know."

"You must!" John Star's voice was a brittle challenge. "You had the full reports, uncensored. Eric must have told you all about it. Let's have it!"

Heavily, the old Commander shook his head.

"Edic didn't know," he said. "Even after the Medusæ had made their agreement to help us, in return for a cargo of iron, they wouldn't tell him anything about it. All I know is what it did to the ships of his expedition when they first tried to land."

"And what was that?"

"Enough," Adam Ulnar said. "His fleet approached the barrier zone without any warning of danger, you see—fortunately Eric had been smart enough to bring his flagship to the rear. Only the two lead vessels got into the zone. They never came out.

"What the barrier force is, his engineer couldn't discover. They believed that it is radiant energy—if so, however, it is something different in effect from any gamma or cosmic radiation known to us. The crews of those two unfortunate ships had no time to signal any reports. The ships fell, out of control. Observers on the other vessels reported that they seemed to be disintegrating—falling apart. Later, a few meteor-like streaks were observed in the planet's upper atmosphere. And that was all.

"Eric kept the rest of his fleet outside the barrier, until he had established radio and television communication with the Medusæ—which took a considerable time. Afterwards, they allowed several of his ships to visit the planet and leave it again—apparently they can open the barrier, at will."

John Star eyed him sharply.

"What else do you know?" he demanded. "The men who landed must have learned something about it?"

The old man clinging to the bars forced a sick, yellow smile.

"The most of them could never tell what they learned." His dull voice held an echo of dread. "They're the ones who came back to die in the mental wards—if they came back at all. You see, there's something in the planet's atmosphere that isn't good for the flesh or the minds of men. A virus, a secondary radiation excited by the barrier rays, or perhaps a toxic emanation from the bodies of the Medusæ themselves—those stricken scientists could never agree on what it was. But they did prove that men can't go there and live. The effects are extremely variable, and sometimes long delayed. But the onset, when it comes, is sudden and terrible."

"Thank you, Commander," Jay Kalam said, and they turned away.

"Wait!" The shaken voice called after them. "You aren't going on—not into the Belt?"

"We're running through it," John Star assured him.

"We shall try," added Jay Kalam, "to get through it at a very high speed. By surprise. Before those radiations— if that is what they are—have time to take effect."

Holding himself upright, with his white and trembling hands on the bars, old Adam Ulnar looked at both their faces. His pale lips twitched. Bowed, now, his shoulders made a weary little shrug, and he finally spoke.

"I can see there's no dissuading you, John. You're the Ulnar breed, and you won't yield to danger. I believe you're really going to try to run the Belt. I really believe you're ready to land on that monstrous planet, a thing that even Eric wouldn't do."

"I am," John Star said.

"I believe you really are." That white, distinguished head nodded slowly, and a feeble spark of pride came back to the stricken eyes. "I admire your resolution, John. At least you'll die an Ulnar's death.

"Now, if you please, John, I've one last request."

"What is that, Commander?" John Star heard a sudden respect in his own voice, and something close to warmth.

"In my desk, in my stateroom, there's a secret drawer," the bleak-faced old man said huskily. "I'll tell you how to find it. It contains a little vial of poison——"

John Star shook his head. "We can't do that."

"We're kinsmen, John." Adam Ulnar's voice held a broken, pleading quaver. "In spite of our present political quarrel, you must remember that once I did a favor for you. I paid for your education, remember, and put you in the Legion. Am I asking too much in return—a few drops of euthanasia?"

"I'm afraid you are," John Star told him. "Because I think we'll need information from you again, when we come to deal with the Medusæ."

"No, John!" the old man sobbed, wild-eyed and frantic now. "Please, John! You can't deny me death——"

"We ought to bring you the bottle, Commander." Jay Kalam gave him a lean dark smile. "Just to see what you'd do. Because you've over-played your role."

Adam Ulnar returned that sober smile. His clutching hands released the bars, and his bent shoulders straightened.

"I was trying to turn you back," he confessed. "I've no need of poison, if you do go on—I believe that death in the Belt is as quick as a man could wish." His voice still was taut and urgent. "But every word I've told you is the truth. You'll never land alive—or, if you do, you'll presently be needing that little bottle yourselves, to escape your madness and your pain.

"Bad luck, gentlemen!"

He dismissed them with a casual wave of his hand, and went back to the papers on his narrow bunk.

The *Purple Dream* drove on.

Barnard's Star burned on their right. A swelling, perfect sphere, sharp-edged against the ebon void. A type-M dwarf, old beyond imagination, so far gone in stellar death that their eyes could safely look upon it, with no filters behind the lenses. But its blood-red rays smote to their very brains, with a stark impact of fateful menace.

Straight ahead was its solitary planet, a dim and fearful crescent, washed with that ominous scarlet. World of the monstrous Medusæ, of that black spider-ship, of the waiting Belt of Peril.

The ship drove on, geodynes singing keen and clear. John Star and Jay Kalam stood before the tele-periscopes, watching for the first sign of danger. The red and cloudy planet swelled ahead.

The night-side of it was utterly black, a round blot on the stars. The day-side was a curved and ugly crimson blade, stained with evil blood, clotted with dark rust. Its orbit lay close to the dying dwarf. And it was gigantic, John Star realized; many times the bulk of Earth.

Jay Kalam drew a long, awed breath.

"The forts!" he whispered. "The stations that make the barrier—that's what they must be. A belt of moons!"

John Star found them. Dim and tiny crescents, red as the monstrous planet. He found three, following in the same orbit high above the murky atmosphere of the mighty world ahead; there must be six in all, he guessed, spaced sixty degrees apart.

A ring of fortress moons! The barrier itself must be invisible radiation, but the perfect spacing of those trailing satellites was proof enough of the Medusæ's hostile and scientific craft. John Star's brooding gaze went back to the larger murky crescent.

"Aladoree—there!" His low-breathed words were choked with a sense of incredulous horror. "Beyond those moons! Hidden and guarded, somewhere on that planet. And tortured, I suppose, for the secret of AKKA. We must get through, Jay."

"We must."

And Jay Kalam spoke quiet orders into his telephone.

"Mortal me!" a thin voice came plaintively back from the bulkhead speaker. "For the sake of precious life, Jay, can't we have a single breath of time? Must we go driving like a pack of reckless fools into new and wicked dangers, with never a blessed pause? Can't you give us a

Alive with pleasure!
Newport

©Lorillard, U.S.A., 1976

18 mg. "tar", 1.2 mg. nicotine
av. per cigarette, FTC Report Dec. 1976.

Newport 20 CLASS A CIGARETTES

Newport

MENTHOL KINGS

True lowers tar to only

5 MGS. TAR

And has a taste worth changing to.

Regular: 5 mgs. "tar", 0.4 mgs. nicotine, av. per cigarette, FTC Report Dec. 1976.

©Lorillard, U.S.A., 1976

TRUE
FILTER CIGARETTES
5 MGS. TAR 0.5 MGS. NICOTINE
TRUE 5 MGS. TAR

moment, Jay—just one single precious moment—to snatch a bite to eat?"

"Give us all the power you can, Giles," Jay Kalam broke in gently. "Because, right now, we're diving toward the barrier zone, depending on surprise and speed."

"Dear life—not now!" gasped Giles Habibula. "Not into that wicked thing they call the Belt of Peril!"

"We are, Giles," Jay Kalam said. "We're going to try it midway between two of their forts, hoping their rays will interfere."

"Sweet life—not yet!" sobbed Giles Habibula. "Give us time, Jay, for a single sip of wine! You couldn't be so heartless, Jay—not to a poor old soldier of the Legion. Not to a miserable, tottering human skeleton, Jay, dead on his feet from toiling day and night to keep his precious geodynes going, and gone to skin and bones for want of time to eat.

"Not that, Jay! Not to poor old——"

But John Star was listening no longer.

Tense at the controls, scarcely breathing, he was driving the *Purple Dream* down toward that vast and evil-seeming crescent of crimson murk, aiming straight between two of those black and tiny moons. And now he saw a fearful thing. Still no visible projectile or ray had come from the fortress satellites, but he saw something happening to the ship—and to him!

The metal bulkheads, and the faces of all the instruments before him, were suddenly luminous. His own skin was shining. Bright atoms were dancing away into the air, swirling motes of many colors. The very metal of the ship, it seemed, was evaporating into iridescent mist. His own body was!

Then he felt it—a sheet of blinding pain.

For a moment he gave way to agony, sick and reeling, eyes closed. He fought grimly to control himself, and lurched unsteadily toward Jay Kalam—who was a shimmering spectre now, clad in a splendid mist of dissolving rainbows.

"What——" His gasping voice came faint and strange, and agony clenched his teeth upon it. "What's this?"

"Radiation——" The bright spectre's voice was thin with pain. "Must dissolve the molecular bonds! . . . Ionized atoms dancing away . . . Everything melting into

atomic mist! . . . Molecular dissolution! . . . Our very
nerves—destroyed!"

"How long can——?"

His voice went out. Red agony surged against his brain.
Every limb and every tissue shrieked. Even the cells of
his brain itself, he felt, screamed protest at this consuming radiation. Every second he thought he had felt the ultimate agony, and every second the agony increased.

He was blind with pain. Pain roared in his ears. Red-
hot needles of pain probed every fiber of his body. But
still he fought to keep the mastery of himself. He stood
rigid over the controls and drove the cruiser down.

Above the agony thundering in his ears, he heard the
whine of the hard-pressed geodynes change again to harsh
vibration. That ugly snarl increased, until the whole ship
shuddered to it. It became terrific. He thought it would
break the very hull.

But the vibration ended suddenly. The ship was deathly
still. The geodynes had failed completely. Only momentum was left, to carry them on through the radiation-
wall.

In the new silence he heard Adam Ulnar screaming in
the brig.

"Disintegration . . ." came the faint, hoarse rasp from
Jay Kalam. "We're going—invisible!"

He saw, then, that the solid metal of the mechanisms
about him was becoming weirdly and incredibly semi-
transparent, as if about to dissolve completely in the glittering mist that swirled away from them, ever denser.

He looked at Jay Kalam, through the haze of shattered
jewels, and saw a ghastly thing.

That shining spectre-shape was semi-transparent now,
bones visible like shadows within misty outlines of flesh.
Fiery smoke swirling away from it. It looked no longer
human; it was grisly death, melting into nothingness.

Yet it still had consciousness, reason, will.

A sound whispered from it, dry and faint:

"Rockets!"

John Star knew that he was another dissolving ghost.
Every atom of his body flamed with unendurable pain.
Red agony blinded him, shrieked in his ears, froze his
body in a final rigor. Yet he moved, before it overcame
him utterly.

He reached the rocket firing keys.

He was sprawled over the control board, the next he knew, weak and trembling. His sick body was limp, dripping with sweat. He dragged himself up, aware that his fearful, agonizing transparency was gone. He saw Jay Kalam, faint and white; saw beyond him a few glistening diamond particles still floating in the air.

"The rockets," breathed Jay Kalam, his voice weak, uncertain, yet gravely deliberate as ever. "The rockets brought us through."

"Through!" It was a dry, hoarse croak. "Inside the Belt?"

"Inside—and plunging toward the surface."

He fought to recover a grip on himself.

"Then we must brake our velocity, before we smash!"

"Giles!" Jay Kalam called into the telephone. "The geodynes——"

"Don't bother me now!" wheezed the faint and plaintive protest. "For poor old Giles is dying, dying! Ah, the wicked agony of it! And the generators are wrecked, burned up! Destroyed by that fearful vibration! They can never be repaired—not even by the rare and perfect skill of Giles Habibula. Ah, poor old Giles—not all his wits and his rare and precious genius can serve him now. Doomed and dying, far from home——"

"You don't mean it, Giles!" John Star broke in. "You can fix them!"

"No, John, the things are finished, I tell you. Burned up and done!"

"That's true," Jay Kalam said. "I checked them. The geodynes are gone. We've only the rockets to keep us from smashing to smoke."

John Star dragged himself grimly to the firing keys, muttering:

"Now is when we need the fuel we left on Pluto's moon!"

CHAPTER FOURTEEN

Corsair Sun

Down upon the huge, expanding, yellow-red planet the *Purple Dream* was hurtling, rocket blasts thundering forward at full power to check her flight—if it could be checked short of catastrophe.

Jay Kalam watched, gravely anxious, as John Star swiftly took the readings from a score of instruments, set them up on the calculators, and snapped down another key.

"What do you find?"

"A close thing," John Star said slowly, at last. "Much too close. At very nearly the same time, three things will happen. Our velocity will be braked, we'll approach the planet, and the rockets will run out of fuel.

"But that dense red atmosphere hides the surface—I can't tell just how far down it is. If it's too near, we smash before our momentum is checked. If it's too far, we'll be falling again—with all the fuel gone. It has to be just right—or else!"

"Then," Jay Kalam calmly observed, "we await the event. How long?"

"Two hours at full power will empty the tanks."

Jay Kalam nodded his lean, grave head, and turned silently back to his tele-periscope. After a moment he tensed suddenly, and turned to point out a new red spark that had crept unseen into the telltale screen.

"Another black flier," he announced. "Out to see the fireworks when we hit, I imagine—they must have spotted us, running past their satellite-forts."

John Star picked it up in his own instrument—a monstrous shape of gleaming black metal; wide vanes moving, strange and slow, about the huge black belly of its hull. Not far above them, it was merely keeping pace with their fall, making no hostile move.

"Waiting to see us smash!" he muttered. "Or to pick us off if we don't!"

"I'm going to get Commander Ulnar," Jay Kalam said abruptly. "I'm going to let him hail them. We've very little left to lose, and everything to gain. Perhaps we can ransom Aladoree. Whatever the Ulnars have offered, the System can afford to raise it—to save her and AKKA."

John Star nodded—perhaps there was a chance. Jay Kalam brought Adam Ulnar to the bridge. The tall Commander was still white and shaken from their passage through the radiation-barrier, but his haggard face smiled faintly.

"Congratulations, John! I never thought you'd get us through."

Jay Kalam told him in a hard, tight voice:

"I'm going to let you talk, Commander. I'll give you a chance to save your life—and to save Aladoree Anthar and her secret for the Green Hall. I'll leave the details to you. But I'm sure the Green Hall would approve any necessary ransom. And I promise you—if you can help us get Aladoree safely back to the System—I promise that you'll go free."

"Thank you, Kalam." The white, distinguished head made him a slight and half-ironic bow. "Thank you for the very touching measure of your trust in me. But it's true that I don't want to die, and true that Eric has blundered very foolishly in his management of the enterprise I planned—for the girl should never have been brought here at all.

"So I'll do what I can."

Sharply, John Star studied that proud face, etched with years but handsome still. For all his hatred of what this kinsman had done, he could see sincerity there, and honor, and reassuring strength.

"Very well," Jay Kalam said. "You can hail them from on board?"

"With the ultra-wave transmitter." The Commander nodded. "The Medusæ, you see, are not sensitive to sound—though Eric's men named them for some terrestrial jellyfish, they're really like nothing in the System. They communicate with short radio waves, directly. I know the code of signals that Eric's men worked out—I used to talk, from the Purple Hall, with the agents they sent to the System."

"Go ahead," Jay Kalam told him. "Get that ship to give us a line, before we crash. Get them to bring Aladoree Anthar safe on board, and to give us what we need to repair the geodynes. And make them open the barrier so we can get away—I don't think we'd survive another passage through it. Promise what you like—but you had better be convincing."

"I'll do what I can."

And Adam Ulnar sat down at the compact panel of the ship's transmitter, his hollowed face visibly strained and eager. He quickly tuned the frequency he wanted, and then began making sounds into the microphone—sounds instead of words, awkward grunts and clicks and whistles.

The reply which came presently from the receiver was stranger still. The voices of the Medusæ were shrill whisperings, dry and eerie, so utterly unearthly that John Star, listening, shuddered to a chill of undiluted horror.

Adam Ulnar, too, seemed to find amazed horror in what he heard. His lean jaw slackened with surprise. He was suddenly trembling, his lax face very white and abruptly pearled with sweat. His staring eyes were black, glazed.

Again he made queer little sounds into the transmitter, his voice so dry that he could scarcely form them. Dry rustlings came back from the receiver. He listened a long time, staring at nothing. At last the alien chirping ceased. Mechanically he reached a white and shaking hand to snap off the transmitter, and he came woodenly to his feet.

"What was it?" breathed John Star. "What did they say?"

"Nothing good," Adam Ulnar muttered blankly. Shakenly he clutched at a handrail to steady himself. "The worst that could have happened. Yet it's something I've dreaded—ever since I heard of Eric's foolish alliance."

His sick eyes gazed at the bulkhead, seeing nothing.

"What has happened?" John Star demanded.

Adam Ulnar rubbed a trembling hand across his sweat-beaded forehead.

"I scarcely dare to tell you, John. Because you'll blame me for it. And I suppose I am to blame—it was I who sent Eric out here with the expedition, so he'd have a chance to make himself a hero. Eric the Second!" He chuckled, without mirth. "Yes, I'm to blame."

"But what have they done?"

His glazed eyes came to John's face in mute appeal.

"Please don't think I planned it, John! But the Medusæ have tricked Eric—and the rest of us, it seems. They bargained to help us restore the Empire, in return for a shipload of iron. Now it seems they intend taking a good deal more."

His gaunt frame shuddered.

"They told me more of their history, just now, than Eric ever learned—and it's quite a history. They're old, John. Their sun is old. Their race was old, on that ghastly planet, before our Earth was ever born. They're too old, John—but they don't intend to die.

"The remarkable motion of Barnard's Star, they tell me now, is a thing of their own accomplishment. Because the mineral resources of their own planet were used up long ago, they've arranged to visit others. In their career across the Galaxy, they live by looting the worlds they pass, and sometimes plant a colony—that's to be the fate of Earth, they tell me."

He shook his white head with a sick, slow motion.

"Please, John," he whispered, "don't think I ever intended that!"

John Star and Jay Kalam stood voiceless with shock. The thing was unthinkable, but John Star knew it must be true. Reason insisted that the Medusæ would scarcely join an interstellar war for a single cargo of iron. And Adam Ulnar's horrified remorse appeared sincere enough.

Dazed, John Star pictured the doom of humanity. The System couldn't fight a science that built these black spider-ships of space and armed them with atomic suns for weapons; a science that fortified a planet with a belt of artificial satellites, and guided a star itself like a red corsair across the Galaxy.

No, the System didn't have a chance—not with the Legion of Space already betrayed by its own Commander's treason, and AKKA already in the hands of the monstrous enemy.

"Please, John!" Adam Ulnar's broken voice was thin with a sick appeal. "Please don't think I intended this. And now, if you please—I really want that little vial in my desk."

Harshly, John Star rasped: "You don't deserve to die!"

"No, Commander," Jay Kalam told him gravely. "You must live—at least a little longer. If we survive the landing, you may yet have a chance to help undo your treason."

He led the stumbling prisoner back to his cell.

Rockets still roaring, the *Purple Dream* fell. Intended only for the delicate maneuvering of takeoffs and landings, the rocket motors were never designed for such a task as this. Braking the terrific velocity which had brought them safely through the radiation barrier was a job for the geodynes—but the geodynes were gone. John Star stood rigid by the controls, fighting for the last ounce of power from the last drop of fuel; fighting to stop the cruiser in time.

The black spider-ship dropped after them. The efficient Medusæ watched—curious, no doubt, to observe the effects of their barrier rays on the wreckage of the ship. And ready, certainly, with some new weapon, if these rash invaders did survive the landing.

Thick red mist came up about the *Purple Dream.*

The black flier following became a dim vast shadow in the murk. All else was lost. And still the cruiser fell, toward the unseen world beneath the red-lit clouds. The rockets paused in their even thunder, came back, barked in a loud back-fire—and stopped.

"The fuel is out," John Star whispered. "Still falling—and nothing we can do!"

Hands knotted with an agony of powerless inaction, he peered into the thick, red-lit mist ahead. His straining eyes made out a surface—something smooth and glistening. It flashed up to meet them.

"A sea!" he breathed. "Going down——"

Panic choked him, but he heard Jay Kalam's voice, soft and calm even in the last moment of their plunging fall:

"Anyhow, John, we've got to the planet where Aladoree is."

CHAPTER FIFTEEN

Under the Unknown Sea

"So we're stuck on the bottom of a mortal sea?" observed Giles Habibula.

His mood was not rejoicing. He had the voice of a well-grown and lusty tomcat protesting a weighty tread on its tail.

John Star nodded soberly, and he continued bitterly: "Twenty long, loyal years I've truly served the Legion, since that evil day on Venus, when——"

He checked himself, with a roll of his fishy eye, and John Star prompted:

"How was it you came to join?"

"Twenty years, lad, old Giles has served in the Legion, as stout and true a blessed man, and—ah, yes, in good life's name!—as brave a soldier as ever was!"

"Yes, I know. But——"

"Old Giles has put his past behind him, lad." His voice turned reproachfully plaintive. "He has redeemed himself, if ever a daring hero did. And look at him now, bless his precious bones!

"Accused for a wicked pirate, when for twenty long years he's never done more than—when for twenty eternal years he's been a noble warrior in the Legion. Ah, yes, lad, look at old Giles Habibula. Look at him before you now!"

His voice broke; a great tear trembled in the corner of his fishy eye, as if terrified by the purple magnitude of the nose below, hesitated and dared and splashed down unheeded.

"Look at poor old Giles! Hunted like a dog out of his own native System. Driven like a rabbit into interstellar space. Hurled headlong into this planet of ghastly danger and crawling horrors. Stuck to spend the rest of his cheerless days of suffering in a wreck on the bottom of an evil sea!

"Pitiful old Giles Habibula! For years he's been feeble,

105

tottering, with gray hairs crowning his mortal head. He's been ill and lame. He's been forgotten, stuck away at a lonely, desolate little outpost on Mars.

"Now he's trapped to starve and die in a wreck on the bottom of a fearful yellow sea! Where's the precious justice of that, lad?"

He buried his great face in his hands, and trembled to sobs somewhat resembling the death-struggles of a harpooned whale. But it was not long before he straightened, and wiped his fishy eyes with the back of his fat hand.

"Anyhow, lad," he wheezed wearily, "let's have a drop of wine to help forget the frightful miseries that are piled upon us. And a taste of cold ham and biscuit. And there's a case of canned cheese I found in the stores the other day.

"And I'll tell you about that time on Venus, lad. It was a brave adventure—if I hadn't stumbled over a wicked reading lamp in the dark! For poor old Giles Habibula was clever, then, and nimble as you are, lad."

"No, we've no way to move the ship," John Star repeated, standing with Jay Kalam, a little later, on the bridge. "She lies in shallow water, though—according to the pressure-gauges, she's less than a hundred feet down."

"But we can't get her to the surface?"

"No. The geodynes are dead, and the rocket-fuel gone —if we had those drums we left on Pluto's moon! And the hull is too heavy to float. Wasn't designed for water navigation."

"Still," objected Jay Kalam, thoughtfully grave, yet with a calm determination that meant more than another's utmost vehemence. "Still, we can't give up. Not so long as we're alive and on the same planet with Aladoree."

"No," agreed John Star, quietly decisive. "If we could release her, just long enough to find materials and set up AKKA, we'd have the Medusæ at our mercy."

"That is what we must do—what we shall do.

"And now," he added, "let's talk to Adam Ulnar."

They found the man sitting wan and dejected on his cot in the brig, still dazed from the shock of the Medusæ's revelation. The regal pride of the Purple Hall had left him. He was staring blankly at the wall, dry lips moving. At first he was not aware of them; John Star heard the whispered words:

"Traitor! Betrayer of mankind."

"Adam Ulnar," called John Star, torn between pity and scorn for the shaken creature who stared up at them with a kind of listless fear. "Are you willing to help undo your crime?"

A little flicker of interest, of hope, came into the dull, tortured eyes. But the Commander of the Legion shook his head.

"I would help," his voice was dully droning, lifeless, "I'd do anything. But it's too late. Too late, now."

"No, man!" shouted John Star. "It isn't too late. Wake up!"

Adam Ulnar got uncertainly to his feet, his haggard face anxious.

"I'll help. But what can be done?"

"We're going to find Aladoree, and set her free. Then she can wipe out the Medusæ with the power of AKKA."

He sank back, and his voice was wearily bitter:

"You are fools. You are lying in a wrecked ship on the bottom of an ocean. Aladoree is guarded in a fortress that would be impregnable to all the fleets of the Legion —if the Medusæ haven't already tortured the secret from her and done away with her! You are idle fools—though not such fools as I was——"

"Tell us what you know about the planet," rapped Jay Kalam. "The geography of its continents. And about the Medusæ. Their weapons, their civilization, where they would be likely to imprison Aladoree."

Adam Ulnar looked at them dully, out of his apathy of despair.

"I'll tell you the little I know—though it will do no good. I was never here, myself, you know. I had only the reports that Eric's expedition brought back.

"This planet is much larger than Earth. About three times the diameter. Its rotation is very slow, its day about fifteen of Earth's. The nights are fearful. A week long, and bitterly cold—a type-M dwarf hasn't much heat left, you know."

His stare was drifting blankly past them; John Star urged him sharply:

"The continents?"

"There is just one large continent—about equal in area to all Earth. There's a strip of strange jungle along the shore, savage and deadly. It grows, Eric said, with amazing rapidity in the long day, and it swarms with fierce, unearthly life.

"Along the east coast, beyond the jungle, is a towering mountain range, more rugged, Eric said, than any in the System. West of the mountains is a vast, high plateau, lifeless, cut up by wild canyons. Beyond is the valley of an immense river that drains almost the whole continent.

"The Medusæ have only a single city left—life is hard on this dying planet, and the most of them have migrated to the other worlds they've conquered—as they mean to conquer ours. That city is located somewhere near the river's mouth—that's as near as I can place it."

"Aladoree?" prompted John Star anxiously.

"She would be in the city, no doubt. A quite amazing place, Eric said, huge by human standards. All built of black metal. Surrounded with walls a full mile high, to keep back the dreadful jungle. There's a colossal fortress in the center, a gigantic tower of black metal. They'd be likely, I imagine, to keep her there—guarded by weapons that could annihilate all the fleets of the System in an instant."

"Anything else you know?" urged Jay Kalam, as the hunted eyes fled back into vacancy.

"No. Nothing else."

"Wake up! Think! The System is at stake!"

He started.

"No—yes, there's one thing I remember, though it won't do you any good to warn you. The atmosphere!"

"What about the atmosphere?"

"You saw that it's reddish?"

"Yes. What—isn't it breathable?"

"It contains oxygen. You can breathe it. But it's filled with the red gas. It does the Medusæ no harm—but it isn't good for men. Its an artificial organic gas, they told me when we talked. They generated it to control the climate—to cut heat radiation at night. They mean to fill the air of Earth with it, no doubt. But it isn't good for men . . ."

He collected himself with a visible effort.

"You remember that wound on your shoulder, John? That was caused by the same red gas. Squirted on you in liquid form. The Medusæ have learned what it does to human beings. The men of Eric's expedition . . ."

The gaunt man shuddered. "Their trouble came from just breathing this atmosphere. It didn't bother them at once, except for a slight discomfort. But later there was a mental derangement. Their flesh began to rot. And there was a good deal of pain. And then . . ."

"Your doctors treated me, after I was burned on Mars," John Star broke in suddenly. "What was that they used?"

"We had worked out a neutralizing formula. But we haven't the ingredients on board."

"We can live, though, for a time, in spite of it?"

"For a time," he echoed dully. "Individual reactions varied, but usually the worst complications were delayed for several months."

"Then it doesn't greatly matter."

"No," Adam Ulnar spoke with a dull and bitter emphasis. "No, you'll find death, if you manage to leave the ship, in a million quicker forms. Life on this planet is very old, you know. The struggle for survival has been severe. The result is a fauna—and a flora—fit to live with the Medusæ. You'll never survive, outside the ship."

"But we're going to try," Jay Kalam informed him.

"The *Purple Dream*," John Star announced a little later when they were all five gathered on the narrow deck just within the air-lock, "is lying on the bottom of a shallow sea. The water is only about eighty feet deep. We can't move the vessel, but we can get out——"

"Get out!" echoed gigantic Hal Samdu. "How?"

"Through the air-lock. We'll have to swim to the surface, and try for the shore—with the water only eighty feet, it's likely enough that we're just off some coast. We'll have to strip for it. And we won't be able to burden ourselves with weapons or supplies.

"We could exist indefinitely here on board. Plently of air and supplies. Perhaps we can survive only a few minutes outside. We may not even reach the surface. If we do, it will be only to meet the dangers of a world where even the air is slow poison."

"My precious eye!" broke in Giles Habibula. "Here we're all stuck to die of slow starvation at the bottom of a fearful sea of evil. And that isn't enough! You want us to swim out like mortal fishes at the bottom of this wicked yellow ocean?"

"Precisely," agreed John Star.

"You want poor old Giles to drown himself like a brainless rat, when he's still got plenty of victuals and wine? Poor old Giles Habibula——"

"You're a fool, John," said Adam Ulnar, with dull and savage emphasis. "You'll never get ashore. You never heard the tales that Eric's men brought back. You don't know the sort of life—plant as well as animal—that fights for survival in the long, red days. How can you live through the nights? You were born on a kind world, John. You weren't evolved to survive on this one."

"Any of you may stay on board, who wish," Jay Kalam interrupted quietly. "John is going. And I am. Hal?"

"Of course I'll go!" rumbled the giant, reddening with a slow anger. "Did you think, with Aladoree at the mercy of those monsters, that I'd stay behind?"

"Of course not, Hal. And you, Giles?"

The fishy eyes of Giles Habibula rolled anxiously; he trembled spasmodically; sweat came out on his face; in a dry voice he spoke, with a sudden effort: "Mortal me! Do you want to go away and leave poor wretched old Giles Habibula here to starve and rot on the bottom of this wicked ocean? Life's precious sake!" he rasped convulsively. "I'll go! But first old Giles must have a taste of food to put strength in his feeble old body, and a nip of wine to steady his torn and tortured nerves."

He rolled unsteadily away toward the galley.

"And you, Commander?" demanded Jay Kalam. "Are you going?"

"No." Adam Ulnar shook his head. "It's no use. Competition has bred some very successful life forms in the seas here, I believe, as well as on the land."

The four entered the air-lock, stripped to the skin, carrying their clothing, proton guns, a few pounds of concentrated food, and—on Giles Habibula's insistence—a bottle of wine; all wrapped in a big water-tight bundle.

They sealed the heavy inner valve and John Star opened the equalization tube through the outer; a thick stream of water roared into the little chamber, flooding it, rising ice-cold about their bodies, compressing the air above them. Merciless pressure squeezed them.

The inrush stopped, with water about their shoulders.

John Star spun the control-wheel of the outer valve, but the armored door stuck fast.

"Jammed!" he gasped. "We must try it by hand."

"Let me!" cried Hal Samdu, surging forward through the chill water, his voice oddly shrill in the dense air. He set his great back against the metal valve, braced himself, strained. His muscles snapped. Agony of effort twisted his face into a strange mask. His swift breath was harsh and gasping.

John Star and Jay Kalam added their strength, all of them struggling in cold water that came to their chins, fighting for breath in the hot, stale air.

The valve gave abruptly. A rush of water swept them back. Air gurgled out. They filled their lungs out of the trapped air-pocket, dragged themselves out through the opening, and swam desperately for the surface.

Dark water, numbingly cold, weighed on them crushingly.

John Star fought the relentless, overwhelming pressure of it; he fought a savage urge to empty his tortured lungs and breathe. He struggled upward through grim infinities of time. Then suddenly, surprisingly, he was upon the surface of the yellow sea, sobbing for his breath.

Flat and glistening, an oily yellow-red under the cold red sky, the unknown sea stretched away into murky crimson distance. It lifted and fell in long, slow swells.

At first he was alone. Jay Kalam's head burst up beside him, dripping, panting. Then Hal Samdu's red hair. They waited, gasping for life, too breathless for speech. They waited a long time, and at last Giles Habibula's bald dome came up, fringed with thin white hair.

They swam on the yellow sea, and breathed deeply, gratefully—forgetful that every breath was slow poison.

The blank surface lay away from them, a waste of silent desolation. The sky was a cold lowering dome of sullen crimson; the sun burned low in it, an incredibly huge disk of deeper, sinister scarlet. A dying dwarf, old when the Sun of Earth was born, it seemed too cold to warm them.

"Our next problem!" panted John Star. "The shore!"

"The bundle," muttered Hal Samdu. "With the guns. Didn't float!"

Indeed, it had not appeared.

"My blessed bottle of wine!" wept Giles Habibula.

Then they were all silent. Some large, unseen body had plunged above the yellow surface near them; had fallen back with a noisy splash.

CHAPTER SIXTEEN

Black Continent to Cross

They waited, treading water, getting back their breath, while they watched for the precious package which held their clothing and weapons and food, and Giles Habibula's bottle of wine.

"It isn't coming up," John Star despaired at last. "We must strike out for the shore without it."

"It leaked, I suppose," said Jay Kalam. "Or hung in the valve."

"Or it may have been swallowed," wheezed Giles Habibula, "by the monster that made that fearful splash. Ah, my precious wine——"

"Which way is the shore?" demanded Hal Samdu.

Away from their bobbing heads reached the oily, heaving yellow sea, unbroken by any landmark. Oppressively low overhead hung the gloomy sky, thick with the murk of that red poison gas. Far across the sea burned the vast, sullen sun, a blood-red ball. A light breeze touched their faces, so faint it hardly scarred the yellow surface.

"We've two possible guides," observed Jay Kalam, keeping afloat with a calm, unhurried efficiency of motion. "The sun, and the wind."

"How——?"

"The sun is low but rising. It must, then, be in the east. That tells us direction.

"As for the wind, there would surely be a sea-breeze on the coast of a continent so large as Adam Ulnar described. At this time in the morning the wind should just be rising from the sea, as the air over the land-mass begins to warm and ascend."

"So we swim with the wind? Toward the west?"

"Our best chance, I think, though the reasoning is based

on a very incomplete astronomical and geographical knowledge of the planet. Too bad we couldn't have got a glimpse of the continent, through this murk, as we fell. For it could easily be that we aren't near the coast at all, but simply over some shoal. But I think our best chance is to swim with the wind."

They struck out away from the red sun. John Star with a steady, effortless crawl. Hal Samdu breaking the water with slow, powerful strokes. Jay Kalam swimming with a deliberate, noiseless efficiency. Giles Habibula puffing, splashing, falling a little behind. For a time that seemed hours, they swam, until he gasped:

"For sweet life's sake! Let's rest a bit! What's the mortal hurry?"

"We may as well," agreed Jay Kalam. "The shore may be within two miles. Or it may be two hundred, or two thousand."

They treaded water for a time, and then swam on again with slow, weary determination.

At first they had noticed nothing unusual in the air. But John Star presently became aware of an irritation of his eyes and nostrils, an oppression in his laboring lungs. He found himself coughing a little; presently he heard the others coughing. The unpleasant fate of those survivors of Eric Ulnar's expedition came to his mind, but he kept his silence.

It was Giles Habibula who spoke:

"This red and fearful air! Already it's choking me to death! Poor old Giles! Ah, it's not enough that he should be flung into the unknown ocean of an alien, monstrous planet, to die swimming like a luckless rat in a tub of buttermilk.

"Ah, mortal me! That's not enough! He must be poisoned with this wicked red gas, that will make a raving mortal maniac out of him, and eat the very flesh off his poor old bones with an evil green leprosy! Poor old soldier——"

A tremendous splash cut short his melancholy wheezing; a huge, tapering body, black and glistening, had plunged above the yellow surface behind him, and dived cleanly back.

"My blessed bones!" he gasped. "Some fearful whale, come to swallow all of us!"

Unpleasantly aware that they were drawing the attention of the unknown denizens of the yellow sea, they all swam harder—until the creature leaped again, in front of them.

"Don't exhaust yourselves," Jay Kalam's calm voice came above their frantic splashing. "We can't distance it. But perhaps it won't attack."

Then Giles Habibula sobbed abruptly: "Another monstrous horror!"

They saw a curving, saw-toothed black fin, cutting the oily yellow surface not far away. It swept toward them, cleaved a complete circle about them, and vanished for a time, only to appear again and cut another circle.

"They're making us a precious circus," wheezed Giles Habibula. "And then, no doubt, a wicked feast!"

"Look, there ahead!" boomed keen-eyed Hal Samdu, abruptly. "Something black, floating."

John Star soon made it out, a long black object, low in the water, still veiled in the sullen, red-yellow murk.

"Can't tell what it is. Might be a log. Or something swimming."

"My mortal eye!" shrieked Giles Habibula suddenly; and he fell to furious splashing, purple-faced, desperately groaning for breath.

"What's the matter, Giles?"

"Some—frightful monster—nibbling away—at my blessed toes!"

They swam doggedly on, toward that black and distant object.

John Star felt a harsh, stinging rasp against his thigh; he saw his own blood staining the yellow water at his side. "Something just took off a sample bit of me!"

"They must be just investigating us," said Jay Kalam. "When they find we don't fight back——"

"That *is* a log, ahead!" shouted Hal Samdu.

"Then we must reach it, climb on it——"

"—before these wicked creatures eat us up alive!" finished Giles Habibula.

Driving leaden-weary muscles to the utmost, they struggled on. John Star was toiling for air, every breath a stabbing pain, every slow stroke a supreme act of will. The others, he knew, were as near exhaustion; Hal Samdu's red ugly face was savage with effort; Jay Kalam's white and set; Giles Habibula, panting, splashing desperately, was purple-faced.

The yellow surface for a time was clear. Then the black, saw-toothed fin came back; it cut the water in a deliberate curve, and came slicing directly at John Star.

He waited until it was near; then he splashed suddenly, shouted, kicked out at it. His bare feeet came laceratingly against sharp scales. The fin turned, vanished. For a while the surface was again unbroken.

On they swam, every breath a torturing flame, every stroke an agony. The black log came near, a huge rough cylinder, a hundred feet long, covered with coarse, scaly bark. On its upper side, at one end, they could see a curious greenish excrescence.

Ahead of them, something splashed again. The curved black fin looped its silent way between them and the log.

They swam on, drawing the energy for every stroke from sheer desperation. The curving rough surface was above them. John Star was all but grasping for it, when he felt sharp jaws close on his ankle. A savage tug dragged him strangling under the surface.

He bent himself double, hands jabbing at a hard, sharp-scaled body, free foot kicking. His hands found something soft that felt like an eye. His fingers gouged into it; jabbed, hooked and tore.

The thing writhed under him, rolling and twisting furiously. He jabbed again, kicked desperately. His ankle came free; he struggled for the surface, strangling. His head burst above the yellow water, and he cleared his eyes to see the curved black fin cutting straight at him.

Then Hal Samdu's giant hand clutched his arm from behind, hauled him up; he found himself seated with the others on the great black cylinder of the log.

"My mortal eye!" wheezed Giles Habibula. "That was a wicked narrow——"

He stopped with a gasp, his fishy eyes bulging; Jay Kalam observed quietly:

"We've a companion on board."

John Star saw the thing he had already observed as a greenish excrescence on the other end of the log. A huge mass of muddily translucent, jelly-like matter, that must have weighed several tons, in color a dull, slimy green, it clung to the black bark with a score of shapeless pseudopods.

Slowly, with baleful, unknown senses, it became aware of them. Semiliquid streams began to flow within its formless bulk, as they watched in puzzled horror; it thrust out extensions, flowed into them, and so began an appalling march down the log, toward them.

"What is the fearful thing?"

"A gigantic amœba, apparently," said Jay Kalam. "Looking for dinner."

"And he'll find it," estimated John Star, "at his present rate of motion, in about half an hour."

The four men, naked, exhausted and defenseless, sat on their own end of the log, watching thin green arms thrusting out, and slow streams of semifluid jelly flowing to swell them. The whole hideous bulk never seemed to move, yet was ever nearer.

How would it feel to be engulfed in it? To be seized by the shapeless, creeping arms, drawn into the avid, boneless mass, inch by inch, smothered and consumed. John Star caught his breath, and tried to shake off that hypnosis of slow horror, and peered around him desperately.

Sullenly red was the sky above. An angry, brighter red, the enormous, sinister disk of the sun burned low in the east. The wind, freshening out of it, ruffled the surface of the yellow sea. Yellow horizons melted into reddish haze. Around and around the log, in endless circles, sliced a curved, saw-toothed fin.

The colossal amœba reached the middle of the log.

"When it gets here," suggested John Star doubtfully, "we might dive off and try for the other end again."

"And be swallowed alive in the mortal water!" predicted Giles Habibula dolefully. "Old Giles is going to stay where he can see what eats him."

"The wind," said Jay Kalam, hopefully, "is drifting us toward the shore—I hope. And it should be near, or there wouldn't be driftwood."

The creeping horror was three-fourths of the way down the log when sharp-eyed Hal Samdu shouted:

"The shore! I see land!"

Far off, under the smoky red horizon at the rim of the yellow sea, was a low dark line.

"But it's miles," said John Star. "We must get past this monster, somehow——"

"We can rock the log," suggested Jay Kalam. "Turn it. And run past while our fellow-passenger is underneath."

"And likely spill ourselves off to feed the wicked things in the water, when it turns over!"

But they stood up, perilously, on the rough bark, and stepped in unison, at Jay Kalam's word, from side to side. At first their huge craft showed no visible motion; the great amœba continued its unhurried flowing.

Gradually, however, under their combined weight, the log began to spin lazily back and forth, each time a little farther. The wet bark was slippery; Giles Habibula sprawled, once, and gasped in terror as John Star dragged him back:

"Bless my bones! Poor old Giles is no nimble monkey, lad——"

The black fin cut close beneath; his fishy eyes rolled after it.

The nearest reaching arm of formless, avidly flowing, green jelly was not five feet away, when the log passed the point of equilibrium; it turned suddenly, and set them scrambling desperately on hands and knees to keep on top.

"Now!" breathed Jay Kalam.

Clinging to one another, they scrambled unsteadily along the wet surface, toward the other end, safe again for a time. But the great mass of hungry protoplasm appeared again above the log, green and dripping. Its senses somehow found them. It flowed again.

Twice they repeated that awkward maneuver, before the log touched bottom.

A black world lay ahead, ominous and dreadful.

The yellow shallows lapped on a beach of bare black sand. Beyond the beach rose an amazing jungle—a dark wall of thorns. Straight, dead-black spines, flaming with innumerable huge violet blooms, bristling with thousands of barbed and savage points. An impenetrable barrier of woven swords, easily a hundred feet high.

Above the gloomy jungle of thorns rose the mountain ranges; immense peaks towered up, rampart behind gigantic rampart, a rugged, precipitous, sky-looming wilderness of crags, bare, grimly and lifelessly black. The last somber wall drew its ragged edge across the crimson, sullen sky midway to the zenith.

Black sand, black jungle of thorns, black barrier of nightmare ranges, under a scarlet sky; the world ahead was shadowed by a spirit of hostile malevolence; it slowed the heart with nameless dread.

"Ashore!" exulted John Star, as they splashed through the shallows, waving a mocking farewell to the amœba on the log.

"Yes, we're ashore," agreed Jay Kalam. "But, you observe, on an eastern coast. The city of the Medusæ is somewhere on the west coast, the Commander said. That means we have this jungle to cross, and those mountains, and all the continent beyond."

"Ah, yes, a black continent ahead, full of mortal horrors," wept Giles Habibula. "Ah, me, and we've no weapons, we're naked as blessed babes. Not even a bite to eat! Poor old Giles, destined to starve on the alien shores of evil——"

CHAPTER SEVENTEEN

The Rope in the Jungle

"Weapons," began Jay Kalam, "are what we must first——"

John Star caught his breath with pain as something jabbed into his bare foot, and broke in with a wry smile:

"Here's one to begin with. Edge like a razor—warranted!"

He picked up the thing he had stepped on, a wide black shell, with a curving edge. Jay Kalam examined it seriously.

"Good enough," he said. "A useful blade."

He looked for others, as they walked up the beach, and found one for each of his companions. Giles Habibula accepted his disdainfully:

"Ah, for life's sake, Jay! Do you expect me, with this feeble thing, to cut a way through those frightful daggers and bayonets waiting for us ahead—waiting to slice us into bleeding ribbons?"

He pointed at the black thorn-jungle.

"And so we're armed," Jay Kalam told him. "As soon as we can cut a spear apiece."

They approached the black, violet-flowering barrier of thorns and spines and hooked spikes. Many of the blades were ten feet long; the close-grained wood seemed hard and sharp as steel. Naked and sensitive as their bodies were, it was not easy for the four to get near the blades they had selected; it proved less easy to cut and shape the iron-hard wood with shells.

Weary hours had passed before each of them was equipped with a ten-foot spear, and a shorter, triangular, saw-toothed dagger. Hal Samdu shaped himself also a great club from a piece of driftwood.

"Ah, so now we set out to cross a whole fearful continent on our bare, blessed feet——" Giles Habibula had begun, with a last regretful look back toward the yellow sea, when his fishy eyes spied something. He ran heavily back toward the beach.

It was their bundle he found, drifted ashore while they worked.

"Our clothes, again!" exulted John Star. "And real guns!"

"And my blessed bottle of wine!" wheezed Giles Habibula, laboring to open the bundle on the sand.

Their hopes for weapons were dashed. The package had leaked; their clothing was sodden, most of the food ruined, the delicate mechanism of the proton guns quite useless from contact with the corrosive yellow water.

Only the bottle of wine was completely undamaged. Giles Habibula held it up toward the red sun, regarding it with a fond fishy eye.

"Open it," suggested Hal Samdu. "We need something——"

Giles Habibula swallowed regretfully, and slowly shook his head.

"Ah, no, Hal," he said sadly. "When it's gone there'll be no more. Not a precious drop of wine on the whole evil continent. Ah, no, it must be preserved for an hour of greater need."

He set it down firmly but carefully on the black sand.

Discarding the useless proton guns, they finished as much of the food as remained edible, and gratefully donned their half-dry clothing—even under the continual radiation of the near sun and the blanket of heat-absorbing red gas, the atmosphere was far from tropical. John Star rudely bandaged the lacerations on thigh and ankle that he had sustained on the way ashore. Giles Habibula stowed the bottle of wine in one of his ample pockets, carefully wrapped against breakage. And they plunged into the jungle.

Thick, fleshy black stems rose close about them, twisted together overhead in an unbroken tangle, bristling with knife-sharp, saw-toothed blades. The dense roof of thorns hid the crimson sky completely; merely a ghastly blood-hued twilight filtered to the jungle floor.

With infinite caution they picked a way under the tangle of blades, and even caution did not save them. Clothing suffered; each of them was soon bleeding from a dozen minor cuts that throbbed painfully from the poison of the blades. And soon they met a danger more appalling.

"One advantage," Jay Kalam was observing, "is that if the thorns hinder us, they also hinder any enemies that— *ugh!*"

A little choking cry cut off his grave voice. John Star turned to see him carried off the ground by a long purple rope. Hanging from the crimson gloom above, it had wrapped itself twice about his body, and clapped a flat, terminal sucking-disk to his throat. Struggling savagely, he was helpless in the contracting, inch-thick tentacle. Swiftly, it drew him up into the tangle of black thorns.

John Star leaped after him, dagger lifted, but already he had been carried out of reach.

"Throw me, Hal!" he gasped.

The giant seized him by knee and thigh, flung him mightily upward toward the red-lit roof of thorns. With one grasping hand he seized a coil of the tough purple cable. Immediately it shortened, drawing him higher, forming another loop to throw about his body.

Hanging on with one hand, he sawed at it with his dagger in the other, above Jay Kalam's shoulder. Tough purple skin cut through; a thin, violet-colored fluid streamed out and down his arm—sap or blood, he did not know. Hard fibers, inside, formed a core that did not cut so easily.

A coil slipped about his shoulders, constricted savagely.

"Thank you, John," Jay Kalam whispered faintly, voiceless, but without panic. "But turn loose, while you can."

He sawed and hacked away, silently.

Suddenly there was red in the streaming fluid—it was, he knew, Jay Kalam's blood.

The purple cable contracted spasmodically, with agonizing, bone-cracking force.

"Too—too late! Sorry—John!"

Jay Kalam's white face went limp.

He made a last, fierce effort, as unendurable pressure forced the breath from his lungs in a long gasp of agony. The live cable parted, they fell.

They were, the next John Star knew, outside the jungle.

He was lying on his back, in a little glade covered with some soft, fine-bladed plant, of a brilliant and metallic blue. Below, over the top of the black thorn-jungle, he could see the oily yellow ocean, a glistening golden desert under the low and sullen sun.

Above towered black mountain ranges. Vast sloping fields strewn with titanic ebon boulders. Bare, rugged, jet-black precipices. Barrier of peaks beyond barrier of somber, Cyclopean peaks, until the jagged dark line of them scarred the red and murky sky.

Jay Kalam lay beside him on the blue grassy stuff, still unconscious. Hal Samdu and Giles Habibula were busy over a little fire by the edge of a tiny, flashing stream that crossed the glade. Incredulous, he caught the scent of meat cooking.

"What happened?" he called, and sat up painfully, his body aching from the inflamed wounds of the jungle thorns.

"Ah, so you're awake at last, lad?" Giles Habibula wheezed cheerfully.

"Well, lad, Hal and poor old Giles got the two of you out of the mortal jungle, after you fell back wrapped in the end of that evil tentacle. It wasn't so far. Here in the valley, Hal threw his spear at a little creature grazing on the blue grass, and I struck sparks with stones to make a fire.

"That's the story, lad. We're through the jungle. But we've got these mortal mountains to climb, when you and Jay are able, and good life knows what dreadful terrors are lying in wait beyond. Ah, if that wicked purple rope is a fair sample——

"Mortal me, lad! This life's too strenuous for such a precious feeble old man as Giles Habibula, that deserves to be sitting somewhere in a blessed easy chair, with a sip of wine to lift his dear old heart from the woe that weighs it down."

He cast a fishy eye at the bulge in his pocket.

"Ah, yes, I've one mortal bottle. But that must wait for the hour of greater need—it will come, soon enough, life knows, with a continent of wicked, crawling horror just ahead!"

Up the mountain barrier they clambered, when Jay Kalam and John Star were able. Over tumbled heaps of colossal black boulders. Up sheer, rugged slopes. Mountain range after wild range they mounted, always to find a wilder, more rugged range beyond.

Slowly the enormous, scarlet sun, which was their compass, wheeled across the gloomy crimson sky, through the long week of its progress. Often they were hungry, and often thirsty, and always deadly tired. The air grew thin and colder as they climbed, until they were never warm, until the least exertion meant exhaustion.

Sometimes they killed the little animals that grazed the blue grass, to cook them while they rested. They drank from icy mountain torrents. They slept a little, shivering in the sunshine, one of them always on guard.

"We must go on," Jay Kalam urged forever. "The night must not catch us here. It will be a week of darkness and frightful cold. We couldn't live through it here."

But it was already sunset when they mounted the last divide. They looked across a vast plateau, lifeless so far as they could see, black and grimly desolate. It was piled with masses of dark rock, riven and scarred from old volcanic cataclysm. A wild waste of utter black. In the darkling sky hung the dying sun, its sinister disk already bitten with fangs of ebon stone.

"We would die, here, surely," said Jay Kalam. "We must go on."

And they went on, breathless in the thin, bitter air, as the sun's red disk was slowly gnawed away by the western horizon, and a chill wind rose about them.

CHAPTER EIGHTEEN

Night and the City of Doom

For hours they hastened on, across that high black plateau, the bitter promise of approaching night increasing in
the air. The huge dome of the sun went down before
them. It was gone. In the lurid crimson twilight they
came to the chasm's rim.

Sheer walls dropped a full thousand feet. A mighty
gorge crossed the plateau, a huge, cliff-walled trench filled
with red, murky dusk.

"A river," Jay Kalam pointed out, "with forest along
it. That means firewood and the chance of food. We
might find a cave in the cliffs. We must climb down."

"Climb down!" snorted Giles Habibula. "Like a lot of
human flies!"

But they found a slope that looked less menacing. John
Star led the descent, clambering down over heaps of
fallen, colossal black rocks, sliding down banks of talus,
scrambling and dropping down sheer precipices. All of
them were bruised and lacerated against jagged rock; all
of them took reckless chances, for the dread night came
swiftly.

Only the faintest crimson glow marked the slash of sky
between the canyon walls when at last they stumbled into
the strip of strange black forest at the bottom. They were
trembling with cold, violent as had been their exertions;
ice-crystals already fringed the river.

Giles Habibula started a blaze, while the others gathered dead wood among the cruel-bladed trees.

"We must find shelter," said Jay Kalam. "We can't live
outside."

With torches they explored the frowning canyon wall.
John Star came upon a round, eight-foot tunnel. He
shouted for the others, and entered, flaring torch in one
hand and spear in the other. The air had an acrid fetor
and he found great strange tracks on the sandy floor.

The cavern proved vacant. At the rear was a twenty-foot hollow.

"Made to our order," he cried, meeting the others in the entrance. "Some creature has lately used it, but it's gone. We can carry in firewood, and wall up the entrance——"

"Mortal me!" shrieked Giles Habibula, who had been cautiously in the rear. "We're trespassing, and here comes the frightful owner!"

They heard a crashing in the fringe of dark trees, as the thing came up from the river. Then torch-light gleamed yellow and green on a crown of seven enormous eyes, glistened red on close-scaled armor, glinted black on terrible fangs.

It met them at the tunnel-mouth; they had no time to choose to fight or not. John Star and Jay Kalam and Hal Samdu braced their long black spears against the floor to face its charge. Giles Habibula shouted, scrambling back behind them and holding up his torch:

"I'll give you light!"

A river-creature, it must have been, by day, wont to hibernate through the dreadful night. It was serpent-like, thick as an elephant, covered with hard red armor; it had innumerable limbs, the foremost armed with savage talons.

John Star's spear, set against the floor, was driven by the force of its charge into the side of its armored snout.

With a screaming, evil-odored blast of air and sound, the creature tossed up its head, splintering the shaft against the roof. A black tongue, hooked with cruel spines, darted at him. He ducked too late. It impaled his shoulder through garments and flesh, yanked him spinning toward black-toothed, yawning jaws.

He struck with his torch the seven great eyes set in a crown of armor, and thrust it ahead of him into that hot, reeking maw.

The monster screamed again. The tongue lashed, flailing him from side to side of the passage; it drew him back, numb, bleeding, half-conscious, into that black, fetid throat.

Hal Samdu's spear came past him, sank deep in the roof of the yawning mouth. He was vaguely aware of the gigantic club, raining pile-driver blows on the crown of eyes and the armored skull. Then he saw the black fangs, closing down.

His shoulder was bound, when he came to; he was lying by a fire in the cave. The others were busy, carrying in firewood, and great pieces of meat from the huge carcass at the entrance.

" 'Tis fearful cold, outside, lad!" Giles Habibula informed him through chattering teeth. "Snowing, with a wicked blizzard roaring down the canyon. The river's already ice. Poor old Giles is too feeble for such a life as this, bless his dear old bones! Killing dragon-monsters in the wilderness of a world where men never ought to be!"

Even by the fire in the cave, the long night reached them with cruel fingers. When they at last emerged again, after the long, grim battle with merciless cold, they found the river a racing torrent. Fed by melting snows, it rose almost to the cave-mouth.

"We shall build a raft," decided Jay Kalam. "And follow the rivers across the continent to the Medusæ's city."

With improvised tools of stone, they laboriously fastened fallen logs together. The slow sun had already reached the zenith when they poled the clumsy vessel out into the rushing stream, to begin the voyage to the black and unknown city by the western sea.

Four painfully built rafts they lost. Two broke up on the rocks, leaving them to struggle ashore as best they might, through angry, icy rapids. One was wrecked by a green, lizard-like water animal. One they abandoned—at the last instant—before it went over a mighty fall.

The onslaught of the red gas in the air was less sudden and severe than John Star had feared. They all developed persistent coughs, but nothing more alarming. He came to suspect that Adam Ulnar had exaggerated the danger.

Week-long days came and departed, and eternal nights of savage cold, when they fastened the raft and came ashore to fight for food and warmth.

Below the thundering fall the canyon was a Cyclopean gorge; the river ran between black and topless walls in perpetual red twilight. Then they came out upon a larger stream, that carried them away from the mountains, and out across an interminable plain. For endless days they floated between low fringes of black vegetation—plants that died in the bitter nights, and grew amazingly again by day.

The river grew wider, deeper, its yellow torrent swifter. The somber, menacing jungles along its banks mounted ever higher, the animal life in water and jungle and air grew larger and more ferocious. With spear and dagger and club, with fire and bow and fist, they fought many times for possession of the raft.

They had become four lean, haggard men—even Giles Habibula was skin and bone and plaintive protest—black from exposure, ragged, unkempt, shaggy, scarred from many wounds. But they had gained an iron endurance, a new courage, an absolute confidence in one another.

Through all of it, Giles Habibula carried his bottle of wine. He defended it when the camp was attacked by a great flying thing, with splendid wings like sheets of sapphire; a thing that sought their bodies with a deadly, whipping sting. He dived for it when the green river-creature destroyed the raft. Many times he held it up to the red heavens, gazing at it with bitter longing in his fishy eyes.

"Ah, dear life, but a sip of it would be precious now," his plaintive voice would wheeze. "But when it's gone there'll be none—not a blessed drop of wine on the whole evil continent. Ah, I must save it for a greater need."

They were drifting one day near the middle of the river, vast now, a deep, mighty yellow flood, ten miles wide. Awesome walls of black jungle towered along its banks; barriers of violet-flowering thorns, interwoven with deadly purple vines; brakes of towering canes that whipped out at anything moving like living swords; gigantic trees laden with black moss that was blood-sucking death. Above the jungle hung the low, smoky sky, the red sun huge and sullen in the west.

Hal Samdu, at the steering-sweep, roared suddenly: "The city! There it is!"

Like another black mountain it rose, dim in the red murk, colossal beyond belief. Above the jungle, its smooth walls leaped up, infinitely, incredibly up, to strange ebon towers and huge fantastic mechanisms. A black metropolis, designed by madmen and built by giants.

Breathless wonder and awed unease overcame the four ragged men on the raft, gazing at the city they had crossed the abysm of space and a savage continent to reach. They stood with heads back, gaping mutely at the unguessable, titanic mechanisms that topped the summits of its walls.

"Aladoree!" muttered Hal Samdu, at last. "There!"

"So Adam Ulnar thought," said Jay Kalam. "In that higher central tower—can you see it, dim in the red, above the rest?"

"Yes, I see it. But how can we get there? What good is my club—against those machines on the walls! We are no more than ants!"

"Ah, that's the word, Hal!" said Giles Habibula. "Ants! We're nothing but miserable creeping ants! Ah, me, those wicked walls look a mile high, indeed! And the evil towers and those fearful machines half a mile more on top of them! Nothing but silly little ants! Except—a precious ant could climb the walls!"

The others kept silent. They stared over the river's yellow, raging floor, over the dark jungle barrier, at the black, unbelievable mass of the city against the sky. Jay Kalam stood grave with thought. John Star pictured the girl Aladoree as he last had seen her, gray eyes demurely cool, hair a sunlit glory of brown and red and gold. Could her quiet, fresh beauty really be still living, he wondered, shut up in the mass of somber metal ahead?

The mighty current carried them on. Beyond a bend they saw the base of the black walls, rising sheer from the yellow river; plunging up a full mile, a vertical, unbroken barrier of dead-black metal.

Hours went by, and the yellow tide bore them on.

The city marched up out of the crimson haze, ever more awful, the bulk of it swelling to blot out half the red sky with gleaming black metal, the titanic machines that crowned it frowning down with the threat of unknown death. A palpable atmosphere of dread and horror hung over that unearthly metropolis, a sense of evil power and hostile strength, of ancient wisdom and monstrous science, for it had endured since the Earth was new.

The four ragged creatures on the raft gazed on those marching walls with a hopeless horror. Their minds sank prostrate with realization that, unless their puny efforts could free the girl imprisoned there, the makers of this pile of black metal had also shaped the doom of mankind.

The city seemed dead at first, a somber necropolis, too old for any life. But presently they saw movement along the walls. A black spider-ship spread titanic vanes, and rose silently from a high platform to vanish in the red sky eastward.

"We must cover ourselves," said Jay Kalam. "They might be watching."

He had them screen the raft with broken branches, to look like driftwood. And the river carried them on toward the mighty wall. They were gazing upward in awestruck silence when Hal Samdu cried:

"See them moving! Above the wall!"

And the others could presently distinguish the creatures that moved, still tiny with many miles of distance—the ancient masters of this aged planet!

John Star had glimpsed one of the Medusæ on Mars, that thing in the gondola swung from the black flier, whose weapon had struck him down. A swollen, greenish surface, wetly heaving; a huge, ovoid eye, luminous and purple. But these were the first he had fully seen.

They drifted above the wall like little green balloons. Their eyes were tiny dark points in their bulging sides—each had four eyes, spaced at equal distances about its circumference. From the lower, circular edge, like the ropes that would have suspended the car of a balloon, hung a fringe of black and whiplike tentacles.

John Star could see the superficial likeness, the dome shape, the fringing tentacles, that had earned them the name Medusæ.

In the distance they did not look impressive. There was about them a certain grotesqueness, a slow awkwardness. They didn't look intelligent. Yet in the way they moved, floating apparently at will above the black wall, was a power and mystery that made for respect. And in the knowledge that they were the builders of this black metropolis was room for awe and terror.

The raft drifted on until the black wall shadowed them. Smooth metal towered sheer to the zenith, hiding the machines and the drifting Medusæ. The raft scraped hard metal where it rose from the water; then the boiling yellow current tossed them back again.

"We'll land," said Jay Kalam, "in the edge of the jungle below the wall."

They threw aside the screening branches, and seized long sweeps; they fought for the shore, where the river drew away from that metal precipice.

CHAPTER NINETEEN

Giles Habibula and Black Disaster

They abandoned the raft when it touched bottom, taking only their crude weapons, and Giles Habibula, his priceless bottle of wine. Hal Samdu stood in the shallows, a giant hand knotted about his club, staring at the dark barrier shadowing the black jungle ahead—staring, helplessly shaking his head.

"How——?"

"There'll be a way," promised Jay Kalam, though even his confidence seemed a little strained. "First, let's get through the jungle."

They attacked the living wall, dared the death that lurked within. Spear-sharp, poisoned spines. Blood-sucking moss. Coiling tentacles of purple vines. Blooms of fatal perfume. Animal death, that crawled and leaped and flew.

But the four had learned in a savage school to meet that jungle on even terms. A dozen hours of swimming and floundering through sucking mud, of hacking deadly vines and creeping through *chevaux-de-frise* of venomous thorns, of meeting with level spear or lifted dagger the hungry things that charged from the undergrowth or rose from the mud or dropped from above, and they emerged from the riverbed upon the higher plain—Giles Habibula still with his bottle of wine.

Close on the right hand rose the wall, sheer and black, a mighty, overwhelming mile of it. The plain reached off to the left, covered luxuriantly with fine-leafed grass, a bright metallic blue. It sloped up in the murky distance to blue hills. From blue hills to black· city ran the aqueduct.

Jay Kalam's thoughtful eyes surveyed it, a straight channel of dull black metal, miles long, which was carried from hills to ebon city on ancient, soaring arches.

"One chance," he said gravely. "We shall try."

They skirted the jungle to keep out of sight, marched

twenty miles, and climbed into the blue hills. They had eaten, slept for a time, but it was still many hours till sunset when they came under the immense dam of black metal below the reservoir.

No guard was visible, but they crept up very cautiously beneath the dam. They climbed slippery, wet walls and flanges of black metal, until they came to the lip of the uncovered channel. Below roared the cold clear torrent from the floodgate, three hundred feet wide, dark and deep.

"The water," Jay Kalam observed laconically, "gets into the city."

He dived. The others followed, leaving all but their thorn-daggers. The clear icy torrent rushed them along the black channel; the mighty dam drew back; the city's ramparts marched to meet them. They kept afloat as the yellow river had taught them, and tried to save their strength.

Ahead, in the black wall, appeared a tiny arch. It grew larger, and abruptly swallowed them up. They were in roaring darkness; the arch framed a bit of crimson sky, swiftly dwindling. The steady current plunged on into utter darkness.

Thunder drummed against their ears, increasing, deafening.

"A fall!" warned Jay Kalam.

His shout was swept away. They shot into a battle of mad waters. Plunging torrents battered them. Merciless currents sucked them down. Savage whirlpools spun them under smothering foam. All in roaring blackness.

John Star gasped for breath, strangled in the foam. He fought the current that carried him down. Down and down! Resistless pressure crushed his body. He endured the agony of suffocation. Desperately he tried to swim, and wild water mocked him. It carried him up—and down again.

When he came up a second time, he contrived to stay afloat; he swam away from the chaos of the fall. They had poured into a vast, cavernous reservoir, completely dark. Its vast extent he could guess only by the rolling thunder of reverberation from its roof.

He shouted as he swam, and heard with keenest joy Giles Habibula's plaintive wheeze:

"Ah, lad, you lived through it! It was an awful time,

lad. A fearful thing, lad, to be diving over mortal water-falls, in this wicked dark.

"But I've still my precious bottle of wine."

Hal Samdu hailed them, then. A little later they came upon Jay Kalam. They all swam away from the thunder, and came at last to the side of the tank which was slick, unclimbable metal.

"Ah, so we must drown, like so many kittens in a blessed bucket!" wailed Giles Habibula. "After all the dreadful perils we've been through. Ah, mortal me!"

They swam along the slimy wall, until they came blindly to a great metal float with a taut chain above it—it must be, Jay Kalam said, the mechanism that mea-sured the level of the water. They climbed the chain.

It brought them up at last, with weary limbs and blis-tered hands, to the vast drum upon which it was wound. There they saw a feeble gleam of red, and they crept to-ward it along the great axle-shaft of the drum, wet and slippery with condensation.

Scrambling over the immense bearing of the shaft, they found a little circular hole in the roof of the tank—it must have been left for attention to the bearings. They climbed through it, Giles Habibula sticking until the others pulled him out, and so at last, on top of the reser-voir, they were fairly within the city.

They stood on the lower edge of a conical black metal roof, a dizzy drop of two thousand feet below them, and the slope too steep for comfort.

Standing there on that perilous brink, John Star felt a staggering impact of nightmare strangeness and bewilder-ing confusion. Buildings, towers, stacks, tanks, machines, all loomed up about him, a black fantastic forest against the lurid sky, appallingly colossal. The tallest structures reached, he soberly estimated, two miles high.

If this black metropolis of the monstrous Medusæ had order or plan, he did not grasp it. The black wall had seemed to enclose a regular polygon. But within all was strange, astounding, incomprehensible, to the point of stunning dismay.

There were no streets, but merely yawning cavernous abysms between mountainous black structures. The Me-dusæ had no need of streets. They didn't walk, they floated! Doors opened upon sheer space, at any level from the surface to ten thousand feet.

The stupendous ebon buildings had no regular height or plan, some were square, some cylindrical or domed, some terraced, some—like the reservoir upon which they stood—sheerly vertical. All among them were bewildering machines of unguessable function—save that a few were apparently aerial or interstellar fliers, moored on landing stages—but all black, ugly, colossal; dread instrumentalities of a science older than the life of Earth.

The four stood there for a little time in a shaken bewilderment, caution forgotten.

"Bless my precious eyes!" moaned Giles Habibula. "No streets. No ground. No level space. All a tangle of wicked black metal. We'll get nowhere unless we sprout some blessed wings!"

"That must be the central tower," observed Jay Kalam, "the black fort Commander Ulnar spoke of. Still miles away."

He pointed to a square, forbidding, tremendous pile, towering up amazingly in the red and murky distance, a very mountain of black and alien metal, landing stages which carried colossal spider-ships and large machines of unguessable use, projecting from its frowning walls.

Weary, hopeless, he shook his head.

"We must get back," he whispered, "and hide till dusk."

"Or the monstrous things," apprehensively promised Giles Habibula, "will see——"

"One, I think," broke in John Star, "already has!"

Hundreds, perhaps, of the city's masters had been in view from the moment they came on the roof, greenish hemispherical domes drifting above the confusion of black metal, dark tentacles dangling. All had been far away, insignificant by comparison with their works. But now one had lifted abruptly over the point of the conical roof.

Giles Habibula dived for the hole through which they had emerged. He stuck; before the others could help him the Medusa was overhead.

The sheer size of it was shocking. Those in the distance had been tiny by comparison only. Its green dome, wet and slowly palpitating, was twenty feet through, the hanging, ophidian tentacles twice that in length.

It was infinitely horrible. Vast, bulging mass, gelatinous and slimy, translucently green. Scores of hanging tentacles, slowly writhing—efficient and quite beautiful, no doubt, in the eyes of their owner.

Gorgon's eyes!

Long, ovoid wells of purple flame. All pupil, rimmed with tattered black membrane. Mirrors of a cold and ruthless wisdom, old when the very Earth was new. John Star was not in fact turned to stone. Yet the sheer, elemental horror of that purple stare set off some primeval fear-response. It paralyzed his limbs with tingling cold, slowed his heart, stopped his breath, drenched him with sweat of terror.

Fear-numbed, they stood motionless, until the tentacles had whipped about them, snatched thorn-daggers from their nerveless hands, and pulled Giles Habibula like a cork from the hole. They were lifted, vainly fighting the hard thin tentacles.

"My mortal wine——" panted Giles Habibula.

It dropped from his pocket. Like a plummet it fell into the chasm below; it fell two thousand feet.

"My blessed bottle of wine!" And he sobbed in the coiling ropes.

Moving by what force they did not know, by what amazing conquest of gravitation, the creature swept aloft with them, above the titanic black disorder of the city, toward—John Star noted it with a certain grim satisfaction—toward the central citadel.

They fought the fear that numbed them.

"Something about that brain," gasped Jay Kalam, even as they were borne away. "Powers that we can't guess. Makes you feel pretty futile."

It carried them into the stupendous building, through a door opening on sheer space, five thousand feet up. Through a colossal green-lit hall. It stuffed them through a rectangular opening in the floor, dropped them without ceremony.

Sprawling in a black-walled room, twenty feet square, they found beside them a man—or what had been a man.

Emaciated, ragged, it was sleeping on its face, breathing with long, rasping snores. John Star shook it, after the Medusa had vanished from above the locked grating overhead, woke it. Stark, feverish terror stared from red eyes in a pallid, haggard face.

It uttered a shrill, hoarse scream of agonized terror; clawed in wild, blind insanity of fear at John Star's hand.

And John Star himself cried out, for the thing was Eric Ulnar.

The handsome, insolent officer who would have been Emperor of the System, become this twisted and pitiful wreck!

"Leave me be! Leave me be!" The voice was thinner and wilder than anything human. "I'll do what you want! I'll do anything! I'll make her tell the secret! I'll kill her if you want! But I can't stand any more! Leave me be!"

"We won't hurt you!" John Star tried to soothe the quivering thing, shocked as he was by the import of its cries. "We're men. We won't harm you. I'm John Ulnar. You know me. We won't hurt you."

"John Ulnar?" Red, fevered eyes stared, wild with a sudden, frantic hope. "Why yes, you're John."

The trembling thing, abruptly sob-shaken, clung to his shoulder.

"The Medusæ!" That wail held more than human woe. "They tricked us! They're murdering mankind! They're bombing the System with red gas, to eat men's bodies away, and make them insane. They're murdering mankind!"

"Aladoree?" demanded John Star. "Where's she?"

"They made me torture her!" sobbed the weak, wild voice. "They want her secret. Want AKKA! But she won't tell. And they won't let me die till she tells. They won't let me die!" it shrilled. "They won't let me die!

"But when she tells, they'll kill us all!"

CHAPTER TWENTY

"A Certain Slight Dexterity"

"My blessed bottle of wine!" sobbed Giles Habibula, plaintively. "I carried it out of the sunken cruiser. I carried it through the jungle of thorns, I carried it up the black and evil mountains. For precious months I carried it on the raft. I risked my mortal life to save it, fighting a wicked flying monster. I dived for it into the horrors of the yellow river. I was near drowning with it in the fall beneath that aqueduct!

"The only bottle of wine on the whole black and monstrous continent!"

His fishy eyes clouded, and the clouds gave forth a rain of tears. He sank down on the bare metal floor of the cell in a stricken heap.

"Poor old Giles Habibula, lonely, desolate, forlorn old soldier of the Legion. Accused for a pirate, hunted like a rat out of his own native System, caught like a mortal rat in a wicked trap to be tortured and murdered by the monsters of an alien star!

"And, ah me! even that is not enough! I'd carried that bottle through a mortal lot of hardship and peril. I'd held it up to the light, many a time, sweet life knows, my old mouth watering. Always I'd save it for the hour of greater need. Ah, yes, for such a time of mortal bleak necessity as faces us now!

"And it must fall! Fall two thousand fearful feet. Every precious drop of it. Gone! Ah, Giles Habibula——"

His voice was overcome by cataclysmic grief, earthquakes of sighs and storms of tears.

John Star questioned Eric Ulnar again. He had slept, that shattered human wreck, his haggard, emaciated body exhausted by the outburst of hysteria. He was calm when he woke, sunk in a sort of apathy, speaking in a dull, weary tone.

"The Medusæ are planning to desert this planet," he said. "They have fought for long ages to keep this mother-city alive. And they've done wonders—making this red gas to keep the atmosphere from freezing, and robbing other worlds to replace their exhausted resources. But now they're coming to final defeat—because the dying planet is spiraling back into the dying star. Even they can't stop that. They have to go."

"They already have an outpost in the System, you say?"

"Yes," continued the lifeless monotone. "They've already conquered the Moon of Earth. They're generating a new atmosphere for it, filled with this red poison gas. And they're building a fortress there, out of this black alloy they used in place of iron, for their base against the Earth."

"But the Legion! Surely——"

"The Legion of Space is destroyed. The last, disorganized remnant of it was annihilated in a vain attack on the Moon. The Green Hall, too, is gone. The System has no organization left. No defense.

"And the Medusæ, from the fort on the Moon, are proceeding with the destruction of the human race. They're firing great shells, filled with the red gas, at Earth and all the other human planets. Slowly, in every atmosphere, the concentration of the gas is increasing. Soon men everywhere will be insane and rotting.

"Only a few of the Medusæ, I believe, have already gone to the System. But their great fleet is now being organized and equipped, to carry the migrating hordes to occupy our conquered planets."

There had been a change in Eric Ulnar's manner. On that first occasion, his voice had been a thin, hysterical scream. Now his dull tones were hardly audible. His face —it still had a sort of pallid beauty from his long yellow hair, worn and haggard and pain-drawn as it was—his face was vacantly calm. He spoke of the plans of the Medusæ with an unconcern that was almost mechanical, as if the fate of the System no longer mattered to him.

"And Aladoree?" John Star demanded. "Where is she?"

"She is locked in the next cell, beside us."

"She is!" gasped Hal Samdu, hoarse with gladness. "So near?"

"But you say she's been——" John Star could not keep a little sob of pain and anger from his voice, "been tortured?"

"The Medusæ want to know her secret," came the lifeless, expressionless reply. "They want the plans for AKKA. Since they can't communicate with her themselves—she doesn't know the code—they made me try to get the secret for them. But she won't tell.

"We've used different means," his dull drone went on. "Fatigue, hypnotism, pain. But she won't tell."

"You——" choked Hal Samdu. "You—beast—coward——"

He charged across the cell, great hands clenching savagely. Eric Ulnar shrank from him, shuddering, cried out:

"Don't! Don't let him touch me! I'm not to blame! They tortured me! I couldn't stand it! They tortured me. And they wouldn't let me die!"

"Hal!" protested Jay Kalam, gravely. "That won't help things a bit. We need to know what he can tell us."

"But he——" gasped the giant, "he—tortured Aladoree!"

"I know, Hal," soothed John Star, holding his arm, though he shared the savage impulse to destroy this no longer human creature. "What he tells us will help to rescue her."

He turned back to Eric Ulnar.

"In the next cell, you say. Is there a guard?"

"Don't let him touch me," came the abject, lifeless whine. "Yes, one of the Medusæ always watches in the great hall above."

"If we could get past the guard, is there any way out?"

"Out of the city, you mean?"

"Yes," Jay Kalam spoke up and his quiet voice held a calm, surprising confidence. "We're going to rescue Aladoree. We're going to take her outside the city, and let her set up her weapon. Then the Medusæ will come to us for orders—unless we decide to destroy the whole city out of hand."

"No, you could never get out of the city," returned the dull voice of that beaten thing. "You can't even leave the hall. It opens over a pit a mile deep. Just a sheer, blank wall below the door. Even if you got down, you'd have no way to cross the city. The Medusæ have no streets; they fly.

"But there's no use even to talk of that. You can't even get out of this cell, or get Aladoree out of hers. The sliding doors are locked. You are unarmed prisoners. Talking of stealing something the Medusæ are guarding in their securest fortress!"

His voice died in dull contempt.

With the impatience of a trapped animal, John Star gazed about the cell. A bare metal chamber, square, twenty feet wide. Ten feet overhead was the rectangular opening through which they had been dropped, closed now with a sliding grille of square metal bars. Green light filtered through the bars from the dim, lofty hall above. His eyes, searching for any weapon or device to aid their escape, found no movable thing in the cell. It was simply a square box of that eternal black alloy.

Hal Samdu was pacing back and forth on the hard bare

floor, his eyes roving like those of a caged breast, sometimes casting a glance of savage rage at Eric Ulnar.

"You can't get out of this cell, even," insisted that flat, no longer human voice. "For they will kill you soon. They will be coming back to make me try again to get the plans from Aladoree. She will tell, this time. They are preparing a ray that burns with all the pain of fire, and yet will not kill her too quickly. But they will let us all die as soon as she tells. They've promised to let me die, when she tells."

"Then," John Star muttered fiercely, "we *must* get out!"

Hal Samdu beat with his fists on the hard black walls. They gave out a dull, heavy reverberation, a melancholy roll of doom; he left blood from his knuckles.

"You can't get out," droned Eric. "The lock——"

"One of us has a certain dexterity," said Jay Kalam. "Giles, you must open the door."

Giles Habibula got to his feet in the corner of the cell, wiping tears from his fishy eyes.

"Ah, yes," he wheezed, in a brighter tone. "One of us has a certain slight dexterity. It came of the accident that his father was an inventor of locks. Even so, it cost him weary years of toil, to develop an aptitude into a skill.

"A blessed dexterity! Ah, as dear life knows, it has never been given the credit it has earned. Ah, me! Lesser men have won riches and honor and fame, with half the genius and a tenth the toil. And to old Giles Habibula his talent and his unremitting effort have brought only poverty and obscurity and disgrace!

"Mortal me! But for that dexterity, I should never have been here, rotting in the hands of a lot of fearful monsters, waiting for torture and death! Ah, no! But for that affair on Venus, twenty years ago, I should never have been in the Legion. And 'twas that dexterity that tempted me then—that, and the fame of a certain cellar of wine!

"Poor old Giles, brought by his own genius to ruin and starvation and death——"

"But now's the chance to make your skill undo all that," urged John Star. "Can you open the lock?"

"Ah, me, lad! The penalty of unjust obscurity! If I had been a painter, a poet, a blessed musician, you would never dare cast doubt upon the power of my art. With my genius, it would be known from end to end of the

System. Ah, lad, it was an ill tide of destiny into which I was cast!

"That even you, lad, should doubt my genius!"

Great tears trickled down his nose.

"Come, Giles!" cried Jay Kalam. "Show him."

The three of them lifted Giles Habibula—now an easier task than it would once have been—so that he could reach the barred grating, ten feet above the floor.

He looked at the black case of the lock, fingered it with his oddly sure, oddly delicate hands. He set his ear against the case, tapped it with the fingers, reached up through the bars and moved something, listening.

"My mortal eyes," he at last sighed plaintively. "I never saw such a clever lock as this. Combination. The case is precious tight. No place to insert an instrument, to feel it out. And the wicked thing has levers, instead of cylinders. Never was a lock like this in the System."

Again he listened intently to tiny clickings from the lock, resting the tips of sensitive fingers against the case, now here, now there, as if vibration revealed the inner mechanism.

"Bless my poor old bones!" he muttered once. "A clever new idea! If we were back in the System, the patents on it would earn me all the fame and wealth that I've been cheated of. A lock that challenges even the genius of Giles Habibula!"

Abruptly he gasped, stooping.

"Let me down! A fearful monster coming!"

They lowered him to the floor. Above, a huge greenish hemisphere floated over the grating. A gross mass of glistening, slimy, translucent flesh, palpitating with strange slow life. An immense, ovoid eye stared at them with such a dread intensity that John Star felt it must be reading their very minds.

A dark tentacle dropped four small brown bricks through the grating. Eric Ulnar, breaking from his apathy, snatched one of them and gnawed it eagerly.

"Food," he whimpered. "This is all they give us."

A cube of dark, moist jelly, John Star found one of them to be; it had an odd, unpleasant odor, an insipid lack of flavor.

"Food!" wept Giles Habibula, biting into another. "Ah, good life's sake, if they call this food, I'll eat my blessed boots first, as I did in the prison on Mars!"

"But we must eat it," said Jay Kalam. "Even if it isn't palatable. We'll need strength."

The greenish, quivering vastness of their jailor presently floated away from above the grating; they lifted Giles Habibula, to resume his battle with the lock.

He muttered in exasperation from time to time; his breath, in the absorption of his effort, became a slow sighing. Sweat stood out on his face, glistening in the dim green light that shone through the bars.

There was, at last, a louder click. He sighed again and raised his face against the bars. Then he shook his head and whispered hastily:

"Life's sake—let me down!"

"You can't open it?" asked John Star, anxiously.

"Ah, lad, so still you doubt?" he breathed, sadly. "The price a man must pay for a precious spark of genius! There was never a lock designed that Giles Habibula couldn't open. Though many an ambitious locksmith has tried, life knows!"

"Then it *is* open?"

"Ah, yes. The bolts just went back. The grate is unlocked. But I didn't open it."

"Why——"

"Because that fearful flying monster is waiting up there in the hall. Hanging still over a mortal queer contraption on a tripod of black metal. Its evil purple eyes would see any move we make."

"Tripod?" shrilled Eric Ulnar, voice edged with a new panic of hysteria. "Tripod? That's the machine they use for communication. They've brought it again, to make me get the secret from Aladoree. They'll kill us all when she tells!"

CHAPTER TWENTY-ONE

The Horror in the Hall

"Lift me," said John Star, and Hal Samdu's great hands swung him up.

Through the square metal bars of the grating, he could see the walls and ceiling of the vast hall, too wide and too high for the scale of human needs. Made all of the dead-black alloy, it was illuminated by little green, shining spheres strung along the middle of the ceiling.

The Medusa was in view, hanging over the cell and a little to one side. A bulging, enormous hemisphere of greenish flesh, slimy, half transparent, slowly throbbing. Ovoid, foot-long purple eyes, protruding a little—hypnotic and evil. Black tentacles dangling, like the Gorgon's serpent-locks.

Beside it was the tripod mechanism. Three heavy, spike-pointed legs, supporting a small cabinet, from which hung cables fastened to little objects that must have been electrodes and microphone, for picking up Eric's voice and the telepathic vibrations of the Medusæ.

At a sign, the giant lowered him.

"There's a chance," he whispered. "If there are no others in sight—and if we're quick enough."

He told what he had seen, outlined his plan. Jay Kalam nodded grave approval. In quick, breathless whispers, they discussed the details, down to the smallest movement.

Then Jay Kalam gave the word, and Hal Samdu swung John Star up again. This time he seized the grating, slid it swiftly and noiselessly back, in a moment was on his feet in the hall above. Without the loss of an instant he leaped toward the tripod.

Jay Kalam meanwhile came through the opening after him, catapulted by the arms of the giant, and helped Hal Samdu to follow.

An instant after the grating opened, the three stood beside it, working with savage haste to dismember the tripod. Even so, the guarding Medusa had already moved.

The green dome of it swept swiftly toward them, thin black appendages whipping out like angry snakes.

Hal Samdu wrenched apart the communicator. One heavy, sharp-pointed leg he thrust to John Star, another to Jay Kalam. The third, with the heavy black case still fastened to it, he brandished like a great metal mace.

Holding the pointed leg like a pike, John Star lunged at a purple eye.

Instinctive terror smote him, the same numbing fear that had struck him twice before from the luminous Gorgon-eyes, the touching off of an age-old response to elemental horror. He felt tingling chills where hair sought to rise, the ice of sudden sweat. Something checked his heart and breath; something froze his muscles.

Immobility of instinctive terror—old inheritance from some primeval progenitor, which had found safety in keeping quiet. Useful, perhaps, to a creature too small to do battle and too slow to run away. But now—deadly!

He had known it was coming. He had braced himself to meet it. He would be ruled by his brain, not by age-old instinct-patterns!

A moment it checked him—just a moment. Then his numbed body responded to desperately urging nerves. He went on, metal point swinging up before him.

The Medusa had taken full advantage of that small delay. The black whip of a tentacle, small as his finger, but cruelly hard, pitilessly strong, snapped around his neck; it constricted with merciless, suffocating force.

In spite of it, he carried out the lunge. Fighting down the blinding agony from his throat, he completed, with every atom of weight and strength behind it, the forward rush, the upward swing.

The point reached the eye, ripped through its transparent outer coat, plunged deep into the sinister purple well of it, between the fringes of black membrane. A pendulous blob of clear jelly burst out, a quick rush of purple-black blood; and the great socket was sunken, sightless, more than ever hideous.

Abruptly increasing its fearful pressure on his larynx, the choking tentacle hurled him forward with a violence that almost snapped his vertebrae, flung him dazed and blind against the metal floor.

With a dogged will that ignored danger and physical pain, he clung to consciousness; he clung to his weapon.

Even before he could see he was scrambling back to his feet, dimly aware of the blows of Hal Samdu's club—great soft thuds against boneless, palpitating flesh.

His sight came back. He saw the giant, head and shoulders towering from a very mass of black and angry serpents, shining bronze with sweat of agony and effort, muscles knotting as he swung the metal mace.

He saw Jay Kalam lunge, as he had lunged, to drive his point deep into a purple eye. Saw him instantly wrapped in ferocious black whips, that squeezed his body and twisted it and flung it savagely against the floor.

Then he staggered forward again. Black ropes caught his knees before he came in thrusting distance, tripped him. They snatched him aloft with resistless strength, whirled him up to dash him down again.

A huge, malevolent purple eye came before him, as he was flung up—one of the two that remained to the creature. It was too far to reach with a lunge. But he threw his weapon, hurled it deep into the shining target with a twisting swing of his whole body, a long sweep of his free arm.

The serpent dropped him to tug at the spear.

On hands and knees he sprawled beside Jay Kalam, who was still motionless, groaning, weapon at his side. John Star snatched it as he got to his feet, straightening fairly underneath the creature, surrounded by agonized appendages.

On the under surface of the hemisphere, a circle of green quivering flesh, he saw a curious organ. A circular area three feet wide, slightly bulging, that glowed with soft golden iridescence. The light wavered, pulsed rhythmically, with the regular palpitations of the slimy flesh.

With the quick intuition that it must be vital, he thrust at it.

Sensing his attack, the creature fought to avoid it. Hal Samdu, dazed, was flung down at his feet. Black serpents struck. A rope whipped about his waist, tightened fiercely. The same weapon that he had flung into the great eye was now grasped in thin coils; it flailed at him, struck his head with a blinding agony.

He drove on; his point pierced the golden, shimmering circle.

The yellow light went out of it at once. And the Medusa fell, a soft mountain of quaking flesh. Only by a desperate, sidewise fling did he get his body from beneath it in time; even so it caught his legs.

The glowing organ, he was later sure, must have been the agency of its remarkable locomotion, perhaps emitting some radiant force that lifted and propelled it; perhaps giving it a grasp, in some manner yet inexplicable, upon the curvature of space itself.

Half under it he lay for a while, unable to extricate himself. Still the creature was not completely dead; the dying serpents writhed about him in aimless agony.

It was Hal Samdu who reeled back to his feet to end the battle with a few mighty blows of his club, and then dragged John Star from beneath.

A moment they stood gazing at that quivering mound of slimy greenish protoplasm, tall as Hal Samdu's head, the yet-twitching tentacles sprawling away from the edge of it, three sightless eyes staring horribly.

Utterly hideous as it was, both of them were moved by a contrary impulse of pity for its manifest agony. For its kind had endured in the face of all adversity, perhaps since the planets of the Sun were born. The death of it was somehow dreadful.

"It had tortured *her!*" gasped Hal Samdu. "It deserved to die!"

They turned from it then, to lift Jay Kalam, who was already returning to consciousness, struggling to sit up.

"Only stunned!" he muttered. "So it's finished? Good. We must get on to Aladoree. Before others come. If it called for aid—Hal, please help Giles and Ulnar out of the cell. Must—work—fast!"

He dropped back again. He had, John Star saw, been cruelly hurt when the tentacles flung him down. His fine face was thin and drawn with pain, his grave eyes closed. Gasping, he lay there a moment, then whispered:

"John? Find her. I'll be all right. We must be quick!"

John Star left him then. He ran around that mountain of slow green death, and found another grating in the floor. He dropped to his knees, peering into darkness but faintly relieved by the green rays that streamed through the bars from the hall. At last he made out a slight form, lying on the bare floor, sleeping.

"Aladoree!" he called. "Aladoree Anthar!"

The slender dim shape of her did not stir, he heard her quiet breathing—it seemed strange to him that she should be sleeping so peacefully, so like a child, when the fate of the System depended on a thing she knew.

"Aladoree!" He spoke louder. "Wake up."

She rose, then, quickly. Her quiet voice showed complete possession of her faculties, though it was dull with a heavy weight of apathy.

"Yes. Who are you, here?"

"John Ulnar, and your——"

"John Ulnar!" Her low, tired voice cut him off, cold with scorn. "You've come, I suppose, to help your cowardly kinsman make me betray the specifications for AKKA? I'll warn you now that you're going to be disappointed. The human race is not all your own cowardly breed. Do what you like, I can keep the secret till I die —and that, I think, won't be very long!"

"No, Aladoree!" he appealed, shocked and hurt by her bitter scorn. "No, Aladoree, you mustn't think that. We've come——"

"John Ulnar——" her voice cut him, hard with contempt.

Then Giles Habibula and Hal Samdu dropped by the grating.

"Bless my eyes, lass! It's a fearful time since old Giles has heard your voice. A mortal time! How are you, lass?"

"Giles! Giles Habibula?"

In the voiceless cry that came up from darkness through the bars was incredulous relief, ineffable joy that brought a quick, throbbing ache to John Star's heart. All the contemptuous scorn was gone; only pure delight was left, tremulous, complete.

"Ah, yes, lass, it's Giles. Old Giles Habibula, come on a wicked and perilous journey to set you free, lass. Just wait a few blessed moments, while he works another precious lock."

Already he was on his knees by the sliding grille, his thick fingers curiously deft and steady, moving over the little strange levers that projected from the case of the mechanism.

"Aladoree!" cried Hal Samdu, an odd, yearning eagerness in his rusty voice. "Aladoree—have they—hurt you?"

"Hal!" came her glad, trembling cry. "Hal, too?"

"Of course. You think I wouldn't come?"

"Hal!" she sobbed again, joyously. "And where's Jay?"

"He's——" began John Star, when Jay Kalam's grave tones, weak and uneven, came beside him:

"Here, Aladoree—at your command."

He reeled to the edge of the grating, sank beside it, still weak and white with pain, though smiling.

"I'm so—glad!" her voice came from darkness, broken with sobs of pure joy. "I knew—you'd try. But it was—so far! And the plot—so clever—so diabolical——"

"Ah, lass, don't weep so!" urged Giles Habibula. "Every precious thing is all right, now. Old Giles will have this door open in a moment, and you out in the precious light of day again, lass!"

John Star abruptly sensed something amiss. Quickly he looked up and down the long, high-walled black hall. The vast bulk of the dead Medusa lay motionless, serpent-locks sprawling and still. The floor of dull green light revealed nothing moving, no enemy. Yet something was wrong.

Suddenly it struck him.

"Eric Ulnar!" he gasped. "Did you help him out of the cell?"

"Ah, yes, lad," wheezed Giles Habibula. "We couldn't leave even him for the wicked things to torture."

"Of course," rumbled Hal Samdu. "Where is——"

"He's gone!" whispered John Star. "Gone! Still a coward and a traitor. He's gone to give the alarm!"

CHAPTER TWENTY-TWO

Red Storm at Dusk

"Ah, now!" wheezed Giles Habibula. "Ready, lass, to come?"

The lock had snapped; he slid back the barred door.

"Please go down, John," said Jay Kalam. "Help her."

John Star swung through the opening, hung by his arms, dropped lightly on the floor of the cell, beside Aladoree.

Her gray eyes watched him doubtfully, greenish in the gloom.

"John Ulnar," she asked, her scornful dislike less open, yet still cutting him deep, "you came with them?"

"Aladoree!" he pleaded. "You must trust me!"

"I told you once," she said coldly, "that I could never trust a man named Ulnar. That very day you locked up my loyal men, betrayed me to your traitorous kinsman!"

"I know!" he whispered, bitterly. "I was a dupe, a fool! But come! I'll lift you."

"I was the fool—to trust an Ulnar!"

"Come! We've no time."

"You must be more clever than Eric, if you have the confidence of my loyal men. You Purples! Are you trying, John Ulnar, to get the better of them and the Medusæ too?"

"Don't——" It was a pained cry.

"Please be quick!" urged Jay Kalam from above.

She came to him, then, still doubtful. John Star slipped an arm about her slight body, lifted her foot, and swung her upward into Hal Samdu's reaching arms; then leaped, himself, to catch them.

They stood in the cavernous hall, tiny in its gloomy silent vastness.

Aladoree was thin, John Star saw, and pale, her white face drawn with anxiety and suffering; her gray eyes were burning with a fire too bright, and ringed with blue shadows. Her startled outcry at sight of the hideous mountain of the dead Medusa showed nerves strained to the point of breakdown; yet her erect bearing revealed courage, decision, proud determination.

Torture had not conquered her.

"We're here, Aladoree," said Jay Kalam. "But we've no ship to leave in. No means, even, to get out of the city. And no proper weapons. We're depending on you. On AKKA."

Disappointment shadowed her worn face.

"I'm afraid, then," she said, "that you have sacrificed your lives in vain."

"Why?" Jay Kalam asked apprehensively. "Can't you build the weapon?"

Wearily, she shook her head.

"Not in time, I think. Simple as it is, I must have certain materials. And a little time to set it up and adjust it."

"We've the thing they used for communication with Eric Ulnar." He pointed to Hal Samdu's mace. "Rather battered now. It was electrical. A sort of radio, I think. It would have wires, insulation, maybe a battery."

Again she shook her head.

"It might do," she admitted. "But I'm afraid it would take too long to straighten and arrange the parts. These creatures will soon find us."

"We must take it along," said Jay Kalam.

Hal Samdu unfastened the device from the head of the tripod, slung it to his body by the connecting wires.

"We must do—something!" cried John Star. "Right away. Eric must have gone to give the alarm."

"We must somehow get outside the city," agreed Jay Kalam. "Aladoree, do you know any way——?"

"No. That way," she pointed, "the hall leads into a great shop, a laboratory, I think. Many of them are always there, working. Eric went that way, I suppose, to tell them. The other end is outside. A mile high! There's no way to get down, without wings."

"There might be," mused Jay Kalam. "I remember— a drain, it looked to be. We must see——"

They ran three hundred feet to a great door at the end of the hall, an immense, sliding grate of heavy black bars, crossed, close-set, fastened with a massive lock. Through the bars they saw the black metropolis again—a storm raging over it.

Looming mountains of ebon metal, fantastic, colossal machines of unguessable function, all piled in titanic confusion, with no order visible to the human eye, no regularity of shape or size or position. No streets; chasms merely, doors opening into breathtaking space.

Now the city was lashed with wild violence. The four had weathered other storms, on their trek across the black continent, always toward the end of the week-long day, when swiftly chilling air caused sudden precipitation. But this was a wilder fury.

It was almost dark. A lurid pall of scarlet gloom shrouded the city's nightmare masses. Wind shrieked. Yellow rain fell in sluicing sheets; it drenched them, stung them with its icy whip, even in the shelter of the bars. Blinding lightning flamed continually overhead, stabbed red swords down incessantly at black buildings that loomed like tortured giants.

Below the door was a mile-deep chasm, walled in completely by black, irregular buildings. John Star could see no way visible to leave its misty, flood-drenched floor.

Aladoree shrank back instinctively from the chill rain that lashed through the bars, from the ominous glow of the sky and the fearful bellow of the wind and thunder. Giles Habibula hastily retreated, muttering:

"Mortal me! I never saw such——"

"The lock, Giles!" Jay Kalam requested urgently.

"Bless my bones, Jay!" he howled above the roaring elements. "We can't go out into that! Into that wicked storm, and a fearful pit a mile deep!"

"Please!"

"Ah, if you will, Jay. 'Tis easier, now."

His deft, steady fingers manipulated the levers of the lock, more surely, this time, more confidently. Almost at once it clicked; the four men set their shoulders to the bars, and slid the huge grille aside.

Staggering against wind and rain that now drove in with multiplied force, they peered over the square metal ledge. The smooth black wall dropped sheer, under them, for a long mile, sluiced with rain. Jay Kalam braced himself against the howling gusts; he pointed, shouted into the roar of thunder:

"The drain!"

They saw it, beside them, ten feet away. A huge, square tube, supported at close intervals by a metal flange that secured it to the wall. Straight into the pit it fell, dwindling to a thin black line, lost at last in the redly flickering murk below.

"The flanges!" Rather by watching his lips than by sound they caught the words. "A ladder. Too far apart. Inconvenient shape. But we can climb them. Down."

"Bless my bones!" howled Giles Habibula, into the tempest. "We can't do that, Jay. Not in this frightful storm. We can't even reach the mortal flanges! Poor old Giles——"

"John——" Jay Kalam's lips moved, his face a question.

"I'll try!" he screamed.

He was the lightest, the quickest, of the four; he could do the thing if any of them could. He nodded to Hal

Samdu, smiling grimly. The giant's hands took him up, hurled him out over the chasm, out into wild rain and bellowing wind.

His arms stretched out, his fingers caught the edge of a metal flange. But the hurricane had his body; it flung him out, over the abysm. Fingers strained. Shoulders throbbed. Muscles cracked. But he hung on.

The merciless gust released him, left him clinging to the flange, drenched and strangled in roaring rain. He tried the flanges, found that they would serve, however awkwardly, as a ladder; he nodded at the others.

He braced himself, then, standing on one leg, the other knee hooked over the flange above, waited, arms free. Jay Kalam was flung out, and he caught him, helped him to a higher position. Then Giles Habibula, green-faced, gasping.

And Aladoree, who said in a queer, muffled tone, "Thank you, John Ulnar," when he caught her in his arms.

Hal Samdu then passed out the gory legs of the tripod, which they slung to their belts. Standing on the narrow ledge, he closed the sliding grate, so that the lock snapped, in hope of confusing pursuit. Then he leaped, through blinding sheets of rain, and John Star leaned out to catch him.

His great weight made an intolerable burden for John Star in his cramped and insecure position. A furious downward gust increased it. John Star felt, as he clung to the giant's wet hand, that his body must be torn in two. But he kept his hold. Hal Samdu caught a flange with his free hand, was safe. And they started down the drain.

The bracing flanges were uncomfortably spaced; it would have been no slight feat to climb down a mile of them under the most favorable circumstances. Now rain fell in blinding, suffocating sheets from the roaring sky; the pitiless wind tore at them. All of them were already half exhausted. But apprehension of inevitable pursuit drove them to reckless haste.

In only one way was the storm an advantage, John Star thought; it had driven the Medusæ to shelter from above their buildings and machines; there seemed no danger of accidental discovery, before pursuit started from above. But that advantage they paid for very dearly in the battle with wind and rain.

They were halfway down, perhaps, when Aladoree fainted from sheer exhaustion.

John Star, just below her, had been watching her, afraid that she would slip from the wet flanges. He caught her; he held her until she revived and protested stubbornly that she was able to climb again. Then Hal Samdu lifted her to his shoulders, made her cling to him pickaback, and they climbed on down.

The great chasm's floor, as they descended, became more distinctly visible through the mist of falling water. A vast square pit, a full thousand feet across. Black, blank sides of huge buildings walled it, without a break. The floor was flooded with yellow water from the rain. All the water on the planet appeared yellow in volume, carrying in solution the red, organic gas.

Anxiously scanning the flooded floor, John Star could see no possible avenue of escape from it—unless they should climb another of the drains that was discharging its flood into the pit. And they were all too near exhaustion, he knew, to make such a climb, even if that could promise safety.

The torrential rain slackened suddenly, when they were near the bottom. The rumble of thunder diminished; the lurid red sky lifted slightly; the cold wind beat at them with decreasing violence.

John Star's feet had just touched the cold standing water on the floor, when Giles Habibula gasped the warning:

"My mortal eye! The evil Medusæ, coming down to take us back!"

Looking upward, he saw the greenish, black-fringed flying domes, drifting one by one from the hall they had left, floating down swiftly.

CHAPTER TWENTY-THREE

Yellow Maw of Terror

Standing in ankle-deep water, as the others were finishing the descent behind him, John Star looked desperately about for some possible way of escape from the pit.

Before him lay the sheet of yellow flood-water, a thousand feet square. Above it, on every side, stood glistening black walls of tremendous buildings, the very lowest taller than the proud Purple Hall. Here and there the high doors broke them, but none that he saw could be reached by any but a flying creature.

Against the little red rectangle of sky above the chasm, the pursuing Medusæ were drifting down, small, darkly greenish disks against the scarlet.

"There's no way!" he muttered to Jay Kalam, splashing down beside him. "For once—none! I suppose they'll kill us, now."

"But there is one way," said Jay Kalam, voice swift and strained. "If we've time to reach it. Not safe. Not pleasant. A grim and desperate chance. But better than waiting for them to slaughter us.

"Come!" he called, as Giles Habibula, the last, clambered groaning and shivering, down into chill water. "No time to waste!"

"Where?" demanded Hal Samdu, splashing after him through the yellow flood, Aladoree still clinging wearily to his back. "There's no way."

"The flood-water," Jay Kalam observed succinctly, "manages to find an exit."

At a splashing run, he led the way to an intake of the flood-drains. A yellow whirlpool, ten feet across, roaring down through a heavy metal grating.

"My bloody, mortal eye!" wheezed Giles Habibula. "Must we dive into the blessed sewers?"

"We must," Jay Kalam assured him. "Or wait for the Medusæ to kill us."

"Bless my dear old bones!" he wailed. "To be sucked

down and drowned like a miserable rat! And then vom-
ited out, sweet life knows, to be torn and swallowed by
the wicked things in the yellow river. Ah, Giles, it was a
mortal evil day——"

"We must lift the lid," urged Jay Kalam, "if we can!"

Hal Samdu had set down Aladoree, who stood shivering
and weary, uncertain. Almost swept off their feet by the
swirling yellow water, the four gathered along one side of
the circular black grating, grasped it, strained their muscles. It did not move.

"A mortal hasp!" cried Giles Habibula, feeling along
the edge.

Staggering in the mad current that buffeted his feet,
Hal Samdu hammered and levered at the fastening with
one of the tripod legs. John Star, glancing up at the
square of crimson sky, saw the dark circles of the
Medusæ, larger now, midway down.

The giant still beat and pried at the hasp, in vain. John
Star tried futilely to help him, and Jay Kalam. The furious swirl of yellow water rushed over it, hindering their
efforts, making it almost impossible even to stand.

"It was Eric Ulnar who warned them," said Aladoree,
her voice icy with a bitter scorn. "One of them is carrying
him. I see him pointing at us."

They renewed their efforts to break the hasp with
clumsy tools, panting, too busy to look up even at death
descending. At last the twisted metal broke.

"Now!" muttered Hal Samdu.

They gripped the bars again, lifted. The grate stirred
a little, to their united strength, settled back under the
pressure of the roaring torrent.

They tried again, Giles Habibula panting, purple-faced,
Hal Samdu's great muscles bulging, quivering with strain.
Even Aladoree added her efforts. Still it did not rise.

The Medusæ were fast drifting down upon them. Stealing an apprehensive glance, John Star saw a full score of
them, some carrying black implements that must have
been weapons, one bearing Eric Ulnar, gesticulating,
seated in a swing of woven serpents.

"We *must* lift it!"

They tried again, in new positions, straining fiercely.
The grating came up suddenly, relatively light when above
the grasp of mad water. They flung it back.

The open pit yawned before them, eight feet across.

Angry, swirling water leaped into it in an unbroken sheet, from every side; it was a yellow funnel, foam-lined. Ominous, furious, deafening, the yell of wild waters came up out of it.

John Star paused, staring into its savage yellow maw with a sickening wave of horror. It seemed very suicide to dive into that bellowing vortex, suicide in a singularly fearful guise. To be sucked down that tawny, foaming throat, whirled helpless through the sewers below, battered against the walls, finally belched into the horrors of the great river!

And Aladoree! It was impossible.

"We can't!" he shouted to Jay Kalam, above the snarling roar of it. "We can't drag her into *that!*"

"Mortal me!" hoarsely breathed Giles Habibula, the color of his face fading to a pallid, unhealthy green. "It's death! Wicked, howling death, and fearful suffocation."

He reeled back, staggering in the water that tore at his feet.

Jay Kalam glanced at the Medusæ drifting down, very close, now, with their black weapons and Eric Ulnar clinging to his cradle of snakes. He looked gravely at Aladoree, a silent question on his face.

She glanced up at them, her pale face momentarily hardening with scorn. Her gray eyes, still cool and steady, though too bright and dark-rimmed with weariness, looked deliberately from one to another of the four, and then down into the thundering whirlpool.

A long moment she hesitated. She smiled then, oddly; she made a little fleeting gesture of farewell. And she dived into that yellow, bellowing funnel.

John Star was dazed by the suddenness of her action, by the cold, reckless courage of it. It was a moment before he could recover his faculties, put down his own horror of that avid, howling maw. He tossed aside his improvised weapon, then; he gasped a last full breath of air, and followed.

Twenty feet down, he fell with the yellow foaming vortex into a plunging river.

The murky red gloom was extinct in an instant. In complete darkness he was whirled along, beneath the black city. After a little time his struggles brought him to the surface. The drain was racing almost full. His fend-ing arm was bruised against the top of the tube. But he was able to inhale a gasp of foul, reeking air.

He caught breath, again, to shout Aladoree's name, then realized the utter futility of that. Whirling ahead of him in the roaring torrent, she could never hear. Nor would it serve any good if she did.

The passage turned presently; he was strangled in the smother of foam below the angle.

Again, after an indefinite time of waiting, fighting to keep afloat, breathing when he could, he was flung into a deeper, swifter current. Here the drain was all but full. The wild water washed and splashed and foamed against the roof of it; it was seldom he could find an open space from which to fill his lungs.

On and on he was rushed, until he felt that he had fought that savage torrent forever; until his bruised, weary body screamed for rest; until his lungs shrieked for pure air again, and not the foul, foam-filled pockets above the thundering tide.

He could not last another moment, he was thinking, when he plunged into a new wider channel. The current sucked him under. For seeming hours, deadly, lung-tortured, he fought for the surface; and he came up under racing metal, no air beneath it.

Somehow, he kept the water from his aching lungs. He let the mad current whirl him on. Could Aladoree, he wondered, have endured all this? And the three behind him, if they had dived before the Medusæ came, could they be still alive?

Abruptly he was in a wild fury of roaring foam. He was drawn down again until a cruel weight of water crushed his chest. Fighting a weary way upward, too nearly lifeless to feel any glow of triumph, he saw light in the water.

Up he broke through yellow foam, gratefully sucked in the clear reviving air of the open—quite oblivious of the red and slowly deadly gas that tainted it.

Above, on the one side, was the sullen sky, washed to its full and sinister brilliance by the storm. On the other was the mile-high metal wall of the black metropolis. He had been discharged into the surging flood of the yellow river.

Boiling, scarred with lighter lines of foam, pitted with vortices of angry whirlpools, its turbid tide reached away from him, ten miles wide, so wide that the low dark line of jungle on the farther bank was all but lost in thick red murk.

For miles below him, it rushed along the base of the mighty wall, until it reached the not less forbidding barrier of the black thorn-jungle.

For months he had voyaged that yellow tide; he had learned to face its thousand perils. But the others had been with him then; they had been on board the raft; they had been armed against the ferocious life of river and air and jungle.

Anxiously, he looked about him for Aladoree—in vain.

When he had breath, he shouted her name. His voice was a thin, useless sound, weak and hoarse, drowned in the roar from the chaos behind him where the flood from the drains met the river's mighty tide.

But he saw her, presently, a hundred yards below him. Her head a tiny thing, bobbing upon the boiling yellow surface. Her body too small, he realized, too frail, too weary, to struggle long against the savage river.

He swam toward her heavily, his limbs all but dead. The turbid current moved her toward him; it carried her farther again, faster than he could swim; wild water taunted him until, in the near-delirium of exhaustion, he gasped curses at it as if it had been sentiently malicious.

She saw him; she struggled feebly toward him, through rough yellow foam, as they raced along in the shadow of the walls. He glanced back, sometimes, hoping that one of the other three might have come through alive, and saw none of them.

Aladoree vanished before his eyes, when he was not a dozen feet from her, sucked down by a pitiless current; she appeared again as he was about to dive hopelessly for her, flung up helpless in the freakish water.

He caught her arm, dragged it across his shoulder.

"Hang on," he gasped. And he added with a last grim spark of spirit:

"If you can trust an Ulnar."

With the brief, wan ghost of a smile, she clung to him.

The yellow, swirling foam bore them on, under the mighty, marching walls, toward the river-bend below. There the thorn-jungle waited.

CHAPTER TWENTY-FOUR

"For Want of a Nail"

John Star had never any clear recollection of that time in the river. In the ultimate stages of exhaustion, driven far beyond the normal limits of endurance, he was more machine than man. Somehow he kept himself afloat, and Aladoree. But that was all he knew.

The feel of gravel beneath his feet brought purpose briefly back. He waded and crawled up out of the yellow water, on the edge of a wide, smooth bar of black sand, carrying the limp girl.

Three hundred yards across the dark bare sand rose the jungle. A barrier of black and interwoven swords, it towered forbidding against the crimson sky. It was splashed with huge, vivid blooms of flaming violet that gave it a certain terrible beauty; and it hid death in many guises.

The open sand, John Star knew, was a no-man's-land, menaced from the river and the jungle and the air. But he had scant heed left for danger. Pulling the exhausted girl safely out of the yellow shallows, into the dubious shelter of a mass of driftwood lodged against a sand-buried snag, he fell beside her on the sand. Fatigue overcame him there.

He knew, when he woke, that precious hours were lost. The huge disk of the red sun was already cut in half by the edge of the jungle; the air already chill with a deadly hint of coming night.

Aladoree lay beside him on the black sand, sleeping. Looking at her slight, defenseless form, breathing so slowly and so quietly, he felt an aching throb in his chest. How many times, he wondered, as they lay there, had death passed by on the yellow river, or stared from the wall of thorns—and spared their lives, and AKKA, and humanity's hope?

He tried to sit up, sank back with a gasp of pain. Every individual muscle in his body was stiffly rebellious. Yet he forced himself up, rubbed his painful limbs until some flexibility returned to them, and got unsteadily to his feet.

First he picked Aladoree up in his arms, still sleeping, and carried her higher on the bar, beyond the unseen peril that might strike from the shallows. He made a flimsy little screen of driftwood, to hide them, and found a heavy club; he waited by her, to watch until she woke.

With wary glance he scanned the tawny river, flowing away until the farther dark jungle wall was dim in red haze. He searched the bare waste of somber sand, the black thorn-barrier behind it; the ramparts of the black metropolis, miles up-river, just visible above the jungle. But it was out of the murky sky that danger came, gliding down on silent wings.

The creature was low when he saw it, diving at the sleeping girl behind her little screen of branches. Somewhat it resembled a dragon-fly grown to monstrous size. It had four thin wings, spreading thirty feet. It was, he saw, like the creature that Giles Habibula had once battled for his bottle of wine.

He caught his breath, startled by its strange and wicked beauty. The frail wings were blue and translucent; they glittered like thin sheets of dark sapphire. Ribs of scarlet veined them. The slim, tapered body was black, oddly and strikingly patched with bright yellow. The one enormous eye was like a jewel of polished jet.

A single pair of limbs stiffened under it; cruel yellow talons spread to clutch the girl's body. And its tail, a thin yellow whip, scorpion-like, armed with a terrible black barb, arched down to sting.

John Star leaped straight in the path of it, swung his club for the jet-black eye. But the brilliant wings tilted a little, the creature swerved up; it struck at him instead of the girl. His blow missed the solitary eye; the thin, pitiless lance of its sting came straight at him.

He flung his body down, twisting his blow to fend away the stabbing barb. He felt the impact as his club struck the whipping tail; the venomed point was driven a little aside, yet it grazed his shoulder with a flash of blinding pain.

Scrambling instantly back to his feet, nearly blind with searing pain, he dimly saw the creature rise and turn and glide back again, on translucent blue-and-scarlet wings.

Again it dived, talons set. This time, he saw, the barbed tail was hanging; his club had broken it.

Staggered with agony, he aimed his blow again at the bright jet disk of the eye. And this time the creature did not swerve. It plunged straight at him, yellow talons grasping. In the last instant, dizzy with pain from its venom, he realized that the talons would strike him.

Fiercely, he sought to steady his reeling world; he put every ounce of his strength behind the heavy piece of driftwood, felt it crush solidly home against the huge black glittering disk. Then his senses dissolved in the acid of pain.

Vaguely, he knew that it was not flying with him. Dimly, he knew that it was floundering on the sand, dragging his body still locked in its talons. His last blow had been fatal.

Presently the death-struggles ceased; the furry body collapsed upon him. The yellow talons, even in death, were set deep in his arm and shoulder. One by one, when the blinding pain began to ebb a little, he strained his fingers to open them, and he came at last to his feet, faint and ill and bleeding.

Even dead, the thing was beautiful. The narrow wings, spread unbroken on the black sand, were luminous sheets of ruby-veined sapphire. Only the reddened talons and the broken sting were hideous—and the head of it, pulped under his last blow.

Weakly, he reeled away from it, too faint even to pick up his club. He sank down beside Aladoree, still quietly breathing in the dead sleep of exhaustion, peacefully unaware of the death that had been so near.

Sunk in a hopeless apathy of new fatigue and pain, at first he did not even move when he saw three tiny figures toiling along the flat black sand. They must be Jay Kalam and Hal Samdu and Giles Habibula; he knew they must have come alive, by some miracle of courage and endurance, through the drains and out of the yellow river. But he was too deep in exhaustion to feel any hope or interest.

He sat there, by the sleeping girl and the brilliant dead thing, aimlessly watching them come wearily over the black bar, out of hazy red distance.

Three strange, haggard men, each of them with a few tattered bits of cloth still clinging to a worn, exposure-browned body. Bearded men, long-haired, shaggily un-kempt. They walked close together. Each of them carried a club or a thorn spear. Their sunken, gleaming eyes peered about with a fierce alert suspicion. They were like three dawn-men, hunting in the shadow of some early jungle; three elemental beasts, cautious and dangerous.

It was strange to think of them as survivors of the crushed and betrayed Legion of Space, the last fighting men of the once-proud System, left alone to defend it from the science of an alien star. Could these shaggy animals decide an interstellar war?

John Star at last found spirit to stand, to shout and wave. They saw him, hurried to him over the bar.

Hal Samdu still carried the black mechanism from the tripod, slung about his great shoulders by its connecting wires. He had dived with it into the drains; burdened with it, he had fought the yellow river.

"Aladoree?" he rasped, hoarse, weary, anxious, stalking up ahead of the others.

"Asleep." John Star found energy for the one word, the gesture.

The giant dropped beside her, eagerly solicitous, a smile of relief on his haggard, red-bearded face.

"You carried her out?" he rasped. "And killed—*that?*"

John Star could only nod. His eyes had closed, but he knew that Jay Kalam and Giles Habibula were coming up. He heard the latter wheezing weakly:

"Ah, precious life! It's been an evil time, a fearful time! Washed through the stinking sewers like garbage, and flung to die amid the wicked horrors of the fearful yellow river. Ah, poor old Giles Habibula! It was a mortal evil day——"

His voice changed.

"Ah, the lass! The lass has not been harmed. And this wicked glittering monster! John must have killed it . . . Ah, old Giles knows how you feel, lad! A mortal bitter time, we've all been through!"

His voice brightened again.

"This dead creature—the flesh of it is good to eat. 'Tis like the one I fought so mortal hard for my bottle of wine —that precious wine I never got to taste! We must have a fire. I'm fearful weak from hunger. Ah, poor old Giles, dying of hunger——"

John Star drifted away, then, a second time, into blissful sleep.

It was colder, when he woke. His body was numb and stiff, though a sheltered fire of driftwood blazed beside him. Dread night was coming apace; the sun's angry disk now completely gone, the sky a low dome of baleful murky twilight. Bitter wind blew across the river, toward the jungle.

Giles Habibula was by the fire, grilling meat he had cut from the dead flying thing. John Star felt gnawing hunger; it must have been the fragrance of the roast that awoke him. But he did not eat at once.

Jay Kalam and Hal Samdu were beside Aladoree, beyond the fire. The little machine that the giant had brought so far, they had taken apart. The pieces of it were spread out before them, on a flat slab of driftwood. Coils of wire and odds and ends of metal and black plastic.

He stood up, hastily, despite the stiffness of his body, and hurried to them. In their absorption, they did not look up. Before Aladoree was an odd little device, assembled from the black metal parts, from rudely carved fragments of wood. She was fingering the remaining bits of metal, anxiously, one by one, rejecting each with a little hopeless shake of her head.

"You're setting it up?" John Star whispered eagerly. "AKKA?"

"She's trying!" breathed Jay Kalam abstractedly.

John Star glanced across the black jungle-top, toward the towers and machines of the black metropolis, remote in the red twilight. It was sheer impossibility, he felt, that the crude little device on the sand should ever do injury to those colossal walls.

"I must have iron," said Aladoree. "A tiny bit of iron, the size of a nail, would do. But I must have it for the magnetic element. Except for that, there's everything I need. But there's no iron here."

She laid down the tiny device, hopelessly.

"We must find ore, then," said John Star. "Build a furnace, smelt it."

Jay Kalam shook his head gravely, wearily.

"We can't do that. No iron on the planet. The Medusæ, you know, first promised to conquer our System for the Purples, just for a shipload of iron. In all our wandering, I saw no trace of iron deposits."

"We can't build the weapon, then," Aladoree said slowly. "Not here. If we could only get back to the System."

"The ship is lying wrecked, somewhere on the bottom of the ocean."

Numbed with bleak despair they stood there, shivering in the chill wind that came up across the river. Over the dark thorn-jungle they stared, at the walls and towers and unguessable mechanisms of the dark metropolis. Old before the dawn of man, it would stand invincible when the last man was gone.

From those far walls and towers, abruptly, green flame burned. They saw titanic forms rising, the black spider-shapes of the Medusæ's interstellar fliers. A monstrous swarm rose up as the far thunder of green-flaring rockets rolled over the jungle and the river, and vanished at last in the blood-red sky.

"Their fleet!" whispered Aladoree. "Flying away to the System, with all their hordes, to occupy our planets. Their fleet, already gone! If we had found a bit of iron—— But it's too late. We've already failed."

CHAPTER TWENTY-FIVE

Wings Above the Walls

"All for the want of a mortal nail!" commented Giles Habibula, in a voice that might have softened the heart of a statue of iron.

"Ah, me! That the lack of a blessed nail could mean so much!"

He was huddled on the black sand, a heap of dejection, carelessly holding a smoking piece of meat on a stick, above the sheltered driftwood fire.

"Poor old Giles Habibula! Ah, that he should live to see such a fearful day! Better—ah, sweet life knows, far better—that he should have died as a blessed babe! Better that the law should have taken its cruel, pitiless course, that time on Venus!

"A fearful reward it is, in dear life's name, mortal fearful, for twenty years of loyal service in the Legion. Accused for a precious pirate. Imprisoned and starved and tortured! Ah, yes, driven out of his own native System, to this hideous world of frightful horror!

"Poisoned by the very mortal air, doomed to howling insanity and death by slow green rot. Hunted by a million mortal monsters. Forced to scuttle like a rat through the wicked black city. Driven like a miserable rat to drown in the stinking sewers. Now face to face with a fearful death, in the cold of the dreadful night. And the one bottle of wine on the whole black continent smashed before he'd had a taste of it!

"Mortal me! It's more than a man can endure. Too mortal much, in life's dear name, for a poor old soldier of the Legion, sick and lame and feeble, with his wine spilled under his very eyes!

"And now, for the want of a nail, the whole human System is lost! Ah, me, for the lack of one precious bit of iron, all humanity doomed to die before the invasion of the monstrous Medusæ! Ah, good life knows, it's a mortal evil time! A mortal bitter time! Poor old Giles Habibula——"

There was a crackling sound from the driftwood fire, a whiff of bitter smoke. He stirred himself abruptly, rose with a final doleful wail:

"Ah, me! Misfortunes never come alone. Now the mortal meat is burned!"

And he went back to the bright-winged thing that John Star had killed, to cut another steak from its furry body.

By the glittering, sapphire-and-ruby wings that lay forlorn on the black sand, the others were standing in a dispirited little group, shivering in the increasing cold wind that blew out of the deepening red twilight.

From the river bar they were staring, beaten and beyond hope, at the walls and towers and machines of the black metropolis, looming weird against the darkling scarlet sky, above the dark thorn-jungle.

An overwhelming sense of failure, of the inevitable doom overtaking them and all humanity, rested oppressively upon them; despair held them in dead silence.

The keen blue eyes that peered above Hal Samdu's red

beard caught a black space flier—a colossal spider-ship of
the Medusæ, riding eerie green jets—moving toward the
somber walls above the yellow river. He pointed, silently
followed it.

"Is that——?" John Star cried, with a sudden painful
leap of his heart. "Beneath it—could it be——?"

"It is," Jay Kalam said gravely, "the *Purple Dream!*"

"Your ship?" cried Aladoree.

"Our ship. We left it wrecked, under the yellow sea,
with Adam Ulnar on board."

"Adam Ulnar!" Her voice was edged with scorn.
"Then he has gone back to his allies."

She looked at John Star oddly.

"It looks," he admitted, "as if he had. He could communicate with the Medusæ by radio. He must have
called them, got them to raise the ship and help repair
it."

They watched the *Purple Dream,* flying under the vast
black vanes of the Medusæ's flier, its tiny torpedo shape
no more than a silver mote. Blue flame burst from its
rockets as it approached the black city, and it slanted
down athwart the red sky, the other huge machine hanging near above it, on green wings of distant thunder. It
slowed; it came at last to rest on a tower of the black
wall, in full, maddening view of them. The black ship
landed close beside it.

For a few minutes they all stared at it, silent with the
intensity of their desires.

"We must get that ship!" Jay Kalam whispered, at
last.

"It would take us to the System," breathed Aladoree,
voiceless. "We could find iron. We could set up AKKA.
We could save at least a remnant of humanity."

"We could try," agreed Jay Kalam. "They would follow us from here, of course. With those weapons that
throw flaming suns. The Belt of Peril is still above us;
we'd have to get through that again. All their invasion
fleet will be guarding our System, now. And the hordes of
them, in that new fortress on the Moon . . . But," he
whispered, "we could try."

"But how?" rasped Hal Samdu hoarsely.

"That's the first question. It's miles to where the ship
is, across the jungle. On top of that smooth wall, a mile

high. Nothing could reach it but a flying thing. And that black flier is beside it, apparently to guard it. How?"

His eyes fell, then, on John Star, who was staring fixedly at the wings of the creature he had killed, glittering beside them on the black sand.

"What is it, John?" he demanded, his low voice strangely tense. "You look——"

"Nothing could reach it except a flying thing?" John Star said slowly, absently. "But I think—I think I see a way."

"You mean—to fly?"

Jay Kalam searched his intent, haggard face; puzzled, he glanced at the long splendid wings at which John Star was staring, sheets of sapphire, veined with red.

"Yes. I used to fly," said John Star. "At the Legion Academy. Gliding. One year I was gliding champion of the Academy."

"Build a glider, you mean?"

"It could be done—I believe it could. Those wings are long enough. Strong. The thing's body was larger than mine. And the wind is blowing across the river, toward the jungle and the walls. There would be rising currents."

"Here are the wings. But the rest——?"

"Not much would be needed. The wings are already ribbed. We need posts to brace them together, but we could cut canes in the jungle. And twist fiber cords to lash them together."

"There isn't much time."

"No. It will soon be too cold to work. Just a few hours. But we've no shelter, no weapons. We'd never live through the night. No, Jay, it seems the only thing."

"Yes!" Jay Kalam spoke suddenly, accepting the idea. "Yes, we shall try. But it's a desperate undertaking, John. You realize that. An uncertain craft—if we can build one that will fly at all. The danger you will be discovered. The difficulty of getting on board; and then getting the better of Adam Ulnar, with only a thorn dagger. Even if you get to the controls, there's that spider-ship on guard."

"I know," John Star said soberly. "But it seems the only thing."

So they set out, in the face of every conceivable obstacle and danger, to do the impossible, first searching for tools, for sharp-edged shells, for rocks that would serve as knives and hammers, for the iron-hard jungle thorns.

Measuring the bright wings, John Star drew on all his old knowledge for a design into which they would fit, sketched it with charcoal on a slab of bark.

Then, in increasing cold and darkness, with the glistening wings, with struts and braces shaped from jungle cane, with twisted fiber cables and members shaped from the tough thorn wood, he labored hour after hour to construct the glider, while the four others roved the beach and the jungle fringe for materials.

They did not rest until it was finished, a simple thing, frail and slight. Merely the four bright wings, braced together, with fiber thongs to fasten them to John Star's body. They bound it on him, and he ran with it a few times down the sand bar, into the bitter wind, the others hauling him with a rope of twisted bark, to try its balance.

He thrust two thorn-daggers into his belt, then, and fastened a long black spear to the frame beside him. He ran down the sand, the others tugging on the rope. He rose, cast it off.

His strange craft came up unsteadily, swerved and dived toward the sand. He righted it with a desperate twist of his body—its only control was by shifting his weight. And he soared up in the strong current that rose over the jungle.

He looked down, once, at the tiny group on the bar of black sand—three ragged men and a weary girl whose hopes had sent him up. Four tiny figures, alone in the red dusk. He waved a hand; they waved back.

Heart aching queerly, he soared on. He could not fail them, for they would surely die unless he took the ship. Jay and Hal and Giles—and Aladoree! He could not let them die, even if their safety had not meant the survival of humanity. Over the black thorns, now. Sheer disaster if he fell here. When he found time to look again, the four were lost in the shadow of the jungle-edges.

His old skill came back swiftly. He found his old elation again in the sweeping, soaring flight; there was a lifting joy even in the difficulty of managing his tricky craft, even in defying the black thorn-jungle.

Keeping within the rising currents above the jungle's edge, he worked steadily up-river, toward black and mighty walls—grown vague, now, in the thickening red gloom, the *Purple Dream* no longer visible. At first he had been doubtful of the frail machine, but he soared with increasing confidence, presently fearing only that the wind should change, or the Medusæ discover him. Then unexpected danger came.

Up from the black forest came gliding another creature, like the one which had supplied his wings. It circled him; it climbed above him; it dived at him again and again, sting and talons ready, until he knew that it meant to attack.

He shouted at it and vainly waved his arms. At first it seemed alarmed, but then it dived again, nearer than before.

He unbound the black spear with cold-stiffened fingers, and set it before him. The thing dived a last time, slender sting curved, yellow talons set. It came straight at him. He met it squarely, spear aimed at its single black eye.

The point went home. But the rushing body struck his fragile craft with a force that made its flimsy structure creak. Flung off balance, John Star slipped toward the jungle, after the body of his attacker.

Equilibrium recovered, just clear of the thorns, he rose again. But the fiber-bound frame had been weakened and warped by the impact. It snapped and groaned alarmingly as he soared, its flight more startling and unstable than ever.

But at last he reached the stronger, gusty current that rose against the walls of the black city. Up he was carried, up, fearful that each moment would see his bright wings folding, his body spinning back to the yellow river.

So he came at last level with the tower. He made out the *Purple Dream,* a tiny spindle of silver, lying on the huge black platform in the vast shadow of the spider-ship that guarded her. The nightmare city stretched away beyond; the machines on the high platforms were an army of black giants, crouching in the red twilight.

Over the landing stage he swept, and down.

The gust carried him too fast, almost he was swept over the wall and into the city; the glider cracked and fluttered. His body was slowed and shuddering with the probing cold, numb and unresponsive.

But his feet touched black metal in the shadow of the *Purple Dream.* He slipped free of the binding thongs, and discarded the bright wings. He ran silently toward the airlock, thorn dagger in hand, alert for the unknown obstacles ahead.

CHAPTER TWENTY-SIX

Traitor's Turn

The air-lock, to his relief, was open, the accommodation ladder down to the metal platform. He was up the steps in an instant, across the lowered valve, and upon the long, narrow deck inside, beneath the curve of the hull, where he came face to face with Adam Ulnar.

At their parting, months before, on the bottom of the yellow sea, Adam Ulnar had seemed a beaten man, shattered, crushed with the discovery that he and his cause had been betrayed by the Medusæ, broken with the knowledge that he had unwittingly betrayed mankind.

He was different now.

Always tall, impressive of figure, he was once more erect, confident, coolly resolute. Freshly shaven, long white hair combed and shining, neatly groomed in Legion uniform, he met John Star with a hearty smile of surprised welcome on his handsome face.

"Why—why, John! You surprised me. Though I had hoped——"

He started forward, extending a well-kept hand in greeting. And John Star leaped to meet him, menacing his throat with drawn thorn dagger.

"Keep still!" he whispered harshly. "Not a sound!"

He felt the contrast between them. A strange figure he presented, he knew; grimy, exposure-blackened, haggard from fatigue, half naked. With shaggy head and many months' growth of beard he must look more beast than man. An uncouth animal, facing a polished, confident, powerful man.

"Adam Ulnar," he breathed again, fiercely, "I'm going to kill you. I think you well deserve to die. Have you anything to say?"

He waited, shuddering and stiff with cold. Suddenly he was afraid that he could not strike this serene, smiling man, whose personality roused instinctive admiration and quick pride in their kinship—for all his black treason.

"John!" protested the other, his voice urgently persuasive. "You misunderstand. I'm really delighted that you came. My unfortunate nephew told me, a little while ago, that you had been here, and had drowned in the sewers. Knowing you and your companions, I could scarcely believe that all of you had perished. I was still hoping to be of some assistance to you."

"Assistance!" echoed John Star harshly, still threatening his throat with the dagger. "Assistance! When you are responsible for everything that's wrong!"

"I want all the more, my boy, to help you, because I realize my own responsibility. It's true that you and I have differing political views. But I never had any desire to help the Medusæ to colonize our planets. I have no other purpose, now, than to undo what I've done."

"How's that?" demanded John Star, with a sick fear that this smooth, compelling voice might win his confidence, and betray it again.

Adam Ulnar made a gesture to include the ship about them.

"I've already done something. You must admit that. I've had the cruiser raised and repaired, in the hope that it might carry AKKA back to the System in time to avert total disaster."

"But the Medusæ raised it."

"Of course. They tricked me; it was my turn—if I could do it. I got back in communication with them, and asked to join them. I agreed to aid them with my military skill, in the conquest of the System. And I asked them to raise the *Purple Dream,* fit it up for my maintenance.

"They raised the cruiser, and repaired her, well enough, but I'm afraid they haven't a very high opinion of humanity. They don't seem to trust me as far as we Purples trusted them. The black flier outside has been standing guard over me, day and night. You know the sort of armament it has—those guns that fire atomic vortices."

"You've seen Eric?" demanded John Star suspiciously. "He's with you?"

"No, John. He isn't with me now. He told me how the Medusæ had made him try to force the girl to reveal her secret. He told me all about your arrival and escape. And he told me how he went back to warn the Medusæ—he didn't think you had a chance to get away, and he hoped to earn their favors."

"The cowardly beast!" mutered John Star. "Where is he?"

Adam Ulnar nodded, a shadow of pain on his handsome face.

"That's what he was, John. A coward. Even though his name was Ulnar. A pitiful coward. He made the first, foolish alliance with the Medusæ, because he was a coward, because he was afraid to trust my own plans for the revolution.

"I knew, then, John, that I'd made a mistake. I knew it was you who should have been Emperor, not Eric. Even then, it might not have been too late—if you had been willing to take the job."

"But I wasn't."

"No, you weren't. And perhaps you were right, John. I'm losing my faith in aristocracy. Our family is old, John; our blood is the best in the System. Yet Eric was a craven fool. And the three men with you—common soldiers of the Legion—have shown fine metal.

"It hasn't been easy for me to change, John. But I had time to think, under that yellow sea. And I have changed. From now on, I shall support the Green Hall."

"Yes?" John Star's voice was hard with skepticism. "But answer my question. Where is Eric? Both of you——"

"Eric will never betray mankind again, John." The voice was edged with pain. "When I found how he had sent the Medusæ after you, when you were escaping—I killed him." He winced. "My own blood as he was—I killed him. I broke his neck with my own hands."

"You—killed . . . Eric?"

John Star whispered the words very slowly, his haggard eyes anxiously scanning Adam Ulnar's face, now stern with its pain.

"Yes, John. And killed part of myself with him, for I loved him. Loved him! You're the heir, now, to the Purple Hall, John."

"Wait!" snapped John Star, savagely, pressing the dagger closer, while he searched the gauntly handsome, pain-shadowed face.

"Very well, John."

With a curious little smile, Adam Ulnar folded his arms, backed to the wall, stood watching him.

"You don't trust me, John. You couldn't, after all that has happened. Go ahead, then; drive your weapon home, if you feel that you must. I shan't defend myself. And as I die I shall be proud that your name is Ulnar."

John Star came toward him, crude weapon lifted. He gazed into the fine, clear eyes. They did not waver. They seemed sincere. He could not kill this man! Though doubt still lurked in his heart, he lowered the black thorn-blade.

"I'm glad you didn't strike, John," Adam Ulnar said, smiling again. "Because I think you will need me. Even though we have the cruiser repaired, there are obstacles ahead of us, yet.

"The black flier, here, is on guard. If we get away from that, they can send a whole fleet after us. The Belt of Peril is still above—it is weaker, I've recently learned, above the poles of the planet, but even there it's a very effective barrier.

"Even if some succession of miracles let us get to the System, humanity is already crushed, disorganized. We would receive no aid; we might be attacked, even, by miserable human wretches already insane from the red gas.

"We'd have to deal with their fleet, and the black fort on the Moon, from which they are shelling all the System with that red gas. Eric says they dismantled all their gas plants here, months ago, and moved them to the Moon— that must be why the concentration of the gas is getting so weak in the air here.

"Already, John, we may be too late. We may be the sole survivors, with no chance of surviving very long, ourselves. If we're going to try at all, we've very little time."

"I'll trust you, Adam," said John Star, striving to put down a lingering doubt. He added swiftly: "We must pick up Aladoree and the others. They're down by the river, without shelter from the cold, or any real weapons. They'd soon die in this night!"

"To move now with that black flier on guard," protested Adam Ulnar, "would be suicide. We must wait some opportunity——"

"We can't wait!" He was harsh with desperation. "We've the proton gun. If we took them by surprise——"

Adam Ulnar shook his head.

"They dismantled the needle, John. Removed it. The cruiser is unarmed. They took even the racks of hand

weapons. Your thorn is the only weapon we have—
against those suns they throw!"

John Star set his jaw.

"There's one way!" he muttered grimly. "A way to
move so fast they'd have very little time to strike."

"How's that?"

"We can take off with the geodynes."

"The geodynes!" It was a startled cry. "They can't be
used for a takeoff, John. You know that. They can't be
used safely in any atmosphere. We'd fuse the hull with
friction-heat! Or crash into the ground like a meteor!"

"We'll use the geodynes," said John Star, harshly. "I'm
a pilot. Can you run the generators?"

Adam Ulnar looked at him for a moment, strangely;
then he smiled, took John Star's hand, and squeezed it
with a quick strong pressure.

"Very good, John. I can operate the generators. We
shall take off with the geodynes . . . I wish you had been
my nephew."

John Star felt a responding emotion, checked by that
little doubt which refused to die. So many had trusted this
tall commanding man; his treason had been so appalling!

They parted. In the little bridge-room, John Star in-
spected the array of familiar instruments; he tested them
swiftly, one by one. All the iron, he saw, had been re-
placed by other metals. But everything seemed to function as it should. He peered through a tele-periscope.

The Medusæ's guarding flier lay beside them, one vast
strange vane extending overhead. Against the dim red
glow lingering in the murky west, it loomed evil and
gigantic; it looked more than ever like some hybrid
spider-thing, swollen to Cyclopean dimensions.

The low, clear music of the geodyne generators became
audible, and rose to a keening whine. Adam Ulnar's
voice came crisp from the bulkhead speaker:

"Generators ready, sir, at full power."

John Star's brief, grim smile at the "sir" was checked
again, by sharp mistrust. Swiftly he estimated the position
of the bar on the river, planning the thing he meant to do.
For the slightest error, he realized, meant instant annihi-
lation.

Fingers on the keys, he peered back into the tele-
periscope.

He remembered the air-lock, then, and touched the

button that closed it. That act, he knew, might betray them. But if he had left it open, mere air-resistance would have torn it away.

Tensely he waited, one second, two, and three, for the motors to work. A long, slender black cone projected abruptly from the huge black sphere of the flier's belly. It swung toward them. A weapon!

Four! Five! He heard the clang of the closing valve and touched a key.

The tower platform and the black flier vanished instantaneously. Yet, since that unimaginable force was applied equally to the entire ship, there had been no perceptible shock; the geodynes had flung them away with a rapidity incalculable—and perilous!

Dim crimson gloom spun about them. A black shadow met them.

Driven with lightning speed to meet this desperate emergency, John Star's fingers leaped across the keys. Years of training now found their test. He had often imagined, in the days at the Academy, that such a thing might be done, half longing for the chance to try it, yet half fearful that the chance might come.

After the merest instant of acceleration, he reversed the geodynes for another split second, to check an inconceivable velocity.

And the *Purple Dream,* a moment before upon the black wall, was plunging down toward the flat yellow river, still at a frightful speed, her hull incandescent from friction with the air. Desperately, he flung down the rocket firing keys, to check the remaining momentum before they struck.

A desperate game, this playing with the curvature of space itself, in the very atmosphere of a planet. Human daring and human skill, pitted against titanic forces. Savage elation filled him. He was winning—if the rockets stopped them in time!

Down on a dark sand bar hurtled the incandescent ship. Down to the bank of a freezing river. Rockets thundering at full power to the last moment, she struck the sand heavily; she plowed into it, steam mantling her red-hot hull.

By the narrowest margin—safe!

Safe, at any rate, until the Medusæ had time to strike. Hot valves flung open. Four passengers came aboard.

Half-naked, haggard passengers, dead-weary, stiff with cold. The air-lock clanged behind them; the *Purple Dream* thundered away again, blue blasts licking black sand.

Geodynes cut in at once, she plowed with an utterly reckless velocity upward through the dim red afterglow. John Star felt a moment of wild triumph, before he recalled the belt of fortress satellites ahead; recalled the six light years of interstellar space beyond; remembered the fleets of the Medusæ, guarding the System, and the occupation force waiting in their new black citadel on the Moon.

Behind, he saw huge machines stirring along the walls and towers of that nightmare metropolis. A full score of the spider-ships lifted on jets of green fire, to pursue. More than a match for the *Purple Dream* in speed, armed with those weapons that fired suns of annihilating atomic flame!

CHAPTER TWENTY-SEVEN

The Joke on Man

The red murk above grew thin. The *Purple Dream* burst upward into the freedom of space, where her incandescent hull could cool. The planet drew away beneath them, a huge and featureless half-moon of dull and baleful orange-red.

Up from it followed the swarm of spider-ships. The recklessly sudden start of the cruiser had left them too far behind to use their fearful weapons at once. But swiftly they closed the gap.

Ahead was the Belt of Peril.

Sinister web of unseen rays spread from the six trailing forts in space. Mighty secret of an elder science. Dread zone of unknown radiation that melted molecular bonds, to let stout metal and tortured human flesh dissolve away into a mist of free atoms.

Remembering Adam Ulnar's new information that it

was weaker over the poles, John Star set his course northward. He drove the cruiser at the utmost power of the
geodynes, sick already with his dread of the barrier, sick
at thought of what Aladoree must suffer within it. But
there was no choice.

The *Purple Dream* plunged into the wall of unseen
radiation, John Star alone on the bridge.

Fiery mist swirled suddenly away from his body, from
bulkheads and instruments. Mist of excited or ionized
atoms, dancing points of rainbow light. White, searing
pain probed his body, screamed in his ears, flamed before
his eyes. Atom by atom, the ship and his body were dissolving away. Limp with suffering, he fought to keep
awareness, to keep the hurtling cruiser within the narrow
passage of partial wave-interference above the pole.

His body, grown luminous and half-transparent, was
immersed in shining agony. He could scarcely move the
keys. Red flame burned away his very brain.

Part of him was startled, inexpressibly, by a sudden
laugh, strange and harsh and wild. A mad laugh. Luna-
tic! It shook him with a sickness of new horror, for he
knew that the one who had laughed was himself.

He had just thought of a terrific joke!

Like those survivors of the first expedition, the sane
part of him knew, he was going mad! Long exposure to
the red climate-control gas had overtaken him at last.
Gone mad! And doomed to die of slow green decay!

He was laughing. Laughing at a monstrous joke. The
joke was the death of the System, by madness and green
leprosy. And its point, the death of those who tried to
save mankind, by the same slow decay. A fearful joke!
So terribly funny!

Millions, all the human billions, laughing foolishly, in-
anely, as their flesh turned to foul green rot and fell away.
And those who had thought to save them—the very
first to die. What a cosmic joke! Men laughing at the face
of red pain. Men and women laughing while their flesh
turned green! Laughing, until their bodies fell apart, and
they laughed at death!

What a universal joke!

His hands slipped away from the keys; he was
doubled up with laughter.

Would the Medusæ see the point, as they rained the
bombs of red gas on the planets? Or was their monstrous

race too old for laughter? Had they forgotten how to laugh, before the Earth was born? Or had those green and palpitating bodies the power of laughter, ever?

He must ask Adam Ulnar. He could communicate with the Medusæ. He could find out. He could tell them the joke—the cosmic joke, a whole race laughing as it died.

He tried to stand up, but laughter wouldn't let him rise. He rubbed his hands together. They felt dry, papery. Already the scales were forming on his skin. His flesh would flake away until his bones were bare. He was a joke, himself! What a joke!

He lay on the floor and laughed.

Dimly, then, he became aware of something he must do. Red flame lapped at his brain; he was sick with suffering. And there were others. Others? Yes, Jay and Hal and Giles. And Aladoree! He could not fail them! But what was the thing he must do?

It was to drive the cruiser on, he remembered vaguely, through the Belt of Peril. Then this intolerable pain would cease. It would leave the others. Aladoree! So beautiful, so weary. He must not let her suffer this!

He fought the laughter. He tried to forget the joke. He battled the agony that consumed his nerves. Doggedly, he dragged his limp body back to the controls.

On through the radiation barrier he drove the *Purple Dream*. He watched the semi-transparent instruments through a haze of colored light. He moved the keys with shining hands. He was shaken again and again with laughter.

He knew, finally, that they were beyond the barrier. The red pain faded; the unearthly luminescence departed from the instruments; the dancing rainbow glitter slowly dissipated from the air. But still he sobbed with laughter.

Jay Kalam came finally into the bridge, haggard and pain-drawn, but calmly efficient. Already, since they had passed the barrier, he had shaved and found a new uniform. He was neat again, lean and brown, gravely handsome.

"Well done, John," he said quietly. "I'll take the bridge a while. I've just been talking with the Commander about our chances of outrunning the fleet behind us. He says——"

John Star had struggled desperately to listen, to keep silent and understand what Jay Kalam said. But the joke

—it was so terribly funny. He burst into mad laughter again, a wild tempest of laughter that sprawled him on the floor.

He must try to tell Jay Kalam about the joke. Jay Kalam could appreciate it. Because, very soon, he would be laughing too, as his own body turned to green decay. But, for the racking laughter, he could not speak at all.

"John!" he heard Jay Kalam cry, aghast. "What's the matter? Are you—hurt?"

Jay Kalam helped him to his feet; held him until he could stop laughing and shake the tears out of his eyes.

"A joke!" he gasped. "An immense joke! Men laughing as they die!"

"John! John!" The grave voice was faint with inexpressible horror. "John, what is it?"

He struggled to forget the joke. There was something else he had to tell Jay, something else not quite so funny. He checked another fit of sobbing laughter.

"Jay," he whispered, "I'm going mad. It's the red gas. I can feel it on my skin, and I can't stop laughing—though I guess it isn't really funny. You must take the controls. And have Hal lock me in the brig——"

"Why, John!"

"Please lock me up. I might—I might even harm Aladoree . . . And go on to save the System."

The laughter came back; he clung to Jay Kalam, sobbing out: "Wait a little, Jay. Let me tell you the joke. So very, very funny. Millions of men laughing—while they die. Little children, even, laughing while their flesh decays. It's the biggest joke of all, Jay. A cosmic joke on the whole human race."

Laughter overcame him. He fell shaking to the floor.

The next he knew, beyond laughter and delirium, he was strapped to a berth in a cabin, and Giles Habibula was bathing his body with a pale, luminously blue solution, evidently the same which Adam Ulnar's close-mouthed physician had used on the wound where the liquid gas had burned him, long ago in the Purple Hall.

"Giles," he whispered, and his voice came hoarse and weak.

"Ah, lad!" wheezed Giles Habibula, smiling. "You know me, lad, at last! It's mortal time you did. You'll laugh no more—promise old Giles?"

"Laugh. What have I to laugh at?" Vaguely he remembered some great joke, but what it was, he could not say.

"Nothing, lad!" gasped Giles, relieved. "Not a precious thing. And you'll be on your blessed feet again, lad, by the time we reach the System."

"The System? . . . Oh, I remember. Does Jay think we can escape the black fleet?"

"Ah, lad, we left them long ago. We flew close to the red dwarf star. They could not follow—its gravitational field stopped their propelling mechanisms. Some of them fell in it. So did we—mortal near! Ah, a wicked fight we had to drive clear of it, lad."

"So I was laughing? . . . I almost remember. I thought that red gas had got me. But that doesn't seem so funny. Am I sane again, Giles?"

"Ah, yes, you seem to be, lad. Just now. Adam Ulnar had this solution. The things made it up, to a prescription he had, while they were repairing the ship. It neutralizes the gas—if one has not been exposed too mortal long. The fearful green scales went from your skin days ago. But we were afraid——"

"Did any of the others——"

The wheezing voice fell. "Yes, lad. The precious lass——"

"Aladoree?" Pain throbbed in John Star's hoarse cry.

"Ah, yes. All the rest of us escaped; we all used this solution. But the dear lass caught it when you did, lad, in that fearful Belt of Peril—the shock of that radiation seemed to bring it on."

"How is she, Giles?"

"I don't know, lad." He shook his head. "The evil green is all cleared from her precious skin. But still she is not herself. She lies, as you lay, in a dead trance we can't wake her from. She was mortal weak and weary, you know, lad, when it took her.

"Ah, lad, it's bad. Mortal bad. If she doesn't wake she cannot build the blessed weapon. And all our trouble has been in vain. Ah, it's a wicked time! I like the lass, lad. Dear life knows I'd hate to see her die!"

"I—I—" whispered John Star, through his agony of apprehension and despair. "I—like her, too, Giles."

And he sobbed.

John Star was able to return to the bridge by the time they entered the outskirts of the System, passing Pluto and

Neptune. All the familiar planets, they saw in the tele-periscope, had turned a dreadful red. Even Earth was a dull spark of sinister crimson.

"Red," breathed Jay Kalam, his lifeless tone edged with horror. "The air of every planet is full of the red gas. I'm afraid we're too late, John."

"Even if we aren't," John Star whispered bitterly, "Aladoree is still no better."

"We'll land on earth, anyhow. Find a piece of iron. And wait. Perhaps she'll wake—before the last man is dead."

"Perhaps. Though her pulse, Giles says——" He broke off, and muttered fiercely: "But she can't die, Jay! She can't!"

They were slipping past the Moon, five days later, to-ward Earth. Aladoree still lay unconscious, her strong heart and her breath grown desperately slow. Her frail body, weakened by exhaustion, by captivity and torture, by months of exposure to the red gas, was fighting des-perately for life itself. The others watched her, kept her warm. They bathed her lax body in the neutralizing solu-tion, helped her swallow a little broth or water when she could. They could do no more.

The Moon was a red world of menace. John Star scanned it through a tele-periscope. Naked since before the birth of Man, its rugged mountains were shrouded now in deadly crimson gas; the new human cities were mounds of lifeless ruin. On a bare plateau of lava, he saw the Medusæ's fortress!

Unearthly citadel! A replica of the black metropolis on their own doomed planet. Tremendous walls and towers of that black, enduring alloy, bristling with fantastic black machines—the instruments of a science that had survived through uncounted ages, had conquered many worlds.

"The hordes of them are waiting there," said Jay Kalam somberly. "Manufacturing the red gas. Bombarding the planets with shells of it. And their invasion fleet is stationed there. If they discover us——"

His voice fell. He had seen the same thing that shocked John Star with horror. A flaring burst of cold green flame above a black landing stage. A black flier rising, follow-ing them toward Earth!

"Perhaps they have already. But we may have time to land ahead of them, and look for a piece of iron."

"But Aladoree is still in that dreadful trance," John Star muttered. "Unless she wakes, to build AKKA, we have no weapon."

On they plunged, toward the red murky Earth, fearfully watching the black spider-ship crossing after them from the newly crimson Moon.

CHAPTER TWENTY-EIGHT

The Green Beast

Into the atmosphere of Earth, red-hazed with poison now, the *Purple Dream* dropped, over western North America, to land at last by the Green Hall, on the brown mesa beneath the mile-high, rugged Sandias.

John Star volunteered to leave the cruiser, to look for iron. There had been none aboard when the ship came back into their possession. Space-craft are non-magnetic, since magnetic fields interfere with the operation of the geodyne; and the Medusæ, refitting the vessel, had removed the few bits of precious iron and steel from the instruments.

"Carry this," Jay Kalam told him, and gave him his old thorn dagger. "And be cautious if you meet men. They may be mad, dangerous . . . And hurry. We must get iron, and slip away, somewhere, before the black ship comes. We must hide, and wait for Aladoree to wake."

Dropping outside the air-lock, John Star paused to stare in horror at what remained of the System's proud and splendid capitol.

The sky was clouded with a scarlet murk, through which the mid-afternoon sun burned with a blood-red, evil light. Bare mesas and cragged mountains were turned strange and grim and incredibly desolate under the dreadful illumination.

The Green Hall had been destroyed by a great shell from the Moon.

On the edge of the grounds, where once had been wide, inviting lawns, a ragged crater yawned, rimmed with torn, raw rock. Beyond the pit the building lay in colossal ruin, a mountain of shattered emerald glass, from which protruded skeletal arms of twisted, rusting steel.

A moment he waited, horror-struck. Then, remembering the urgent need of haste, he plunged forward through a rank growth of weeds, through the bare skeletons of trees that the liquid gas must have killed, across dead lawns piled with rocks flung from the crater and shattered fragments of green glass.

Curious, he soon had cause to reflect, how hard it is to find even a nail when it must be had. He found assorted metal objects: a bronze lamp-stand, a little figurine of cast lead, the charred, twisted aluminum frame of a wrecked air-sled. Even a great steel girder flung from the building, many times too heavy to carry.

He hurried on, desperately searching the devastated grounds for any fragment of iron small enough to move, with an occasional anxious glance at the lurid sky. If the Medusæ *had* seen them, if the black ship was coming to attack them——

He stumbled around a great heap of broken green glass, and came face to face with green horror.

It had been a man. A gigantic man. It must have survived through the days of terror by sheer brute strength. Nearly seven feet tall, its body half naked, half clad in the ragged, filthy fragments of a Legion uniform—the uniform of the Green Hall Guards. Its skin was a mass of bleeding sores, scabbed and crusted horribly with hard green flakes. Red-rimmed eyes, green-clouded, hideous, stared from the horror of its face, half sightless. Its lips were gone. With naked fangs it was gnawing avidly at a fresh red bone that John Star knew, shudderingly, from its shape, to be a human humerus.

Sight of this man-beast, crouching, gnawing, snarling, sickened him with pitying horror. For it meant far more than one man's fate. It epitomized the doom of all humanity, under invasion by an older and more able race—a wise, efficient race, now proved by the crucial test better fitted to survive.

Involuntarily he had cried out at sight of that green, doomed beast. Then, realizing the danger, he tried to slip away. But it had already become aware of him. It made a curious, half-vocal, questioning sound—hoarse and flat and queer, for its vocal cords were evidently too far decayed for articulation. The red-rimmed, clouded eyes peered hideously, and found him. It came toward him, lumbering, shambling, bestial.

"Stand back!" he shouted sternly, tension of panic in his voice.

The effect of his sharp command was curious. For that shambling thing straightened suddenly to military erectness. It came to attention. Stiffly it raised an unspeakable, green-crusted paw in salute. But that was no more than a mechanical reaction left over from its forgotten humanity. It slumped back into the same stooping posture; it lumbered on toward him.

"Attention!" he shouted again. "Halt!"

A moment it paused, and then came on faster. Formless, protesting sounds spewed from its lipless mouth. And John Star stood, faint with horror, trying to understand its cries, until it uttered an abrupt, eager, animal squeal, and broke into a crouched and stumbling run.

He knew, then, that it was stalking him for food.

Swiftly he looked behind him for a path of escape; he realized with a wave of sick apprehension that it had trapped him. Its animal cunning was not yet gone. Mountains of broken green glass hemmed him in. He must face it.

True, he had the black thorn. But he was not so strong, he knew, as he had been before his own long sickness. And this avid, mewing animal was well over twice his weight. The green decay, apparently, had not yet greatly wasted away its strength.

He hoped, as they came to grips, that the tricks of combat he had learned in the Legion Academy would make up his disadvantages. But as one horny, green-scaled paw seized his dagger wrist in a clever, cruel hold, he knew that it had once been another Legionnaire. Its crazed brain had not forgotten how to fight.

The dagger dropped from his paralyzed grasp. Foul green arms locked him in a crushing embrace. Then it tried an old trick of his own. A knee in his back, the other locked over his thighs; his shoulders twisted, twisted, until his back would break.

He struggled vainly in the merciless hold, blind with pain and panic. The hard green scales were harsh against his body; fetor of decomposition sickened him. His efforts failed, and he felt a giddy sickness.

Naked fangs slashed at his shoulder; the thing made an eager whine. It was hungry.

Sheer desperation brought his old cool composure back, then. Through the mist of agony he imagined himself back at the Academy. He smelled the reek of leather and rubbing alcohol and stale sweat. He heard an instructor's bored, nasal monotone: "Twist your body, *so;* drive your elbow into the plexus, *so;* slip your arm here, *so;* then lock your leg and turn."

He did it, as the dry old voice whispered in his memory, hardly aware where he was, knowing only that the torturing pain would cease when he had done it, and he would be free to search for a nail.

Snap!

He rose slowly, beside that quivering mass of greenish decay. He staggered on again among the shattered Green Hall's ruins, scanning the battered earth. He must hurry! If the black flier came. . . . It was a child's toy that caught his eye. A rusty, broken little engine that could no longer move its tiny burden—but might yet save the System.

He tore the shaft out of it, assured himself that it was good gray iron, and hastened back toward the cruiser.

Clambering over a heap of broken green glass, he looked up, and saw the black spider-ship. It was slanting down, across the red and murky sky, already very near.

At a dogged, weary run, he staggered back into view of the *Purple Dream*. Tiny torpedo shape of silver, a pygmy in the shadow of the huge, black-vaned machine plunging down on hot green jets above the dark Sandias. It was still beyond the yawning crater, a quarter mile away.

Hopelessly, a needle-pain of exhaustion stabbing at his heart, he stumbled on. The cruiser was unarmed; the weapons on the black flier could annihilate it in an instant.

Wondering dimly, as he ran, he saw a little group appear on the lowered valve of the air-lock, and hurry down the accommodation ladder. Jay Kalam and Hal Samdu and Giles Habibula, he recognized them, carrying the inert figure of Aladoree.

The valve closed above them; and Adam Ulnar had not appeared.

They ran away from the cruiser; evidently it was about to take off with Adam Ulnar at the controls. But why? Still running grimly on, John Star remembered his old doubt. Had his famous kinsman turned again? Had he put the others off to go back to the Medusæ? John Star could scarcely believe that. Adam Ulnar had seemed sincere. But——

Then the *Purple Dream* moved.

It plunged forward in the fastest take-off he had ever witnessed. It leaped away so swiftly that his eyes lost it. They caught it again, flashing toward the spider-flier, its hull already incandescent.

Even as he realized that it was driven, not by the comparatively feeble rockets, but by the terrific power of the geodynes, it struck the round black belly of the enemy craft with a burst of blinding light.

Flaming, the black invader fell with a curious deliberation out of the red sky. It struck the barren slopes of the Sandias, rolled down them, still looking queerly like a black and monstrous spider in the slow agony of death.

John Star's old, haunting doubt was gone.

"You are the last Ulnar," Jay Kalam greeted him with a solemn new respect, when he came up to the lonely little group on the edge of the mesa. "Adam Ulnar said he was trying to pay a debt. And he told me to tell you, John, that he hoped you would be happy in the Purple Hall."

John Star dropped on his knees by the limp, white-faced girl on the ground, whispered anxiously:

"Aladoree! How is she?"

"Ah, me, lad," dolefully wheezed Giles Habibula, fixing a pillow under her head, "she seems no better. No better! It's the same evil trance she's been in for mortal weeks. She may never wake. Ah, the poor lass——"

He flung a tear out of his fishy eye.

They tried to make her comfortable, under a little shelter made from the branches of a shattered tree. They found rude clubs to defend her if the green beasts should find them. Hal Samdu and Giles Habibula went to search for food and water; they returned in the dim and lurid sunset, empty-handed.

"Mortal me!" wailed Giles Habibula. "Here we are lost in a fearful desert, all death and dead ruin, without food or drink for ourselves or the lass! Ah, me! And frightful, mewing creatures are roving all about us, hunting for mortal human food. Ah, it's a wicked time!"

The Moon came up in the scarlet dusk, a huge and blood-red globe, above the rugged ramparts of the dark Sandias. And they saw, against its pocked and sinister face, a little cluster of tiny black specks, creeping about, growing, expanding. A little swarm of black insects that became steadily and ominously larger.

"A fleet coming down from the Moon," whispered Jay Kalam. "Since that one ship did not return . . . A whole fleet of their spider-ships, coming to make sure we are destroyed. They'll be here in an hour."

CHAPTER TWENTY-NINE

AKKA—and After

"She must wake," whispered John Star. "Or she never will!"

"I'm afraid so," agreed Jay Kalam. "I imagine they'll destroy the very mesa, with those atomic suns. To be sure we trouble them no more . . . But there's no way—"

"She must wake!" John Star muttered again.

With a sort of fierce tenderness, he lifted Aladoree from where she lay. Her body was limp, relaxed. Her eyes were closed, her pale, full lips parted a little, her fine skin very white. He could scarcely feel her pulse; her breath was very slow. Deep, deep, she was sunk in the coma in which she had lain so long.

So lovely and so still! He held her fiercely in his arms, staring up in mute, savage defiance at the red and black pocked Moon. She must not die! She was his! Forever—his! So warm, so dear! He would not let her die.

No! No, she must wake, and use her knowledge to build the weapon and destroy the menace of that red Moon. He must wake her, so she could be his forever!

Unconsciously, he had been whispering it to her. And he spoke louder now, in a desperate appeal. He called to her, trying without actual hope to shout through her coma, to make her realize the desperate need that she should wake.

"Aladoree! Aladoree! You must wake up. You must. You *must!* The Medusæ are coming, Aladoree, to kill us with the opal suns! You must wake up, Aladoree, and build your weapon. You must wake up, Aladoree, to save what's left of the System! You mustn't die, Aladoree! You mustn't! Because I love you!"

He always believed that his appeal reached through to her sleeping mind. Perhaps it did. Or perhaps, as a medical scientist has suggested, it was the irritating stimulation of the red gas itself that roused her, outside the *Purple Dream.* That does not greatly matter.

She sneezed a little, and whispered sleepily:

"Yes, John, I love you."

He almost dropped her, in his eager start at her response, and she came wide awake, staring about in amazed alarm at her strange surroundings.

"Where are we, John?" she gasped. "Not—not back on that planet——"

She was gazing in horror at the red Moon in the red-bathed sky.

"No, we're on the Earth. Can you finish the weapon, quickly, before the Medusæ come? We brought the parts you made by the river."

She stood up, looking dazedly around her, clinging uncertainly to John Star's arm.

"Can this be Earth, John, under this terrible sky? And that the Moon?"

"It is. And those black specks are the spider-ships of the Medusæ, coming down to kill us."

"Ah, the lass is awake!" wheezed Giles Habibula, joyfully.

And Jay Kalam hurried forward with the small, unfinished device that Aladoree had built back on the other planet, useless for want of a little iron.

"Can you finish it?" he asked, still calmly grave. "Quickly? Before they come?"

"Yes, Jay," she said, equally calm, seeming to recover from her first bewilderment. "If we can find a bit of iron——"

John Star produced the broken shaft of the toy engine. She took it in eager fingers, examined it swiftly.

"Yes, John. This will do."

Dusk was red in the west. Ghastly night came down. Under the red, rising Moon the four stood silent about Aladoree and her weapon, tense with hope and dread. They were alone on the mesa, cold in that dreadful light. Behind them was the murdered Green Hall, a stark skeleton of dead human hopes, terrible and quiet against the murky afterglow. Before them the mesa sloped up to the rugged Sandias, beneath the baleful Moon.

Silence hung over them—the awful silence of a world betrayed and slain. Only once was it broken—by a fearful, hideously half-vocal howl of agony and terror from the ruin.

"What was that?" the girl whispered, shuddering.

It was something no longer human, stalked by another hungry beast, John Star knew. But he said nothing.

Aladoree was busy with the weapon. A tiny thing. It looked very simple, very crude, utterly useless. The parts of it were fastened to a narrow piece of wood, which was mounted on a rough tripod, so that it could be turned, aimed.

John Star examined it—and entirely failed to see the secret of it. He was amazed again at its simplicity, incredulous that such a thing could ever vanquish the terrible, ancient science of the Medusæ.

Two little metal plates, perforated, so that one could sight through their centers. A wire helix between them, connecting them. And a little cylinder of iron. One of the plates and the little iron rod were set to slide in grooves, so that they could be adjusted with small screws. A rough key—perhaps to close a circuit through the rear plate, though there was no apparent source of current.

That was all.

Aladoree made some adjustment to the screws. Then she bent over, sighting through the tiny holes in the plates, toward the red Moon, with the black specks of the enemy fliers against it. She touched the key and straightened to watch, with a curious, lofty serenity on her quiet, pale face.

John Star had vaguely expected some spectacular display about the machine, perhaps some dazzling ray. But there was nothing. Not even a spark when the key was closed. So far as he had seen, nothing had happened at all.

For a strange moment he fancied he must still be insane. It was sheer impossibility that this odd little mechanism—a thing so small and so simple that a child might have made it—could defeat the Medusæ. Efficient victors over unknown planets and unknown ages, what had they to fear?

"Won't it——?'" he whispered, anxiously.

"Wait," said Aladoree.

Her voice was perfectly calm, now without any trace of weakness or weariness. Like her face, it carried something strange to him. A new serenity. A disinterested, passionless authority. It was absolutely confident. Without fear, without hate, without elation. It was like—like the voice of a goddess!

Involuntarily, he drew back a step, in awe.

They waited, watching the little black flecks swarming and growing on the face of the sullen Moon. Five seconds, perhaps, they waited.

And the black fleet vanished.

There was no explosion, neither flame nor smoke, no visible wreckage. The fleet simply vanished. They all stirred a little, drew breaths of awed relief. Aladoree moved to touch the screws again, the key.

"Wait," she said once more, her voice still terribly—divinely—serene. "In twenty seconds . . . the Moon . . ."

They gazed on that red and baleful globe. Earth's attendant for eons, though young, perhaps, in the long time-scale of the Medusæ. Now the base of their occupation forces, waiting for the conquest of the planets. Half consciously, under his breath, John Star counted the seconds, watching the red face of doom—not man's now, but their own.

". . . eighteen . . . nineteen . . . twenty——"

Nothing had happened. A breathless, heartbreaking instant of doubt. Then the red-lit sky went black.

The Moon was gone.

"The Medusæ," Jay Kalam whispered, as if to assure himself of the unbelievable, "the Medusæ are gone." A long moment of silence, and he whispered once more: "Gone! They will never dare—again!"

"I saw—nothing!" cried John Star, breathlessly. "How——?"

"They were annihilated," said Aladoree, strangely serene. "Even the matter that composed them no longer exists in our universe. They were flung out of all we know as space and time."

"But how——?"

"That is my secret. I can never tell—save to the chosen person who is to keep it after me."

"Mortal me!" wheezed Giles Habibula. "Ah, the blessed System is safe at last. Ah, dear life, but a mortal desperate undertaking it's been to save it. You must be precious careful not to fall into hostile hands again, lass. Old Giles will never be able to go through all this again, sweet life knows!

"Ah, me! And here we're left in the middle of the desert, in the wicked dark—and the Moon will never rise again!"

His voice had snapped the tension that held them.

"John——" breathed Aladoree.

No longer was it the voice of a goddess. Its awful serenity was gone. It was all human, now, weak and shaken, appealing. John Star found her in the darkness. He made her sit down, and she sobbed against his shoulder, with happy sobs of relief.

"Ah, lass," groaned Giles Habibula, "good cause you have to weep. We all may perish yet, for want of a mortal bite of food!"

The *Green Defender*, newest cruiser of the Legion of Space, flashed down to the Purple Hall, on Phobos, nearly a year later. Though one red gas shell had fallen on that tiny moon of Mars, during the Medusæ's bombardment, the great building had not been injured. The neutralizing solution had cured those affected by it; it had dissipated, combined into harmless salts, until the dark sky of the little world was free from any stain of red.

The cruiser dropped on the landing stage that crowned the central purple tower. The new Commander of the Legion came gravely down the accommodation ladder, and John Star came eagerly to meet him. Greetings over, they paused, looking down at the luxuriantly green convexity of the little planet, with grim memories of the last time they had been together here, when they took the *Purple Dream*.

"Not much trace left of the invasion," remarked Jay Kalam.

"No, Commander," replied John Star, with a little smile

at the title. "Not one case of the madness left uncured, in all the System, I understand. And the red gone from the skies. It's already history."

"A splendid estate, John." With admiration, Jay Kalam's glance roved the richly green, curving landscape. "The finest, I think, in the System."

John Star's face clouded.

"A responsibility I had to assume." His voice was almost bitter. "But I wish I were back in the Legion, Jay. With Hal and Giles. I wish I were back in the guard of Aladoree."

Jay Kalam smiled. "You're—fond of her, John?"

He nodded, simply. "I was—am. I hoped—until that night, when she used AKKA. I realized then what a fool I was. She's a goddess, Jay. With the secret she has a power—a responsibility. I saw that night that she had no time for—for love."

Jay Kalam was still gravely smiling.

"Did it ever occur to you, John, that she's just a girl? Even though it may be interesting to destroy a planet, she can't be doing it all the time. She's apt to get lonesome."

"Of course," John Star admitted wearily, "she must have other interests. But she was—simply a goddess! I couldn't ask her. Anyhow, it could never be me!"

"Why do you think that, John?"

"For one thing, my name. Ulnar. I couldn't ask her to forgive that."

"But the name needn't worry you, John. The Green Hall, recognizing your distinguished service, has officially changed your name to John Star. That's one thing we came to tell you."

"Eh?" he gasped.

Then Aladoree came through the air-lock, Hal Samdu and Giles Habibula behind her. Her face sedate, gray eyes cool and grave, the clear sunlight working miracles of red and brown and gold in her hair, she looked at John Star in demure inquiry.

"Since the Purple Hall is now the strongest fortress in the System," Jay Kalam explained hastily, "the Green Hall requests you to assume the responsibility of guarding Aladoree Anthar."

"If you are willing, John Ulnar," added the girl, eyes twinkling.

His throat was dry. He searched in a golden mist for words, uttered them with an effort.

"I'm willing. But my name, it seems, is John Star."

Still grave, but for her eyes, she said: "I shall call you John Ulnar."

"But you said——"

"I've changed my mind. I trust one Ulnar. More than that, I——"

She was suddenly too busy to finish the sentence.

"Ah, me!" observed Giles Habibula, approvingly watching the two.

" 'Tis evident we're welcome, with the lass. Mortal evident! Especially the lass! Ah, and it looks like a good enough place for a poor old soldier of the Legion to pass his remaining years in peace. If kitchen and cellar bear proper proportion to the rest of the building.

"Ah, Hal, if you can forget your precious pride in all those medals and decorations that Jay has showered on you since the Green Hall made him Commander of the Legion, let's look about for a mortal bite to eat."

SCIENCE FICTION MASTERPIECES